MLS

WALTER'S SUITCASE

a novel by

Sheryl Coley

DEDICATION

<u>Chad, Adam and Erica</u> – you inspire me and keep me going every single day. Thanks for the freedom and encouragement to pursue this goal.

<u>Linda, Jerry, Ron and Thaynle</u> – Thank you for your time and encouragement. I have truly appreciated your insightful comments and your valuable feedback throughout this process. You were the first to read this book and you gave me the confidence to finish it and share it.

Table of Contents

Dear Sunny,   Dec. 12th, 1986

    I have been looking for you for several years now. I have
tried various agencies in hopes of finding you. I was so happy
that one of them has finally tracked you down, and right in
time for Christmas too! It has been so long since I have seen you
or talked to you. I truly hope that you are doing well. Please
call me collect as soon as possible. I would like to fly you out
here to New Jersey for a visit. There is so much to say but I will
save it for your call and visit.
    Love,
    "Nana"
    Cora Britt
    279 W. Lukeview Rd. #41
    Dover, New Jersey, 07802
    (273) 649-1382

CATALYST
August 17, 1988

I watched her take small shallow breaths as she laid in her hospital bed. She hadn't moved on her own in a week. Wires and tubes, strung like garish Christmas lights, decorated the room. The strong chemical smell of sanitizer permeated everything and burned my nostrils. The doctors and nurses were surprised by her tenacity, but that was who she was. I knew she needed rest, though.

I picked up the old brush from the bedside table and began to brush her white hair, at least the parts I could reach. It was a color that people always commented on. Not a yellowed or aged white but a beautiful shiny hue that looked like spun silver. She had been a redhead in younger days. Mine was a boring mousy brown.

Her rose-toned porcelain skin remained soft, but deep lines and wrinkles marred it now. Her features were sinking on her face as the life force drained out of her. I had brushed out her hair as best I could many times in the last few weeks. My ritual that I performed as I maintained my vigil by her deathbed. No sense lying to myself, I knew what the eventual outcome would be for my biological grandmother.

She was ninety-three years old and I was grateful to have reconnected with her in the last couple years of her life. Most people did not get that proverbial second chance like I had. It was a blessing and a curse to find family I didn't know until after I had crossed into adulthood. I had only faded, black and white memories of her from when I was very little. The memories played out like an old movie where the actors looked vaguely familiar, but I couldn't remember their names.

It was selfish of me, but the reality did not match up to the fantasies in my head. She had lived her life and she did not want to rehash all the highs and lows of it. Especially not the lows, and that hurt most of all.

I was an outsider looking in at what should have been rightfully mine. My heritage. I wanted so badly to know it all, but she only allowed me to see a little of our shared history. Only the pieces that didn't hurt her heart. The rest was neatly locked away. I resented her for it, but I would never tell anyone how I really felt. I would be that dutiful granddaughter to this woman that I barely knew. I always had to be the good girl that my adopted parents had raised me to be. That nagging voice in my head chided me for my selfishness. That voice in my head that was so good at making me feel so bad.

After I finished brushing her hair, I put down the brush and grabbed the jar of cold cream off the bedside table. I opened it and gently rubbed some on her cheeks and forehead. She had taken good care of her skin when she was able. I took a tissue and wiped off the excess like I had seen her do a hundred times before. Then I sat back down and picked up her copy of *The Book of Virtues* by William J. Bennett.

I started reading to her from the tattered book. She had written all over the margins. It was one of her favorite books. I had spent a lot of time reading to her in the past weeks. She loved to read books, newspapers, magazines; whatever she could get her hands on.

She constantly clipped little articles, to fold up and insert them between the pages of her many books back at her apartment. I doubted that she would ever find a particular piece again with her filing system. It sometimes maddened me when I opened a book and a clipping fell out, succumbing once again to her literary booby-traps.

2

I smoothed down the wrinkled pages of the book I was reading to her, trying to flatten them. A couple of the pages were completely torn out of the book and simply resting, inserted between other pages. It was one of her favorites and she had several editions, but she always returned to this copy.

She began to stir as I read. The monitors and alarms confirmed the activity. Her eyes fluttered open and she tried to prop herself up on an elbow without success. She let herself bounce back down to the pillow. Her wild gaze fell upon my face. Her red-rimmed eyes appeared an electric blue color, now that they were open. She watched me for the longest moment. I could see no recognition in those wide eyes. It made me sad and sorry for being cross with her.

"What about Walter?" she croaked. "I only see sister Sadie and Hoyt...where is he?"

"Shhh, shhh. It's okay," I said trying to comfort her.

She hadn't been conscious for so long that I was amazed to be having a conversation with her. I grabbed a cup of water and put it up to her lips but most of it dribbled down her chin and she coughed as she tried to push the cup away with a weak hand.

"But we are all supposed to go together...Mother and Father are waiting. He is always making us late," she said in her southern drawl that was gaining prominence as she faded away.

"It's okay...just rest. You need rest."

"Oh, there he is. I see him now. He's down at the water...but the glare is so bright...I can hardly look. Walter! Walter!" I saw a flash of light out of the corner of my eye, but when I turned to look there was nothing there. It must have been a reflection from a car in the parking lot as it passed by.

"Oh...and look. There's little Bobby. What a sweet smile...he's gotten big..."

Then she went silent and just stared up into my eyes. I knew this time that she was seeing me and that she knew me. Cora was back with me. She raised a hand as if to brush my cheek, but it was too late, and she was too weak. Her hand fell back to the bed and her eyes rolled upward. I heard her exhale one last time. Alarms were beeping, and monitors were flashing. A nurse ran into the room and looked over the equipment. I wanted to yell for her to do something, but I couldn't get any words out. All that would come were the tears. Me and my useless tears.

Like that, Cora was gone. She had left on her own terms without any drama. Drama was not her style. Drama was for Sadie and Walter, not Cora and Hoyt. She had been the last one left of the four siblings. Drama was not my style either. I stood up, brushed her cheek and walked out to the nurse's station, not bothering to worry about my tear-stained face. I knew that she had really seen me in that final moment and that was enough, even though the voice in my head said otherwise. She said, *you should have done more,* and she blamed me for everything.

I was surprised to hear my grandmother mention Bobby in her last moments, but I really shouldn't have been. The mention of his name had stirred something strong in me. Bobby was one of those pieces that hurt her heart. I realized I had pushed his memory aside just like she had. Buried him long ago. His name made me uncomfortable.

I was so little on the Bad Day, but I do remember it too clearly. That was the first time that Ivey spoke to me, if only in a hushed whisper. She scared me back then. She blamed me of course. Now she was only a daily nuisance that I tried to ignore, just like I tried to forget about Bobby.

🌴 🌴 🌴

I found myself once again back at my grandmother's little apartment that we had shared for the last two years while I attended college. Just like my graduation two months prior; the funeral had come and gone without much fanfare. At her age, there were few of her peers or family around. It was up to me to deal with her

4

belongings and I had to have everything out of her apartment by the end of the week.

My biological mother came over the day after the funeral and took what she wanted. She hadn't been to the hospital once while Nana was there. She looked old and haggard as she stared down at her feet. She wouldn't make eye contact and she barely spoke. She cried, and I did the best I could to comfort her. It was like comforting a stranger.

She didn't want much. A book, the TV and a motorized recliner. Her boyfriend helped load everything into his beat-up old car, except for the recliner, they said they would find a friend with a truck and come back for that later. They said to leave it at the curb. They were taking it all to the room they shared in some nearby boarding house.

I had never been there in the two years that I lived with my grandmother. I had never been invited. I told her to stay in touch as they departed, but I doubted that would happen, unless she needed something. The rest was left to me.

I decided to get a rental truck and load everything up myself. I packed it all, not bothering to sort any of it. It was still too painful. It took me all day to do it. There were lots of books. The apartment manager helped me with the larger items. He was a nice man who had done a lot for my grandmother over the years. Probably much more than her own troubled daughter, or granddaughter for that matter.

I decided to make one final pass through the small apartment. Then I would use the bathroom and head out. Maybe I could find some fast food on the way out of town. It was 6:30 PM and I hadn't eaten much since breakfast. I went room by room double checking everywhere. My footsteps echoed on the worn hardwood floors. The place felt abandoned. Funny how easy it was to pack up a lifetime. Her's had only taken one day and that seemed wrong.

I was back in the living room when I noticed the small coat closet door. I thought I better double check that as well. It ran under the hallway stairs outside of the apartment, so the ceiling sloped down to nothing with the angle of the stairs above. The stairs led to the apartment above Cora's. There was no light in the closet, so I grabbed a flashlight.

I had missed something. At the very back of the closet, there was an old, brown leather suitcase. It had blended into the walls in the darkness. I thought about just leaving it. It might not have even belonged to Cora. Maybe it had been left by the tenant before her. It would have been easy to do. Then I thought better of it.

I grabbed it and brought it out to the fading light of the living room. It had several worn travel stickers on it. There was a piece of paper taped on it and in my grandmothers handwriting it was labeled *Walter*. I assumed it was the same Walter she had been looking for in the hospital as she left me.

She was the last, and then there were none. Gone and forgotten so fast. Her siblings were the ones that she had thought of in her final moments. In the lonely hospital bed, she thought of them even though they had all been gone for so many years. Her siblings and Bobby.

I loaded the old battered suitcase into the front of the rental truck. It felt heavy. I was glad I had grabbed it. I would sort through everything once I was home; now was not the time.

I turned in the key to the apartment manager. He was a nice family man and I found myself strangely emotional as I told him goodbye. It had been a long few weeks, I guess. *You're such a sap,* Ivey told me.

I loaded up and headed out of town. I was anxious to get back home to my sleepy little Midwestern town where fate had seen fit to spit me up when I was only four years old. I wanted to leave my emotions behind me in New Jersey.

THE NIGHT BEFORE
December 17, 1988

I was meeting David for dinner to tell him that night that I was leaving the next morning. I don't know why I was so nervous. I guess I was worried about his reaction. I had only been back in Buffalo, Wyoming about three and a half months. Since my grandmother had died, and I had packed up all her stuff. But I had not seen David in person yet since I had been back.

We had been apart most of the past two years while I was away at school on the east coast and living with my grandmother. It didn't bother either of us that we hadn't got together yet. He knew I was busy getting settled. It bothered my adopted mother more.

David was always the one constant I could fall back on. He had finished college and found work back home before I had. It was a comfortable relationship. When we were together, we had fun and when we weren't, we each had our own lives to live.

We had met when we were young and stupid college kids who weren't even old enough to buy a beer. That was at State before I left for the east coast and changed majors. I could count on one hand the number of boyfriends I had before David. He was an utterly normal guy unlike any of my ex's and I liked that. He was better than I deserved, which the voice in my head liked to remind me of constantly.

I found an open parking spot in front of the restaurant. That was a miracle on a Friday night, even in our tiny western town. David lived a couple towns away in a much bigger city. Cities didn't overlap in Wyoming like they did in New Jersey. I locked the car and headed inside. He was already at a table with an open bottle of white wine and two menus. He didn't like wine, but he knew that I did on occasion. One of the waitresses was smiling down at him, with her hand resting easily on his shoulder. He stood up when he saw me, then he gave me a hug and pulled out the chair for me.

"Hi Sunny. This is Sheila, we went to high school together. Sheila this is Sunny." I smiled at her and extended a hand. I mentally noted that he did not introduce me as his girlfriend. I guess I deserved that for not getting together with him sooner. *Bingo!* Ivey agreed.

"See you later David. Stay in touch," Sheila said with a wink after shaking my hand. She never even looked at me. David turned toward me. Sheila was into him and giving off the vibe. Why not. He was a successful good-looking guy with no ring on his finger. *Who deserves better than you...*

"How have you been?" he asked me as she left us.

"Great. How are you?" I asked awkwardly. "Sorry I have been so busy since I got back. How is work going?"

"It's going great. I love it. I just took over some new accounts today. Business is booming, and they need to hire more staff already...since I started that is. How about you? Are you ready to start working?"

"Well, about that...I decided to take a little more time off...sorry...I meant to talk to you sooner about all this. You know I received some money after my grandmother passed. I decided to spend some of it to get away on a trip. I need some more time to clear my head before jumping into the real world. I'm just not ready yet," I said as I poured a glass of wine for myself.

"Oh. Wow. This is a surprise, but I totally get it. You've had a lot to deal with. Finding your grandmother and then losing her. Graduating college. Moving home. I understand. Don't worry, your boss and I will be here waiting when you get back," David said with a wink.

He was always my cheerleader; it was part of what attracted me to him in the beginning. He rolled with the punches. He took whatever I threw at him with little reaction. Sometimes I did secretly wish for him to be more reactive, not so even-keeled about everything. More passionate. It could be maddening to have someone always agree with whatever I said. *Only you would feel that way* my inner voice told me.

"So where are you going?" he asked.

"The Bahamas…for two weeks. I leave in the morning."

"Wow. Well, do you need a ride to the airport or something?"

"No, Dad is taking me. The flight is early."

"How are your parents with all this?" David asked. He meant my adopted parents.

"Not that good actually. They don't understand why I am doing this, and I don't completely understand it myself, to be honest. They want me to get on with it and start working. I did take my sweet time in getting my college degree, so to them, I am already behind schedule with life in general. They think I've goofed off long enough. Most people graduate college before the age of twenty-six."

"Well…I hate to say it, but Christmas is in a week. Maybe you could wait until after that?"

"I know. I know, but I have to do this now. I don't want to push back jumping into the real world any longer than I have too. They should appreciate that, at least," I pleaded, trying to make him understand my crazy logic.

David grabbed my hand. "Well then, you do this, and you don't feel guilty about it. You wouldn't be doing it if it didn't need to be done. You have always done what's right. Take some time for yourself."

He knew exactly what to say even when I didn't know what I needed to hear. I felt my eyes start to burn. I did not deserve him, or maybe he really did deserve better as the voice in my head, Ivey, had chided. She had been bugging me for so long that I thought it best to name her.

9

Luckily the waiter showed up then. I was not being honest with David or my parents and I felt bad about that, but it was too hard to explain. I knew that none of them would understand. David would say he did but that would not be the complete truth. I didn't want to make a liar of him.

This trip was not just about me taking a vacation…it was about that old battered suitcase of Walter's that I had found in the little coat closet under the stairs, back at my grandmother's apartment.

The contents of that suitcase had fascinated me, especially one letter in particular. I had become obsessed with all of it as I poured over the contents nightly since I had come home. I don't know what I thought I would find in the Bahamas, but I had to go see for myself. I had to see if I could find Angela Merriweather and give her the letter, no matter how crazy of an idea it was.

"Let's get some dessert. I want you to have a great time on your trip and just relax. Have some fun," David said.

I smiled back at him. I had not come clean on everything, but it had been good to talk to him anyway. It was getting late and I needed to leave. I needed to finish packing and I had to get up early. I told David I should invite him over, but Dad was coming to get me at four in the morning. We made plans to get together when I got back. He told me to call him from paradise. He told me to be safe then he kissed me on the cheek, and we walked out hand in hand when dessert was done.

ARRIVAL
December 18, 1988

Of course, my adopted Dad was early to pick me up. He was always early and a morning person on top of it. I had not had my coffee yet. The anticipation of the trip helped some. I could grab a coffee at the airport. I dragged my heavy suitcase out and threw it in the back of Dad's old pickup with the dent in the side. Then I went back into my apartment and grabbed my purse, as well as Walter's old beat up suitcase. I locked the door and headed to Dad's truck. He looked at me funny as I got in with the ragged old case, but he didn't say anything.

We drove along in silence, thankfully. It was still dark out, but the sky was just starting to lighten a little. Looking back on the past few months, it seemed like so much had happened since I had arrived home from the east coast.

I thought back on the day I drove the large rental truck into the driveway of my adopted parent's big barn shaped house…

🌴 🌴 🌴

I drove up to the house I had grown up in. The house was a cream color when I came back from finishing college and burying my grandmother. It had been dark brown when I had left for New Jersey. I had only been gone for two years. Dad was outside sweeping the driveway when I pulled up. I ran over to him and hugged him. He had retired but mom was still working. He was ten years older than her, but I knew she resented him for retiring without her even though she would never admit it out loud. It was surprising that she did not bring it up, but she would find other ways to twist the knife.

"How was your trip," Dad had asked, still holding me in a big bear hug.

"Long!" I exclaimed.

"We got to get that truck unloaded. I cleared a spot in the shop for your stuff. Your grandma's stuff I mean."

Dad was a man of few words and I was grateful for that. I backed the truck up through the narrow gate, into the backyard. Dad had a large shop in the back with an overhead garage door on it. We opened the truck and began to unload boxes and furniture into the shop.

I was going to stay with mom and dad for a while until I found my own place. I had about a month until I was supposed to start working for the company that I had interned with over the past summer. I figured it would give me time to move and unpack and deal with all my grandmother's belongings.

"Did we get it all?" Dad asked.

"I think so."

I grabbed a broom and swept out the back of the truck. Dad leaned against the side of the rental truck with sweat dripping down his face and staining his T-shirt with the pocket. He always had a pocket to cram full of paper and pencils. When I was done, he called mom and told her we would meet her for dinner after we dropped off the rental.

Dad hopped into his pickup to follow me to the truck rental place. I climbed into the truck and saw the old leather suitcase on the passenger seat. I grabbed it and jumped out, running up to the front door of the house that was never locked. I looked at Dad and held up a finger, signaling just a minute. I went inside and took the suitcase upstairs to the bedroom I would be using and dropped it on the bed. Then I was back out in the truck and driving off.

We returned the moving truck and I jumped in with Dad. He wanted to stop off at The Lantern Lounge for a beer since we had some time before we had to meet Mom for dinner. Dad's hangout of the month. We sat and drank a beer in silence and then Dad ordered a second.

"So, have you talked to David yet?"

"Umm…yeah…I called him when I got back to town."

"How's he doing?"

"Good."

"Did you talk to your boss yet? Are things lined up at your office?"

"Yes…and no. I talked to Tim. I told him I needed some more time, just to get settled and find a place," I said as I took a swig from my frosty beer mug.

"Oh. Well, you can stay with us as long as you need too. I know you have been busy with graduation…and your grandma. Mom and I really want to help."

"Thanks, Dad. I know I can always count on you. I'm just glad I got to spend some time with her before she passed away."

It still made me feel awkward to talk to my adopted parents about my biological family. It felt like a betrayal to the ones that had raised me. I hoped that was all in my head because I didn't want to hurt them.

"Well, just give it time. I am glad you're taking a little time off though, I have plenty of projects you can help me with," dad said with an evil grin.

"So much for time off!"

"We better go meet your Mom," Dad said as he threw down some money on the bar. "And whatever you do, take your Mom with a grain of salt. You know how she is. She has been chomping at the bit to get your life in order now that you're back."

We walked across Main Street over to the local café. Mom was already sitting at a table. The hostess said, "Hey Big Jack," as we walked in. He was well known in our little city. He had seen the inside of most of the bathrooms in town as the resident plumber. I gave my adopted mom, Margie, a big hug and sat down.

"Hey sweetie, how is everything going? We have missed you. And just when is that boyfriend of yours going to pop the question now that you are done with school and back home for good?" Mom asked.

Before I could even answer, she had moved on to talk about her job and all the things she had to deal with that day. It was truly okay with me. The beer had made my head feel fuzzy and I wasn't much in the mood for talking. Listening was good. Mom had a whole entire conversation by herself with the occasional head nod from Dad and me. Sometimes I wondered how those two ever got together in the first place. I think Mom was lucky that Dad was around to keep her grounded.

"Well?" Mom asked. "What about David? Has he talked about any plans for the future? No living together in sin of course. You need to do this the right way. He should come over for dinner this weekend. I would love to see him."

"I just got back...I don't know. I've been driving cross country for two days now. Please, can we talk about this later?" I asked, looking away. I was so frustrated with her. If only she would sort out her thoughts before she blurted them out. I could never come up with a good way to give her a subtle hint to back off.

"Gosh...sorry. Don't get your panties in a bunch. I just got carried away."

"Well...I'm sorry too. I'm just so tired from the long drive."

Dad grabbed the check and headed up to the cashier. Mom tried to suggest that we go dutch and Dad turned and glared at her. He paid and came back to the table. He told Mom we would see her at home. She said bye and headed to the door. Then Dad turned and looked at me and mouthed "sorry". We headed out the door behind Mom. It was a silent ride home. We were all in a better mood back at the house that evening. After some small talk and television, I headed up to my room.

I dug out some sweatpants and a T-shirt from my suitcase to wear for bed. I hadn't done laundry in a while, so it was hard to find something that had only been worn once. I performed my daily rituals of teeth brushing and face washing. I was too tired for a shower. I took my hair out of its usual ponytail and let it fall on my shoulders. It had been such a dusty and bumpy ride in the moving truck. Sleeping at rest stops had made the trip even longer. I was ready to collapse.

I climbed under the covers, but then I noticed Walter's old suitcase was still sitting on the foot of the bed. I looked at it closer, thinking they must have traveled lighter in those days. I would never fit all my clothes in a suitcase like that unless it was only an overnight trip.

The brown leather had cracked in places. I wondered if there was any way to repair it or at least patch it. Colorful travel stickers covered it, from places like the Bahamas, Spain and Cuba.

I was tired, but suddenly, I was curious as well. I pushed the quilt down and pulled the suitcase closer. It took a few minutes for me to haggle the locks open. They weren't truly locked, just latched. I slid the two keyed buttons outward and the latches snapped up. One caught my finger. I put the sore finger in my mouth; it smarted badly. I opened the suitcase with the other hand. A jumble of papers, photos and other odds and ends fell out. What a mess.

I started to pick through it. I had been shocked to see all my grandmothers' belongings squeezed into the rental truck, but this was so much more impressive. It was hard to believe all the items that came out of that old suitcase. My great uncle's life was spread out before me on the bed. I found his birth certificate, his death certificate and everything in between.

There were letters, news clippings, photos, military records, canceled checks, a glass paperweight with his photo, a tuxedo bow tie and even a small reel of an old 8mm movie. I found a marriage license too. I thought he had never married, but he had wed, during the forties according to the marriage license. Did he ever have kids, I wondered? There were none I knew about.

I stayed up much later than I had planned to that night. Every time I looked through the suitcase, I found something new. A rare glimpse into a part of my family history and a forgotten era. I could not get enough…

🌴 🌴 🌴

"You sure you want to start spending all this money you just got?" my adopted dad said, bringing me back from my reminiscing. Bringing me back to the start of my adventure.

"Well, it's kind of late for this conversation now. The money is already spent, no refunds. Besides, I'm not spending all of it. I just want a break before starting my job. Is that so bad to want some time off? Come on…you and Mom already gave me all the lectures. Let me leave on a good note, okay?"

"Just be safe, alright? A woman traveling alone can be an easy target."

"You forget that I wandered the streets of New York City and New Jersey for two years, on my own. The real big city, Dad."

"Well, I guess all my years of hard work paid off. I'm going to miss you. I might have to get David to help me with Mary's bathroom job."

"I am sure he would be glad to help, Dad."

"Don't forget to give us a call once in a while…let us know you are still breathing. And you better call on Christmas day…or else. I don't know why the heck you have to take off right before Christmas."

"I will call. I love you Dad."

Dad got out and helped with my suitcase. He gave me one of his big bear hugs and then he stuffed some cash in my hand and said to buy myself lunch with it. He pulled out a small can of pepper spray on a keychain and pressed that into my hand with an apologetic smile. I stuffed the mace in my pocket and then I lugged my stuff in through the big revolving door. As I circled around, I looked back and saw Dad in the pickup with the window down, watching me go. He waved.

I checked in my bag and found my gate. When it was time to board the plane, I made my way down the walkway with Walter's old suitcase and a coffee in hand. I found my seat and put the suitcase in the overhead bin. I could sit down and relax. I had a good book with me. It was about a detective in the near future that travelled the Midwest region. He was so good at putting together the clues with his loyal companion, a dog named Watson. Pure fantasy but so fun.

Between the book, two naps and two airplane changes; the trip went by rather quickly. I did find myself a nice lunch during one of the layovers, as I had promised Dad. Then I was getting off the plane and going to retrieve my suitcase in the Bahamas on the Island known as Euphoria. The air smelled different, warmth and humidity embraced me.

My natural curls turned into a frizzy mess almost instantly. I had not found any hair product that was strong enough to tame it. I waited for my suitcase and then worked my way to the hotel shuttle. Lots of locals tried to sell me shell necklaces and homemade soaps as I walked through the airport. The clean flowery smell of the soaps drenched the air as I passed by. I said "no" about a hundred times.

I found my bus quickly, ready to leave the airport behind. The sun hovered low on the horizon, preparing for its descent. The familiar orange orb seemed bigger on Euphoria than it had back home.

The bus bounced along through narrow streets. The city looked ancient and run down. Lots of people stood on corners; talking and laughing. Maybe they wanted to escape the heat of their little cottages with the paint peeling off the siding. I had only seen the ocean from the plane so far. This dirty, dusty city was not the paradise I expected.

We turned down one especially narrow, garbage-littered alley. I thought the bus might get stuck between the walls. I became alarmed when some bicycle riders pulled out in front of our bus full of tourists. The bus screeched to a halt. I remembered a similar scenario in one of the many books I had read, but unlike my novel, the bikers finally moved on instead of pulling out an Uzi and spraying the bus with bullets.

Finally, the bus crossed a bridge and I found my paradise. It was night and day from the dirty city streets of the Island to the resort property where I would be staying. I was grateful. As we crossed the bridge and entered the grounds of the hotel property, I got a good look around; it was incredible. Like nothing I had seen before.

The resort was on its own little isle that was connected to the rest of the Island via the bridge we had crossed. There was only one way in or out. All the buildings were wild tropical colors of blues, corals and yellows with white trim. Christmas decorations and lights adorned the buildings. They seemed out of place amongst the palm trees and sand.

Lush palm trees, gardens with pools and fountains adorned the property. The man-made pools blended in so seamlessly with the organic vegetation that it was hard to distinguish what was natural and what was not. The resort sprawled along the edge of the ocean. I loved the salty smell of the beach. The aqua waters of the ocean dominated the scenery.

The bus unloaded, and people dispersed. I found my building and headed inside. I had decided to splurge when I booked the room. I had heard there was a convention of some sort going on, but they still had a couple of unsold rooms left. The weather at this time of year could be questionable but I hoped for the best. There were indoor activities if it did rain, and besides, I wasn't here for sight-seeing.

My building was the tallest of them all, and judging by the clientele, it had to be the most expensive. It was called Triton's

Tower. I felt under-dressed and out of my league. The surroundings quickly distracted me from my ineptitude.

I walked up to the massive registration desk in the white pristine lobby, checked in and received my keys. I would be glad to get up to the room and put down the old suitcase along with the rest of my stuff. I had been worried about misplacing Walter's suitcase the entire trip, but I was more worried that it would be too fragile to turn over to the baggage crews of the airlines. A bellhop escorted me to my room.

My room was not on the top floor, but the view went on forever as I looked out the wall to wall glass, and past the balcony rail from nine floors up. I could see for miles. Cruise ships glided along on the horizon. They looked miniature from my vantage point, like they belonged in a bottle.

I gave the bellhop a tip and an awkward thanks. He set everything down and exited without a word, as he backed out the door. I did some quick unpacking. I freshened up a bit, changed into shorts and then decided to go walk around the property and down to the beach. I wanted to explore. There was still enough daylight for that and besides, I was tired of sitting all day. It would feel good to stretch my legs a little and loosen the knots that had grown in them.

I headed back down to the lobby and out the glass doors. The sound of the ocean waves lapping at the shore was a constant whirr everywhere I went. I walked down by the swimming pools and aquariums teeming with sea life, lost in the beauty of it all. People wandered around, seeming so peaceful. Everyone seemed to move at a different pace here. I found my way to the sand and breathed deep. I took off my shoes and wiggled my toes into it.

I thought back on my time spent with my grandmother. She had made this trip possible for me. I was grateful to spend time with her but somehow it still felt unfinished. Nana had wanted to get to know the adult I had become and not dwell on that aching past we shared. I really should stop blaming her for that. I had my own buried secrets as well.

Besides, why would she want to think about her abusive alcoholic husband or the painful life of her mentally unstable and only child, my mother? My mom who only brought her heartache. She had tried so hard to tuck those things away. I am sure it had been a hard and lonely life for my grandmother, but it can be so difficult to change paths once you have set out. She had done all she could for me after we reconnected. And yet, I still felt frustration. I had more intimate access to the details of my great uncle's life through his suitcase. A man who died before I was even born…but still, he was family.

I had tried to ask my biological mother questions about our family one of the few times I saw her. She was never around, even though she lived near my grandmother's apartment. That had been a complete dead end. She had grown up in a much more secretive era. Dirty laundry was not to be aired in those days. Everyone seemed to develop amnesia when it came to bad family history. She kept herself in a drug and alcohol induced haze of forgetfulness to make sure of it. Besides, why would she tell me anything? We were strangers and she made no effort to change that.

My grandmother would have liked it here on this Island. She had traveled to many places throughout her life. That much I had learned. I wondered if she ever came to visit Walter while he was here? Or did she prefer to keep her distance from him and his lifestyle? From what I knew of her, the latter was probably true. She was like me. She liked to live properly. Following the rules was the thing to do, especially back then.

I would imagine it would have been disgraceful for a married but separated woman to travel alone to such a hedonistic place. The Island was called Euphoria after all. When my mom was born, my grandmother and grandfather soon stopped living together but they never divorced. That would mean an outward declaration to the world that they had failed. Better to keep it quiet and just live apart. He was another relative that had died before I was born.

A few people walked along the beach, stopping to stare out to sea and take in the view. The sun was starting to sink below the horizon and there was a beautiful multi-colored glow. I heard some commotion from further down the beach. I looked to my right and saw a man and two kids. The man was obviously frustrated with the boys. He dramatically waved his arms around. One boy was maybe twelve and the other around fourteen. I overheard enough to know that the man was trying to take a photo and the kids were not cooperating.

I tried to keep my head down and avoid eye contact. I did not want to get in the middle of the blow-up. I was in the act of turning around to go back the way I had just come from when I was stopped cold as the man addressed me.

"Hello there? Hello Miss. Can I trouble you for some assistance? Would you mind taking a picture of the three of us? With the sunset in the background."

"Umm…okay, I guess. Sure," I said, as he tossed me his camera, which I proceeded to fumble and drop into the sand. I quickly scooped down to pick up the silver square; hoping he hadn't seen me drop it and hoping it still worked. It was one of those disc cameras with the round negatives. He had already turned back to the boys, who were not having any of it.

"Can we just go back to the hotel now?" asked the older child.

"No. We are not leaving this beach until I get one decent photo of all of us together. Eyes open, nice smiles, looking at the camera, etc., etc. Is that too much to ask? I don't care if we have to sit here all damn night!" yelled the frazzled adult.

I moved closer with the camera. I put it up to my eye to see if I was close enough. When I was finally face to face with the group, I did a double take. The man looked to be around my age, maybe a little older, and he was good looking. Model or actor good looking. He ran a hand through his jet-black hair and tossed his head back like he was in a shampoo commercial. He looked like the kind of guy that did not need an introduction. He also seemed a little young to be the father of the two boys, but maybe he had an early start at parenthood.

"It would be a true miracle if we could take one nice photo together," he said as he turned to glare at each kid in turn. They were glaring right back. I think they had their fill of photos for the day.

"Okay, well…you both look like Al Pacino in Scarface. That's good, you have the tough guy faces down. Now, how about a sweet one for grandma?" I asked. No response from the kids. "Okay, now smile like you just saw Bo Derek or Kim Basinger walk by," I said hoping my lack of knowledge of current pop culture had not betrayed me.

That elicited a little smile as they both turned to look at each other and then looked back at me. They had recognized the names. I snapped several quick shots with the fading sun and ocean in the background. The man was a professional at posing for a camera. I thought there might be a few good shots of all three of them by the time we were done.

"Well…one of these should work," I said as I handed back the camera.

"Thanks," the man said and then he flashed me a brilliant, glowing white smile. "Brooks. Brooks Laughton. I am at your service Milady." he said grandiosely.

"You are welcome and…anytime," I said awkwardly looking down at my toes.

I waved and walked off feeling good for helping. The walk and ocean air had done me some good. I made my way back to my room and off to a dreamless sleep.

THE LETTER
December 19, 1988

I slept in late. The long trip the day before had caught up with me. I found some breakfast and a coffee downstairs and then I was back in my room with the suitcase and its contents spread out before me on the bed, as I had done so many times before, back in Wyoming. I was able to sort and organize a little more each time I went through it. I sat there for a couple of hours looking through photos and letters, with the sunlight and fresh air filtering through the open balcony glass.

I was getting a better picture of who my great uncle was. He was born July 5, 1912. He went to college for 2 years at NCSC at Raleigh; at least those were the initials back then. I knew from my grandmother that the family hailed from North Carolina. My grandmother had gone to college as well, in the thirties. The family must have had money back then to be able to send a female to college in the dirty thirties. It was not a common occurrence in those days.

Walter joined the Navy in 1932. He traveled around the world in the military. He must have had a photo from every bar and nightclub he ever graced with an appearance. He was in uniform in some of the photos. There he was, smiling big at a table of soldiers, all with a girl on their arm in a bar or supper club. The scenery changed but otherwise, the photos were always the same.

In those days they must have had a photographer at every club that would help the soldiers commemorate their big night for a price.

They would get a nice glossy print in a cardboard sleeve with the logo and name of the club on the outside. Walter had a lot of these mementos.

There was a folded-up map that had writing and red lines showing the campaigns that his unit participated in during World War II. There was a letter from the Navy Department with a Presidential Unit Citation, including an insignia. He was in the military for more than ten years but not active duty the entire time.

His occupation on the military forms was listed as hotel work. I found a few letters and documents from many different hotels all over the country and beyond, but the one hotel that seemed to stand out from the rest had to be the Montague. Located on the Island of Euphoria in the Bahamas, the Island that I currently found myself on. There were more photos, letters and documents from here than any other place. He was listed as the Vice President and General Manager of the hotel on several of the documents.

The pictures from that period told quite the story. Parties and Bingo in the famous Jungle Room of the hotel, with celebrities and royalty. Golfing with the rich and famous amongst the palm trees. There was my Great Uncle Walter in almost every photo, with that winning grin. It looked like a wonderful life.

I picked up the letter and reread it. It was the most interesting piece in the suitcase. It was in my Uncle's handwriting. The return address was G. Walter Fender in Chandler, Arizona. The intended recipient was a Ms. Angela Merriweather in the Bahamas. I had carefully opened the letter with a butter knife when I read it for the first time back in Buffalo, Wyoming.

A letter written by a relative I never knew. A letter that had been written but never sent...

24

November 2, 1960
85 degrees and sunny

Dear Ms. Merriweather,

Hello from an old acquaintance. I would imagine that you are quite surprised to hear from me of all people. I am terribly sorry for the way things ended and my sad departure from Euphoria. My current health situation is not so good. I feel I must make amends for many things in my life at this time. Arthur was a great man. I regret what happened between the three of us. I should have done more. My guilt still haunts me daily. I have never spoken of it to anyone and I would guess you have kept this secret as well. Unfortunately, we can never go back, no matter how much we wish it, to that more innocent time.

Could you find it in your heart to forgive me for my inaction and let time heal this wound? This is, of course, a hypothetical question that I know I may never receive an answer to. Just know that you have my sincere apology for the past and best wishes always.

Sincerely,

G. Walter Fender

I was puzzled by the letter. The most curious thing was that the letter had been dated November 2nd of 1960. That would mean the letter was written just days before Walter's death. Written but never sent. What could have moved him to write such a moving apology at the end of his life and more than three years after leaving the Bahamas?

It was the mystery that I felt obliged to investigate. The mystery that had pushed me into taking this trip. Maybe I could find Angela. She must have been important to my great uncle and she obviously deserved an apology from him for something that happened between them on this Island. It was conceivable that she was still around. This was one small act that I could do for the family I never really knew. It was crazy, but this letter was why I had come all the way to the Bahamas. I wanted to find Angela and deliver it to her in person.

A rereading of the letter stirred me into action. I grabbed the phone book off the credenza. Of course, there was no Merriweather in the phone book, but I did find a street map. I had her address from the envelope of the letter. Based on my bus ride yesterday, I guessed that the address was not in the best part of town, but it was daylight and I figured it would be safe to go snooping around during the day. I put the letter into one of my bags, the larger one, and checked to make sure the mace that Dad had given me was packed along with some other essentials. I opened the room safe. I grabbed some cash and one credit card to take with me.

I took a hotel shuttle across the bridge to the heart of the City. I exited the bus at a tourist area of local shops and street vendors. It was very near to my destination. I took my time walking around and stopping to look at the local wares. The sunshine felt warm on my shoulders. I bought a few trinkets for friends and family back home. I also purchased a folded-up map of the entire Island from a little corner shop.

I consulted my map and decided to go look for Ms. Merriweather's house. As I walked away from the market area the buildings became more run down and garbage fluttered around in the streets. I unconsciously found myself walking faster. I located the street I needed and turned right. Loud music blared from an open second-floor window. Two more blocks down, and then a left turn, and I was there. 545 E. High Street was the address.

I found the house, and it was no surprise, that it was as run down as the rest of the surrounding neighborhood. I don't think anyone had cleaned or painted it since my Uncle had lived on the Island. It may have been nice at one time when it was brand new, but it was hard to see it. The paint was so faded that I wasn't sure what the original color had been. It had mutated to a dingy and colorless gray.

I marched up to the front door and willed myself to knock before I lost my nerve. No response so I knocked again, louder. This time I heard movements from inside. The door slowly creaked open.

"Yeah?" the resident inside questioned. All I could see was an eyeball through the crack in the door. It was a younger, local female judging by the accent and voice.

"Hi. Um…I was looking for someone. Does Angela live here? Angela Merriweather?"

"Who?" she said angrily.

"I'm looking for Angela Merriweather…do you know her?"

Laughter.

"I am sorry to bother you, but do you happen to know an Angela that used to live here at one time? I have something for her."

"Look…she don't live here. I lived here for two years now. I ain't buying whatever you trying to sell me, believe that. Girl Scout cookies…Avon…whatever. I ain't buying. Now get out my face," she hollered, and with that, she slammed the door.

I stood on the doorstep staring at the weathered wood of the door for a few seconds before I turned to go back toward the tourist market. What a way to start but did I really think it would be so easy? Did I really think I would find Angela? I would just give her the letter and she would empty her soul to me and tell me all about Walter and their days at the glamourous Montague Hotel? She is probably long gone just like Great Uncle Walter. Probably died before I was even born too. That would be my luck. All this way for nothing.

I was halfway back to the tourist market when I heard a loud noise that startled me out of feeling sorry for myself. I turned to look. It was just some kids across the street kicking a bottle around. The oldest couldn't be more than thirteen.

I turned back and picked up the pace until I heard another noise directly behind me this time. The kids had crossed over to my side of the street. There were five of them. The youngest was dragging a hula hoop and a couple of them had no shoes. The oldest kid ran in front of me and I stopped.

"Hey lady. Hello. Can we carry your bags for you or give you free directions? You shouldn't be hanging out around here by yourself. There are some bad dudes that live in this neighborhood," the kid said with a wide grin.

He was a tall, skinny dark-skinned kid. His clothes were patched up hand me downs that were a size too big. He wore a faded Yankees baseball cap on his head, with the bill pulled down low.

"Thanks, but I am just going back to the market down the block. I'm Sunny, what's your name?"

Instead of responding, they all took off running after two of the younger kids grabbed my purse and bag of souvenirs from behind. DAMN IT! I didn't even bother to try and chase them. They were gone from sight in a matter of seconds. Well, at least I only had one credit card in my bag. Most of my money and other cards were back in my hotel room safe. But even worse than losing a credit card and my can of mace was the fact that I had just lost the letter for Angela.

I made my way dejectedly back to the market and waited for a hotel shuttle. I explained to the bus driver that I had my purse stolen and I didn't have my shuttle pass, which was required to use the bus.

He gave me the benefit of the doubt and I slunk into the nearest available seat. All the passengers were watching me.

† † †

I got off the bus in front of my hotel and went to the customer service desk. The girl at the counter was not phased at all by my story. Probably a common occurrence with all the gullible tourists. She was helpful and gave me a new room key and let me use the phone to cancel the lost credit card. She said maintenance would be by shortly to switch out the lock on my door for security measures.

I felt like an idiot. I decided to go back up to my room for a bit. I needed something to eat and then maybe I would go down to the beach. Maybe that would improve my mood. I was angry and wanting to give up on Walter. This was all a big waste of time.

I walked over to the elevators and found an open door. There were already some people in the elevator. I recognized one of them as the man I had taken a picture of the previous night on the beach, the one with the two boys. I managed a weak smile and then I quickly looked away. His sons were not with him.

The others on the elevator surrounded him and chatted amicably with him. He seemed to be the center of attention. One man pulled out a piece of paper and asked for his autograph. Brooks obliged and then everyone exited the elevator on the fourth floor, except for Brooks and me.

"How's the photographer today?" he asked. He had recognized me. Most of the time it seemed like I disappeared into the scenery. People were always reintroducing themselves to me, even after we had already met on a different occasion.

"Great...just another day in paradise, sunny and seventy-eight degrees," I said, and then giggled stupidly, laughing at my inside joke. Uncle Walter's letters always included a weather report.

"Really? Cause you look like someone just ran over your cat."

That made me laugh even more. He gave me a strange glance.

"So, are you a celebrity or something? I noticed you signing an autograph for that man," I said, as I tried to change the subject. I didn't want to bore him with my wreck of a day.

"Well, actually, I am. I've been in several movies."

"Really? What movies? Not sure if I will recognize them though. I am more of a book person. I don't get to very many movies."

"*Doomsday Apocalypse? Ghost of the Battle-bot? War Zone of Terror 2000?*"

"Ahh...nope."

"*Creature from Death Island?*"

"Nope."

"Well, you aren't really my target audience, are you," he said with a wink. It was more of a statement than a question. "And what about you? Why so glum...really?" he persisted.

"Well, it is a long story...no...not really a long story. Just a little boring and too painful to tell without bruising my ego and making me feel like a complete fool. I would not want to do that in front of you..." I said as my cheeks turned red. "You or anyone for that matter," I said trying to cover my tracks.

"Hey...no judgment here...promise."

"Well...it all started with a suitcase...and then a letter for an Angela, that had never been delivered. I stupidly thought I could make things right for something that happened thirty years ago...but you don't care about all that. Anyway, my great uncle used to live and work on this very Island way back when, at a local hotel. He died before I was born. I inherited his belongings when my grandmother, his sister, passed away recently..." I did not want to talk about my rejection and robbery and besides my inner voice was yelling at me to shut my mouth. *Why would this complete stranger be interested in your excuse for an adventure,* she asked me?

"Sorry to hear it. This is your stop," he said as he moved into the doorway to keep the doors from closing. I walked out past him noticing that his room was on the top floor. It must be nice to be in one of the suites on the fifteenth floor. I bet the view was incredible. Brooks was living the life of the other half as Walter had at one time.

"Hey…just out of curiosity…where did your uncle work? I was born on this Island. I know a lot about this place."

"He worked at the Montague Hotel. I was hoping to go see it while I was here."

"Interesting…I know the place. Guess you should have done your homework before coming all the way down here, though. That hotel was demolished a few years back. It was condemned at first and then they finally tore it down. All that is left are a few crumbling foundations."

"Well the way this day is going, that is exactly what I would expect to hear. Strike three. I was really hoping to find something, anything really. Just trying to connect with my past. Stupid, huh?"

"No, not really. What did you say your Uncle's name was?"

"Great uncle. It was Walter… G. Walter Fender that is."

He stepped quickly out of the elevator, surprising me a bit with how fast he moved. I stepped backward.

"Hey…there is a bonfire down on the beach tonight. You should check it out. I will buy you a drink, even though you have no idea what good cinema is," he said with a grin and a wink. "What did you say your name was?"

"I'm Sunny McQueen," I said, extending my hand.

"Of course you are. See you at eight, down on the beach."

He reached out to shake my hand and then he stepped back into the elevator and the doors slid shut. I smiled and walked down the hallway to my room. My feet never touched the hallway carpet. My cheeks felt warm and good old Ivey was silent for a change.

🌴 🌴 🌴

It was all too soon eight o'clock in the evening and I was in my hotel room with all my clothes dumped out onto my bed in a panic. I hadn't really packed much but I hoped casual attire would be

31

SHERYL COLEY

appropriate for a bonfire on the beach. I found some cut-off jeans and a tank top. I added a white hooded sweater. The breeze off the ocean might be cool at night. I was anxious. I decided to let my hair have a break from my usual ponytail and I even added some makeup which I had not applied since I left home. I didn't wear it very often anyway. I wanted to drink a couple of beers and forget about my waste of a day. I would start fresh tomorrow.

I tried not to dwell on the fact that I was excited about Brooks invitation to the bonfire. It made me feel like a silly school girl. I was too old for that and I had a good boyfriend back home. David was everything a person should want. He was safety and security. But if I were to put into words what I was to him, it seemed much less. I was a puzzle piece that fit into his perfectly planned life. Just a link in the chain. That's not to say he didn't love me, but he just took me for granted.

Brooks seemed exciting and edgy, the opposite of David. I could not deny the boost to my ego. I was entitled to a little fun on this trip, wasn't I? It wasn't like I was going to date Brooks and dump David. But I couldn't deny my attraction for Brooks even though I tried to play it down.

I took a last look in the bathroom mirror. I would have to do. Go have some fun I told myself again. My inner antagonist laughed. I hated her. I found my flipflops and my small bag, which I had refilled with essentials from the lobby store to replace what had been stolen. Then I headed out the door and down to the beach.

There were people everywhere, laughing and dancing. An Island band was playing loud music. Steel drums. I found myself swaying to the tunes floating in the air and smiling. There were three big bonfires going with chairs set up all around. I was not sure if I would be able to find Brooks, but I did find a bar cart. I ordered a local bottled beer and took a big drink. It was a Kalik Crisp and it went down smoothly.

I kept moving and circled my way around all three bonfires, and then I ordered another beer. I sat down on an open beach chair

32

with my new drink. The soft breeze caressed my cheeks and tousled my hair back. The moonlight danced off the ocean waves. I watched all the tanned bodies moving about and chatting happily in the warm glow of the fires. I felt like an outsider eavesdropping on a conversation. Maybe I was wrong to come. Maybe I should have stayed in my room where I would be alone. That was where I felt the most comfortable. Then I wouldn't feel like a fish out of water.

I was just thinking about finding another beer and possibly a bathroom when I saw Brooks Laughton through the flames. His eyes sparkled in the glow. He was talking to a gorgeous blonde in a bikini. He had a hand nonchalantly resting on the small of her back and his other hand held a cocktail glass. I couldn't look away. They looked beautiful together, two perfect people. So far out of my league that they may as well be in a different universe.

He caught sight of me then. Without taking his eyes off me he leaned in to whisper in her ear and then kiss her cheek, smiling all the while. Then he started making his way over to where I sat. It took a few minutes as he was stopped by many of the partygoers along the way. He must have known everyone on the beach and he knew they were all watching him as he sauntered across the sand. He was used to being watched. I was really rethinking coming down to the party. Why did I think he would want to hang out with me; and yet here he was walking my way.

"Well there she is…the world's biggest action movie fan!" he said as he casually plopped down into the empty chair beside mine. "I hope your day has improved since we last met." He flagged down a server and motioned for a round of drinks for the two of us.

"Yes, much better," I said as I looked down at my toes.

"Great. I was starting to wonder if you were going to stand me up for our first date," he said, with a frown and a wink.

"Looks like you found a replacement," I said cattily, surprising myself and immediately regretting it. But he only laughed.

"The blonde? She was an extra in one of my movies. There's an acting convention going on at this resort and you have just crashed the beach party."

"Oh," I said still feeling like a fool and wishing I had never brought up the blonde. What right did I have to be jealous? We were both silent for a moment. I looked down at my un-manicured toenails as I wriggled them around in the sand. The server showed up with another round.

"So…how are your boys doing? I haven't seen them today. Do you need me to coax another photo out of them?"

He laughed again.

"Well, …they're actually my cousin's sons. Marlena Manderson, she's like a sister to me. I'm an only child. No brothers or sisters. She let me fly them out for a few days before the convention started. They flew back home this morning. I miss them already. Good kids…just don't ask them to take a damn photo."

Then it was my turn to laugh. He stood up and grabbed my hand pulling me up off the chair. His hand was warm and soft and easily wrapped all the way around mine, making it feel small.

"Well, I won't forget her name. Manderson is the name of the town that my aunt lives in, back in Wyoming."

"I should have known you were from the Midwest. Come on then. Let's mingle."

I let him lead me around the bonfires and introduce me to many of the people enjoying the party. There was a reggae song playing. It was nice. I knew I would never remember any of their names even if they were famous, but they were all so friendly. I imagined that this would have been what Walter's life was like here on the Island. Party after party with celebrities and the rich and famous all around. Brooks ordered another round for us and the people we happened to be chatting with.

My head was starting to spin, and it was getting late. I felt a little sad because no matter how hard Brooks tried, I didn't feel like I really belonged, deep down.

"Brooks, this has been amazing, but it is getting late and I have had a very long day. I think it is time for me to head up to my room," I said.

"No…don't leave yet. Can we go somewhere a little quieter maybe?"

"Okay…for a bit. I really appreciate you introducing me to literally everyone on this beach!"

He grabbed my hand again and pulled me along the beach and back towards our hotel. I liked the feel of his warm sheltering hand around mine. We entered the lobby and then he turned toward a quiet lounge that was just to the right of the lobby area. Soft elevator music wafted out of the dim, smoky bar. There was a huge grand piano sitting in the middle of the bar with seating and booths on three sides and the bar on the fourth. The fallboard of the piano was down, and the bench was empty. The entire hotel was out on the beach at the bonfire, so we had the place mostly to ourselves. We found a small table and Brooks ordered a couple more drinks. Mine sat untouched.

"So…I was just curious. I wanted to hear more about your uncle. I have been thinking a lot about what you told me in the elevator," he said.

"Well, it's really a long and boring story."

"It sounds fascinating to me. Go on. Tell me more."

"Well…I was adopted and when I reconnected with my biological grandmother, she was ninety-one years old already. That was Christmas of nineteen eighty-six. I got to spend a couple of years getting to know her before she passed. I ended up with all her belongings after she died. That's how I got the suitcase that belonged to my great uncle. His whole life was crammed into that one piece of luggage.

"I found everything in it, but the strangest thing…the thing that really peaked my curiosity was a letter that he had written but never sent. It was written days before he died. It was addressed to a lady here on the Island. Of course, I opened it. I figured it was okay since it was almost thirty years old and my uncle was long gone. The letter was an apology from him to this lady, Angela…but for what I don't know.

"I guess I just thought that I could come down here and find her and deliver the letter myself after all these years. Maybe she would tell me about him. I really thought it would be that easy but of course, she didn't live at the address anymore, and she is not in the phone book either. Strike two was getting robbed by some school-age kids who stole my purse which happened to have the letter in it and a credit card…and some money. They even took some damn souvenirs that I had just bought."

"What horrible luck," he said as he took a swig of his drink.

"Yeah, I know. I thought this trip might be a way to learn more about my real family. I know very little about any of them and they are mostly gone now except for me…and my biological mother. But she is a whole other story and it's worse than the one I just told. You know, I think maybe I made a big mistake coming here and I need to get my head out of the clouds. It's hard to stay positive when I keep taking the wrong turn at every corner and it has only been day one of my search. Sorry…I've been rambling. It's really not much of a story."

"Actually, it is a great story. I must admit…I have my ulterior motives here. This could be huge. You have the makings of a blockbuster for sure. You must promise me that you will keep me posted on whatever else you do or find while you are here, okay? Anything at all. Even the smallest detail. I am thinking this story would make an incredible movie project. Of course, we would need to get some writers involved, but I am getting ahead of myself. We also need some big action to push this story over the top…but there is definitely something there…I'm sure of it."

I was a little shocked. I had not expected anything like this. I didn't really know if I agreed with him since everything had gone wrong so far, but something about his excitement made me hopeful.

"Now Sunny, please keep this quiet for now. There are a lot of Hollywood types bumbling around this Island right now. I don't want any of them getting wind of this. Just promise you will keep me in the loop, okay. One other thing – what was the name of this lady that your uncle's letter was addressed to? You did say…Angela?"

"Oh…yes, it was Angela Merriweather."

"Well, we will have to change the names to protect the innocent of course," he said with a wink.

That made me laugh out loud, but I agreed to it. How could I not? With that, he stood up and kissed my cheek and then exited the bar. I guzzled half the beer he had bought me and then made my way to my hotel room, feeling excited, and also a little confused.

THE MONTAGUE HOTEL
December 20, 1988

I was dreaming of Bobby again. He started visiting me after I had reconnected with my grandmother. That connection had pulled him out of the depths. He would sneak in at night sometimes. Usually early morning, right before I would wake. He scared me in my dreams. His face was not that of the sweet little boy that I barely remembered. It was twisted and tortured. The eyes were too big in his head and open in a look of constant surprise. He kept them so wide open so that he didn't miss anything, at least that's what I used to think when we were little. But in my dreams, it became a grotesque caricature.

The memories that I had of him were faded old photos. Worn images. Not real memories of living interaction. He would come, just before waking to startle me out of my sleep. During that in-between time where dreams could be whisked away so easily like a dropped glass that shatters to the ground. Lost forever. Maybe it was better that way than to remember his face too clearly.

I threw a pillow at the glass patio doors to distract myself from thoughts of Bobby. The bright sunlight streaming through the glass was making me mad. I guess I should have closed the curtains last night. I sat up still in the same clothes I had worn to the bonfire. My purse was draped across my shoulder. My head was pounding. I needed a big coffee and some food. My inner demon laughed at me and told me I deserved a good hangover for thinking I was in Brook's league.

I stumbled into the bathroom and took a long steamy shower. Then I slipped into some shorts and a button-down plaid camp shirt. I put in my usual ponytail and no makeup. I was feeling better after last night's distraction, but I wanted to get back to business. I grabbed the phone book and plopped down onto the bed. An idea had come to mind as I had showered up.

I found a listing for The Island Historical Society. I looked up the address on the map. It was near the tourist market that I had visited yesterday. Nothing like returning to the scene of the crime, at least that's what they always did in the best detective novels. This time I would be much more cautious though, plus, the Society was closer to the market than Angela's house had been. Not so far off the beaten path. I could even replace the stolen souvenirs. Just thinking about it raised my blood pressure.

I would stop at the kiosk in the lobby and rent a scooter for the day instead of taking the bus. The weather was beautiful and there were some other places I was hoping to check out. I would need to replace my street map as well. That had been in my missing purse also.

I grabbed my little bag and draped it over my shoulder and then went to the door. I stopped short when I saw an envelope on the floor. Someone had slid it under the door. It was addressed simply, "*S*". I opened it and slid out the cardstock note.

Yacht party tonight – glamourous Hollywood types
Will you be my date? 6 PM at the dock
Stop in the boutique downstairs – ask for Karen
How goes the sleuthing, Sherlock?

B

I couldn't stop myself from smiling. At least it was not until six. That would still give me lots of time to do some searching. It was hard to refute the boost to my ego, but why would Brooks want to hang out with me when Bikini Blonde was around? There was something there between us though – a spark of something; a connection. He seemed genuinely interested in what I had to say. That was rare. I liked hanging out with him, I had to admit it. But I still felt uncertain.

I walked to the elevator and down to the lobby. I found the boutique. I never would have shopped at a place like it; too fancy and too expensive. I went up to the counter and asked for Karen. She came over to the counter smiling. She looked me up and down in a judgmental way and the smile faded. She cut an impressive figure with her big blonde hair, phony blue eyeshadow, and neon pink lips.

"You must be Sunny. Brooks said to help you out and let me say, you're going to need a lot of help. Go try this on. Brooks picked it out himself. Dressing rooms are at the back," she said dismissing me as she handed me a garment bag on a hanger.

I made my way to the back and found an open dressing room. I went in and closed the curtain. I placed the bag on a hook and unzipped it. It was stunning. A beautiful, yet simple, flowy white cocktail dress. It had a low neckline and bare shoulders. There was no price tag. I had many reservations about accepting such a gift from someone I barely knew, but I decided to go along with it anyway. The only bad thing about the dress was that it was the wrong size. I had to go ask Karen for the next size up. She smirked and rolled her eyes. She went into the back and came out with the next two larger sizes.

I took them back to the changing room and undressed. I slipped on one of the dresses trying desperately not to rip it. It was beautiful and very flattering although part of my bra was showing because it was so low cut in the front and on the sides. I would have to find some different things to wear underneath. Last time I wore anything like this was prom, only not nearly as glamorous or exposing. My prom dress had big, pink, puffy shoulders. I felt like I had to turn sideways to go through doors when I had worn it. This dress made me feel like a real princess. Karen helped me find the appropriate undergarments and then she said she would have everything delivered to my room right away.

My next stop was the customer service kiosk in the lobby where I rented a scooter for the day. Then I was ready to head out across the bridge and back to the real Island. Key in hand, I walked out of the lobby to find a scooter waiting out front. There was a helmet on the seat. I put it on and hopped onto the motor bike. I headed out of the resort property and on to the small bridge, crossing over to the mainland. I remembered the route from the bus rides. The hot air felt unusually still. The sun beat down, softening the asphalt.

I parked on the same street as the now familiar tourist market. I would grab some souvenirs after I checked out the Historical Society, but I did decide to grab a new map first. I went back to the little shop where I had bought my first map. I recognized the clerk that was working. He looked at me funny but never said anything. I was sure he remembered me from the day before. I went back outside and unfolded the map to study it. Over the top of my map, some movement caught my attention and I looked across the street.

It was one of the juvenile delinquents from yesterday. The oldest one. He had a little folding card table set up on the edge of the tourist market and he had some things spread out on the table. My souvenirs. He was trying to sell them to people passing by. He was smiling big and making wide gestures like a game show host talking to his contestants. I was fuming, but I made myself stop and calm down. I had the advantage. He hadn't seen me yet. I kept my map up and headed down the street, so I could cross and circle around. I would approach him from behind. None of the other kids were around either, that was good.

He was talking to some tourists as I walked up behind him and grabbed the back of his tank top. He turned to look at me and there was recognition, along with fear on his face. His customers started yelling at me. He threw his hands up and slid himself right out of the shirt that I had a hold of, but the element of surprise was in my favor. He stumbled and crashed into the card table as he tried to escape. Souvenirs went flying and he fell to the ground.

"He is selling you stuff he stole from me yesterday!" I shouted at his customers. Then I stooped down to grab him by the shoulders. The tourists took off deciding it would be best to stay out of it.

"You have some nerve kid!" I yelled as I glared down at him. He wouldn't even look at me.

"I'm sorry…you can have all your stuff back…at least what didn't sell already…"

I looked around at my scattered souvenirs. Half of them were broken. I didn't really care about the stupid souvenirs anymore, but I was mad because he had taken advantage of me. As I glared down at him, I noticed that there was something wrong with his right hand. It was deformed, and the fingers were curled up. My anger began to subside. He saw me looking at his damaged appendage and he moved it around behind his back.

"Why are you doing this? Why aren't you in school? I want to talk to your parents, kid."

"No…please don't. They will tan my hide, and good," he said as he finally looked at me. That had hit a nerve.

"Well, why aren't you in school, kid?"

"We're on break now."

"Okay…well, I might consider not telling your parents on a couple of conditions," I said, as an idea began to form.

"Anything, what?"

"Okay. First, I need your help…I need your help finding some places while I am here on the Island. Would you do that? Would you be my tour guide?"

"Sure…okay."

"Second, I need you to promise me that you will stop stealing."

"Okay, I promise," he said very convincingly, but I had my doubts.

"Oh…and third, I want the rest of my stuff back. My purse and all the contents."

"Hey, you said two things," he said as he shook a finger at me.

"Alright, see that constable across the street? I bet he can help me find your parents."

"Okay, okay, but I don't have the rest of your stuff. The other kids took it. I just wanted the souvenirs to sell, see?" he said gesturing toward his knocked over table with his messed-up hand.

I let go of him and stood up slowly. I half expected him to bolt but he didn't.

"What is your name, kid?"

"Charles, ma'am."

"Well, Charles…I'm Sunny. Pack up your stuff and stash it, then meet me at the Island Historical Society in about an hour or so. You might even earn some cash instead of having to steal it, understand?"

"Yes, ma'am!"

"Keep the souvenirs too."

I wasn't sure if I would see him again or not, but it would be helpful to have someone familiar with the Island to help me find some places. I hoped I had won him over. He was packing up as I headed down the street to the Historical Society. Maybe I would see him again…

🌴 🌴 🌴

The Historical Society landed right in the middle of a block of row houses which all looked identical. A small sign jutted out perpendicularly from the front façade of the building. That was the only thing that differentiated it from the others. I opened the screen door and proceeded in through the large wooden door behind it.

The building had been opened up on the inside. It was all white walls and pale wood floors. Large glass windows adorned the front of the building, toward the street. The second-floor structure above had been painted black and track lights hung down. There were some partial height walls down the middle that held various displays. There looked to be a small office with a window in the back-left corner and maybe a workroom on the other side.

A portly gentleman in polyester pants and a short sleeve shirt with oversized tie stumbled out of the office. He was finishing a bite of lunch.

"Welcome to the museum. My name is Roger Hodair," he said with a thick British accent. "May I be of some assistance?"

"Hi. Well...I...maybe, yes."

"Which is it, then?"

"Okay. Let me start over. Hello, my name is Sunny McQueen, and this may sound a little strange, but I recently inherited some belongings of my great uncle's. He lived on Euphoria back in the Fifties. I've been looking through his stuff and I have become fascinated with it all. I know...sounds kind of crazy. Just looking to see if I could find more information. I have been obsessed with it, actually. He worked at the Montague Hotel. Do you know the place?"

"Ohhh yes, how interesting. Yes, I know of the hotel. It was only torn down three years ago, but it had been abandoned many years before that. It was an opulent and glamorous place back in its' heyday, in the Forties and Fifties, that is. That hotel was *The Place* to see and be seen. This Island was the gem of the Bahamas back then. Not too many people come here now, but they are trying to restore the Island back to its former glory with all the fancy new resorts. We have a whole catalog of press releases and many odds and ends from the hotel," he said as he leaned in close to me and put a hand on my shoulder. I could smell the garlic on his breath.

"Would you like to look through our archives? Maybe do some further research?" he asked.

"That would be a dream come true. As I said, I would love to learn more about the hotel and my uncle's past. Would you really let me look through your files?"

44

"Of course. That is why we are here. It has been years since anyone has looked through those archives. I will have to track them down for you. I would be interested in seeing your Uncle's items as well. Maybe you have some things that we don't. Did you happen to bring his belongings?"

"Yes."

"Grand. We can make a trade. Not literally, of course, I would never part with the museum pieces, but maybe I can make some copies of your items if you will allow me that liberty. The hotel was built in 1929 and it is of great historical importance here on the Island of Euphoria. England colonized this Island long before that. There are over seven hundred islands and cays that make up the Bahamas. Very few are inhabited though.

"Soldiers stayed at the hotel during World War II. The hotel was the Island Stock Exchange building as well, at least for a time. There is a great deal of rich history there. I was so disappointed when they tore it down. We tried to raise funds for preservation efforts, but it was just too big of a task. It was a terrible loss for the Island, historically speaking."

"That is amazing. I would love to learn more about the place. I am just here for a couple of weeks though. How about I come back tomorrow? I will bring my great uncle's suitcase."

"Of course. Come back first thing in the morning and we will get started right away. I'll set out some of the archives for you. What was your Uncle's name by the way?"

"Great uncle. His name was Walter Fender…G. Walter Fender."

"Oh yes, he was the Vice President and General Manager back in the Fifties."

"Yes. So, you know him?"

"Of him, my dear. He is in almost every picture and press release from those times. His name was on all the brochures. He was very popular with the ladies, eh? At least that is what I have heard…that's how the rumors went. He was even around during the Murray Scandal…the biggest scandal of the hotel…the biggest unsolved mystery of the Island's history for that matter. It was big news even over in Miami at the time.

"Murray had money. Miami was the jumping off point for travelers coming to our Island back then. The case was never solved but there were many theories and many suspects. They even brought some detectives from Miami down to the Island. Of course, they didn't have the forensic capabilities that they do now. Maybe the crime would have been solved if they did. Rumor has it, his wife and family didn't want a big investigation. They were afraid of what might be dredged up if you know what I mean. Murray was one of the investor-slash-owners of the hotel. He would fly down almost every weekend for some fun in the sun. He and your Uncle were chums, very tight. Parties and ladies every chance they got."

"Walter was my great uncle," I corrected, not knowing what else to say. This was all interesting, but I wasn't sure how to process the news.

"Well, Murray was new money, he struck it rich in Canada – owned an oil field. He invested heavily down here on the Island due to the favorable tax situation back then. Quite the philanthropist around here too. Oh, and definitely a ladies' man like your Uncle.

"There wasn't much left that was identifiable when they found his body in one of the penthouse suites at the top of the hotel. He had been doused with petrol and set on fire. Lucky the whole bloody building didn't burn down. The Montague was touted as completely fireproof when it was built though, and it proved true. It was built a couple of years after a bugger of a fire at the Royal Colonial Hotel. Peculiar thing is, the Royal still stands after being rebuilt, and the Montague is gone forever now."

My buddy Charles happened to crash through the door right at that moment. The museum curator looked up, surprised to see the street kid. He pushed his thick glasses up on his nose.

"No public loo's in here," Roger said directly to Charles.

"Hi Charles," I said, moving toward the door. "He's with me. Right on time, Charles. Thanks so much for your time, Mr. Hodair.

I will see you first thing in the morning. Goodbye now," I said as I grabbed Charles by the shoulders and pushed him back out the door he had just entered through.

🌴 🌴 🌴

We were out in the dazzling sunshine, but I could see some clouds building in the distance. My mind was racing. It was time that I paid a visit to the Montague Hotel, or at least what was left of it. I had no idea what I would find there, but I wanted to see the place for myself.

I couldn't wait to come back to the Historical Society in the morning. Roger Hodair was a treasure trove of knowledge and anxious to share. I was lucky to have found him and I was eager to see what else I could learn. It was already noon. I needed to find some lunch and then go to the hotel. Then I needed to get ready for the party with Brooks.

"Hey, ma'am, where we going to?"

"Follow me," I said as I walked over to my moped. I handed Charles the only helmet and then hopped on the bike. I motioned for him to climb on the back. He looked at me funny but shrugged and climbed on. He managed the helmet surprisingly well with his one good hand. I wondered if he had been born left-handed or if he became left handed due to necessity. I didn't ask.

I drove a few blocks with the island breeze in my hair and Charles' hands resting on my shoulders. I pulled over to the curb when I spotted a street vendor. We got off and I bought a couple of sandwiches and two bottles of Coke. We walked across the street to a neighborhood park and sat down on a bench. We ate in silence. Charles was a fast eater. He gulped down the coke, which he had saved for last and then let out a loud belch and smiled. His smile was infectious.

"Thanks for coming, Charles. I wasn't sure if you would."

"Well, you did say there would be cash, right?"

"Yes, of course."

"Then I'm your man."

"Do you know where the old Montague Hotel used to be at? The one they tore down a few years ago."

"Sure, but why you want to go there? There ain't nothing there now."

"That's okay, I just want to see where it used to be."

"Well...okay. It's past the cruise ship docks, by the beach on Bay Street. It's your dime lady."

"Thanks, my man," I said as I pulled down the bill of his raggedy Yankees cap. He smiled in response with a completely unguarded expression. I liked it. I finished my sandwich and we took off on the bike again.

Charles tapped my right or left shoulder depending on which way we needed to turn. We drove a couple of miles inland toward the center of the Island and then turned West toward the coastline. As we moved closer to the ocean, I could smell it rising in my nostrils. That salty smell mixed with hot tar and bleached wood. Charles gestured and hollered in my ear for me to stop when we reached our destination.

The old hotel ruins sat on an overgrown grassy area. We were on a street that separated the abandoned hotel property from the beach so there was a wide-open view of the ocean from where the Hotel used to stand. A few people wandered along the shoreline in their shorts and flip-flops, a mixture of tourists and locals. I could see the towers of the hotel I was staying at a long way down the seashore. The towers were so big that it was hard to miss them from almost anywhere on the Island I guessed.

The crumbling gray concrete dock of the Montague Hotel stood out in stark contrast to the vibrant towers. I recognized the dock from images I had seen. Back in the day, it was full of life. Fisherman would lay out their fresh catches along it to be sized up and prepped for cooking. Tanned tourists stood on the dock, staring wistfully out to sea in the vintage photos from the suitcase.

It was afternoon by then and clouds were moving closer to shore. Charles hopped off the bike and replaced the helmet with his crumpled baseball cap. He set the helmet on the seat of the bike. I was surprised that nothing had been rebuilt on the site. It was prime oceanfront property. Charles tapped me on the shoulder and I turned to look at him.

"This place is no good," he said. I could see he was scared.

"What's wrong," I asked with concern.

"Obeah people marked this place. Look at the trees. Something is wrong with this place. They only do that when there are bad spirits around. Look around, they put stuff in the trees to ward off the evil. I've seen this stuff before, definitely Obeah."

I turned and took a closer look. What I hadn't noticed at first glance, I now saw clearly. Old dolls, small bottles and other odds and ends hung in the trees. Not the trees right on the boulevard but the trees that were further in on the property. All the thick vegetation made it seem dark, like a forest. Hardly any sunlight reached the ground through the canopy of trees.

"Can I have my money now? I gotta go."

"Sure. Thanks, Charles. Do you need a ride? Will I see you tomorrow? I might have need of your help again."

I handed him five dollars. He said thanks and took off running, never answering my questions to him. I yelled after him. He didn't know where I was staying at or when I wanted to meet him next. He rounded a corner and was gone without looking back. I kicked a tree branch laying on the ground in frustration. What the hell was Obeah anyway?

"Hey! What's Obeah?" I yelled at the deserted street.

Oh well, I was here, and I wasn't going to waste the trip. I walked onto the property and made my way around; the trees scratched at me as I pushed my way through. It was hard to believe that there had ever been a building in the middle of what was now a jungle.

I felt like someone was watching me thanks to the creepy dolls hanging in the trees. They watched me with their vacant eyes. I bumped my head on a couple of the bottles. I found parts of the concrete foundation and I followed it around to get a sense of the footprint of the building. The place was big. I stumbled on to some tennis courts and I almost fell into a swimming pool that had a small murky pond at the bottom. I wasn't sure what I expected to find but I was feeling disappointed again. It was another dead end.

I was thinking that it was time to head back to the hotel, the nice new hotel that I was staying at when the wind really kicked up. It stirred the bottles and they made an eerie tinkling sound as they bumped against each other. I tried to retrace my steps. The wind had blown in more clouds. The clouds had darkened the afternoon sky considerably and it was even gloomier in the thick tree growth. I worked my way around the building remnants trying to get back to my starting point.

The wind gusts were growing stronger and the bottles were getting louder. It was disorienting. If I could just stay on a straight path, I should get to a street eventually. Suddenly, I noticed some lights sparkling around me. It looked like the bottles in the trees were beginning to glow. Something soft and furry brushed against my leg and I jumped. I heard a loud crash a little further away from where I was standing. That was when I lost myself and began to run in the opposite direction.

I had to get away from the lights and the noise and especially the creature that had rubbed up against me. My heart was racing. I fell a couple of times tripping over vines and roots snaking in different directions along the ground. I heard more noises, like someone or something was following me through the over-growth. And then a loud bang. I ran faster.

At last, I burst out of the trees and was back on Bay Street about a block down from where my moped was parked. I ran to it. I heard more loud noises. I jumped on the bike knocking the helmet to the ground and not caring. I started it and took off before I had my balance. The bike and I both crashed to the street a few feet away from where I started. I jumped back up and was off again.

My knee was hurting. I knew it was bleeding, but I didn't want to look at it. I did look back over my shoulder once and I could still see a glow in the trees even though my mind was telling me that was not logically possible. I faced forward and pushed the moped faster. I felt safer once I made it to the main road that went over the bridge and back to my resort complex...but I was still shaking.

Someone or something had been in the trees with me, I was sure of it. But once back amongst people and vehicles, I was starting to feel a little silly. Maybe I overreacted. It could have just been a stray cat or dog or something, but *what about the lights* my mind asked? It was a different voice, it was not Ivey's. It was more rational.

🌴 🌴 🌴

I drove the scooter up to the front door of the hotel that I was staying at. I stopped and took a deep breath. I looked down at my knee. It was a bloody mess. The valet came over and grabbed the bike without asking about the helmet that I had left back on Bay Street. I took my bag off and let it hang down to shield my knee as I limped through the lobby and over to the elevators. I was wishing I had my bigger bag, the one that had been stolen. My heart was still beating hard when I got back to my hotel room.

I walked in and saw the white party dress hanging up near the door. Damn it. I had almost forgotten. I still had plenty of time to get ready. I thought about skipping the party, but I didn't really want to do that. Besides I needed a drink badly to calm my shaking hands. I took a long hot shower. My knee didn't look quite so bad once I washed the blood and dirt off. I did my best to bandage it up. I had some things in my travel bag to patch it with. Then I slipped into the clothes that Karen had delivered and made my best attempt at some hair and makeup. My curls would never cooperate with the humidity of the Island. I went for the sloppy bun. I still felt unsteady.

I made my way back down to the lobby. It wasn't six o'clock yet, so I grabbed a sandwich and some fresh fruit from the hotel store and ate it in the lobby. Then I found my way into the piano bar, the one that Brooks and I had gone to. Time for a shot of courage and a chaser before the party. The dark wood and crowded little tables felt somehow comforting. It smelled like cherry pipe tobacco. I walked over to the bar. I was the only one there besides the bartender and piano player. The piano player was playing a tune I knew but I couldn't remember the name of it.

"What will it be, Miss?"

"A shot of something…something strong."

"Boy…that leaves it pretty wide open…"

"What do you usually do shots of? I will take one of those and a beer…Kalik Crisp please…and charge it to room 902."

He delivered the drinks. I slammed the shot down fast. It tasted like cough syrup and it felt warm sliding down my throat. I sipped at my beer listening to the soft piano music. I finally felt calmer. It was getting close to six. I got up and fished some dollars out of my purse for a tip. I put a couple down on the bar and then a couple into the cliché oversized brandy snifter on the baby grand piano.

I walked outside and down to the dock. There were lots of people milling about and I was extremely grateful for the party dress when I saw them. Some were boarding the ship, and others were standing around with cameras, hoping to get a shot of somebody famous. The boat at the end of the dock was more like a cruise ship than a yacht. It was white and grand with strings of lights hovering over the top deck. I had never been on a boat like it. I was excited to go on board and look around.

Someone grabbed my hand from behind and spun me around. It was Brooks. He looked so handsome. His jet-black hair was slicked back, and he wore a dark tuxedo to match. He flashed me a big smile. He reminded me so much of my smiling Uncle in the black and white photos just then. He did his dark hair the same way. Old Hollywood style.

"Wow, you clean up good, Nancy Drew," he said. His charm was hard to resist. He was not alone though. There was a blonde supermodel on each arm. He gave them both a kiss on the cheek and they headed up the gangway to the boat, all smiles. He made me feel so confused. I wasn't used to how the whole party scene worked, I guess.

"And how was your day?" he asked as he kissed my cheek.

"It was okay. I found the Island Historical Society. That was probably the highlight of my day."

"Well you look amazing in that dress," he said as he spun me around again, but he stopped me mid-spin.

"What the hell happened to your leg?"

"Nothing…really…just a scooter accident. I want to thank you for the dress. It is just beautiful," I said feeling my cheeks burn and trying to change the subject. The smile was gone from his face and I looked down at my shoes. I didn't know what else to say.

"Let's go get a bloody strong cocktail. Then I will introduce you to everyone on this damn boat…at least the good ones. Then you will tell me all about your day. No details left out. Come on."

He was true to his word. We boarded the boat and it headed out to sea shortly after. There were musicians playing Christmas music. People were talking and laughing, dressed in their formal dinner attire. The soft lighting from the chandeliers bathed them in their diamonds and gems, making them sparkle like glitter in sunlight. We drank champagne from crystal glasses and snacked on fancy finger foods that I didn't know the names of, served on silver platters.

Brooks introduced me to royalty, celebrities and a host of others. A few faces I remembered from the bonfire on the beach. He made sure my champagne flute stayed full. I drank so much champagne that I almost began to feel like I belonged. Maybe I could get used to this if I kept hanging out with him.

I thought I had met everyone on the boat but then I saw a tall, muscular man striding toward us like he was on a mission. He was not the typical partygoer in his worn pullover and stocking cap. He wore jeans with a frayed blow-out at the left knee. He must have boarded the wrong boat, I thought. He had a big camera with lots of attachments hanging around his neck.

"Damn it!" Brooks exclaimed when he saw him. He grabbed my hand and started in the opposite direction, but he was too late.

"Well, hello, Brooks. Merry Christmas and Happy Boxing Day and all that. I'm afraid I left your gift at home, though. I didn't know they let you back on the Island. Did the statute of limitations run out?" the stranger asked in a condescending tone as he extended his hand. He was slightly taller than Brooks and he was handsome in a masculine, unkempt way that was the opposite of Brooks classic, well-manicured, pretty-boy looks.

Brooks mumbled a response and stuck a hand out to shake.

"And who is this beautiful creature with you? Not your typical plastic blonde, like the ones I usually see you with. Take that as a compliment, Miss," he said as he grabbed my hand and kissed it.

"Sunny McQueen, this is Carter Davis. He and I grew up on the Island together. Carter, this is Sunny."

Carter took off the stocking cap and bowed with a wave of his hat. His shaggy dirty blonde hair needed combing.

"Now don't you have someone's grandmother to go photograph? You know, you could have at least dressed for the occasion instead of sticking out like a sore thumb," Brooks said snidely as he regained his composure. I had not seen this angry and annoyed side of Brooks before.

"Well I was actually here for *The Tabloid* and I know how much you like to make the pages. How about a big smile…you and Queenie? Any publicity is good publicity, right? Although your fans will be pretty shocked to see you with a brunette on your arm."

"Well, good to see you, old chap, but we were just heading up to meet the Captain of the ship. He was going to let Sunny steer, I was going to surprise her."

"Oh…but Queenie has an empty glass. She can't meet the Captain with an empty glass. You must first remedy this situation, old chap. Off you go," Carter said smiling but his eyes bored intently into Brooks. Brooks glared back at Carter and then looked at my champagne flute. He dejectedly hurried off with it. Carter turned to look at me, with a frown on his face.

"May I take your picture," he said to me as he slid his stocking cap back on his head.

"Well, sure, I guess so," I said, taken off guard. His arrogant attitude had left with Brooks. They had been trying to one-up each other and I didn't like it.

"Okay. Over by the railing, foot up on the bottom rail. Head down looking at the sea." There were still streaks of color in the sky, but the light was beginning to fade.

"Queenie, you do hang with some odd company, I must say." I could sense that he was choosing his words carefully. "Okay, now, your back to the railing…arch your back…turn your head to the left…look up at the sky. Perfect. Beautiful." He came over to me and repositioned me. He leaned in close and deeply inhaled, close to my hair. I felt myself tensing up at the awkward gesture. I felt on edge. He snapped a few more photos then he moved close again and grabbed my shoulders. He was looking down into my eyes with a soft expression on his face. He smiled.

"You seem like a nice girl, so be cautious Queenie, okay? Brooks Laughton doesn't do anything that's not in his own best interest. Please don't take this the wrong way but I am truly having a hard time seeing what you two would have in common. You have piqued my curiosity. Don't let him use you, okay?" he said as he brushed my cheek with a light kiss. Brooks came stumbling back over to us, with a couple filled glasses in hand, as the ship ran into some choppy waters.

"Carter, you are a true asshole. Always have been always will be. I was gone for five minutes and you are already kissing my date? Some things never change do they."

"Cool your jets, Haircut. I was just thanking Sunny for letting me take her picture. In fact, I have a little studio in the city, back on the Island. That is my real passion, not taking photos of self-indulgent phonies. But unfortunately, *The Tabloid* pays better. Queenie – would you come down to my studio and let me take some more photos of you? I know some great locations around Euphoria. I have an exhibit coming up and I think I just found my muse," he said. I could hear that the brashness had come back into his voice.

"Wow, that would be an honor, but I am not a model. I am the opposite of a model. You flatter me, but you really need some better material."

"Nonsense, you are real and beautiful. I am so tired of these dime-a-dozen plastic princesses flying in from California, or wherever they come from," he said with a meaningful glance at Brooks as he handed me his business card. I was feeling like a mouse between two cats. Maybe if I said yes to the photos Carter would leave us alone, but I couldn't do it tomorrow, I had to be at the museum. Or maybe I would just blow him off completely…

"Okay, thank you but not tomorrow. It would have to be the next day."

"10 AM, then?"

"Perfect."

Carter willfully leaned in for another kiss on my cheek as he glared at Brooks. Then he slipped away through the crowd.

"Wow! I am so sorry. That guy is such an asshole. I always seem to run into him whenever I come back to the Island. Not sure how he always finds me? He makes good money at being a paparazzi stalker, though. He plays the part perfectly. He's probably just trying to get a story about me for his rag of a magazine. Just be careful around him and don't let him use you to get at me, okay?"

"Yes, okay. He seems harmless enough, really."

"He was nothing but an immature jerk when we were growing up. I think he is jealous that I made it off this rock and he never did. Bad things always seem to follow whenever he's around. Let's head up to the bridge to meet the Captain. What do you say? Sorry,

Carter had to spoil my plans. The Captain said we could steer the ship. I really wanted to surprise you," he said, with a disarming grin.

"That sounds amazing. Lead the way," I said, feeding off his contagious excitement.

The view from the bridge was breathtaking. The boat was pointed back toward the Island by then, it was a glittering beacon in the distance. I am not sure how much steering I really accomplished but it was fun to pretend. Everyone knew Brooks, including the Boat's captain. The local boy who made the big time, how could they not? Eventually, we said our goodbyes to the crew and made our way to the bow of the boat.

I was cool in my thin gown with the breeze off the ocean washing over me. Goosebumps rose on my arms. Most of the guests had moved inside for warmth but there were a few stragglers around on the deck. The stringed lights over our heads cast a warming glow around us. Brooks had found us both another glass of champagne. I leaned on the polished wood railing and looked down into the dark churning waters below as they were sliced in half by the ship's prow. I felt fuzzy and tired.

"So, Miss. Drew, I must hear all about your adventures today and how you got that scraped up knee."

I told him the whole story of my day starting with running into Charles who had stolen my stuff the day before, going to the Historical Society and then having Charles take me to the site of the Montague Hotel. How I became scared by the lights and sounds at the hotel property. My frustration came back in the retelling of it.

"I can't believe that you found the kid who stole your belongings. What are the odds? So, he had your souvenirs, but what about your other items, like your purse...and the letter? Did you get those back?"

"No, he said his friends that were with him had that stuff, but I wasn't totally sure if I believed him to tell you the truth."

"Well, how do you get ahold of him? Did he give you a name or number or something?"

"No number, just a first name. I am not sure if I will see him again, but I hope I do. He's a good tour guide and he fits on the scooter with me," I said with a chuckle.

"And did you find anything new at the museum?"

"Well, the curator was very knowledgeable. He went on and on about the Hotel and its history. He even knew of my Great Uncle Walter and his time there. He told me a crazy story about an unsolved murder mystery. It was one of the owners of the hotel. They found his body in one of the rooms. The curator is letting me dig into the archives tomorrow. Is it getting juicy enough for your blockbuster? You asked for more action and intrigue."

"Very intriguing but I was hoping to distract you away from all that sleuthing tomorrow. We have the morning off from the convention and some of us are taking helicopter tours of the Island. I would love to have you join us."

"Wow, that sounds incredible, but I really need to go to the Historical Society tomorrow. The curator will be expecting me. I'm sorry. You've been so kind to me and it's been a wonderful evening, here on this boat with you tonight. I feel like a princess. Why have you been so nice to me?" It was out before I could stop myself and I felt horrible for saying it. I think Carter had planted a seed of doubt or at least curiosity in my mind. I could see I had hurt him.

"Look...Brooks...I'm sorry. Forget I said that."

"Only if you come with me tomorrow," he said, and the smile was back as he poured on the charm. I laughed at his tenacity.

"I am afraid I will have to sit this one out. I am only here for a short time and I really need to keep going with my search. I have no idea what I'm looking for, to tell the truth, but this whole adventure has given me a purpose. I feel like it's a way to contribute something to my family. Even if it is only something small. It's a way to connect even though they are gone. Everyone deals with a situation like this in their own way. My grandmother was the only one I got to spend any quality time with. But she wasn't very forthcoming with family history," I said, thinking I must have sounded like a broken record with my talk of reconnecting with my family, but he was a good listener.

"Okay, but I want the movie rights...don't forget...and you absolutely must keep me posted on your adventures. Keep it on the down low, just between us, okay?"

"Yes, of course," I said as my teeth began chattering.

"You're cold. Do you want to go inside?"

"No, I like it here. The Island is so beautiful at night."

"Well, here's my jacket," he said as he slid it off himself and onto my shoulders.

His left arm draped across my back and stayed there. We rode back to the dock that way, in silence and leaning against the railing. My thoughts swirling like the waters beneath the boat. I thought about my grandmother again. Looking into Uncle Walter's life was a way to have some connection, but that was not all. If I was honest with myself, I was fascinated by the glamourous lifestyle that he lived. I always felt like a foreigner everywhere I went. I preferred a good book to human company.

I envied the people who were the life of every party they went to. Entertaining and telling stories came so easily to people like that, people like my great uncle and Brooks Laughton. I could see it in all the letters and pictures in Walter's suitcase and yet my uncle ended up alone and a penniless alcoholic on top of it. How does that happen? Could I say that I would do it differently if I had the opportunity? If I wasn't so uncomfortable in my own skin? I didn't know but the voice in my head had her answer.

The boat finally reached the dock. It was late, probably close to midnight or even later I guessed. Brooks and I walked down the gangway.

"Good luck with the sleuthing tomorrow. If you change your mind about the helicopter tour you know where to find me, okay? Just ring my room. Room 1509. I want to hear how it goes tomorrow if you don't."

"Thanks for a great evening," I said. This time I kissed his cheek. He smiled, surprised. I hesitated for a moment, thinking he was heading back to the hotel also, but he just stood there on the beach.

"Well, see you later...oh, your jacket," I said.

"Keep it. You can leave it at the front desk in the lobby for me, okay?"

"Thanks."

I turned to go and walked across the sand. When I got to the resort grounds I turned and looked back just in time to see Bikini Blonde walking over to Brooks. They strolled off down the beach hand in hand as they greeted each other. I wasn't the only one watching them either. Standing on the deck of the ship looking down, stood Carter Davis with a champagne glass in hand.

I felt anger and embarrassment rising inside me and then I thought why am I being so stupid? Brooks didn't owe me anything, but I was confused anyway. Why was he being so nice to me? I pulled his jacket tighter around me and stuck my hands in the pockets walking off toward the hotel lobby.

There was something in the pocket. I pulled it out and looked at it. I had to move closer to one of the walkway lights to read it. I found a book of matches advertising some local investigation and security agency. That seemed odd. I guess I wasn't the only one that was sleuthing. Or maybe Brooks had hired them for security while on the Island.

I could see that what with all the paparazzi around. I dropped the matches back into the pocket and continued on to the hotel, stumbling a little along the way. I dropped off the jacket as Brooks had suggested and then I went up to my room. I took a hot shower and climbed into bed. I drifted off fast, within seconds of my head hitting the pillow.

60

78 DEGREES AND SUNNY
December 21, 1988

The sunlight through the glass woke me again. I really needed to remember to shut the curtains before going to bed. It was another beautiful day in paradise. It made me think of how Walter always included the date and temperature on his letters. Was it meant to be an enticement for the reader or a mockery to tease them with? 78 degrees and sunny. I would never be able to ask him that question. My stomach rumbled. I craved food, coffee and maybe a gallon of water.

I showered to wake myself up and refresh. It was still early enough that I could hear morning traffic and horns beeping in the distance. Commuters on their way to work. I had hoped to be at the museum already. I threw on some shorts and an oversized T-shirt and then put my hair up with a banana clip. I sighed as I looked at the mirror. The banana clip made my curly hair look like a horse's mane. I grabbed my stuff, including Walter's suitcase, and I was out the door.

I had requested the moped for the week and it was waiting downstairs for me when I went out the lobby doors. No one had asked about the missing helmet, but there was a replacement on the bike seat. I managed to grab some coffee and a bagel on my way out the door. I found some ibuprofen as well at the hotel store. Then I strapped the old suitcase on to the back of the moped with some bungee cords that were in one of the bike compartments.

The ride felt exhilarating, as the breeze washed over me. It woke me up. I was finding my way around pretty well, at least around my little corner of paradise. I pulled up in front of the Historical Society and parked the bike. I hopped off and unstrapped the suitcase.

I walked inside, and Roger came out of the back office to greet me. A man who had been in the office with Roger turned to look me over and then he exited out the back of the building. He wore a dark suit and dark sunglasses inside the museum. Something about him made me suspicious. I shrugged it off. I needed to lay off the mystery books. All the sleuthing was going to my head.

This time Roger had some breakfast in hand. He wiped a greasy hand down his pant leg as he came over to me and extended the hand out for me to shake. I reached out my hand and he grabbed it and pulled me in for an awkward hug. Evidently, he really was not used to visitors.

"Well hello, Sunny. It is Sunny, right? This whip smart mind never forgets any bits or bobs. That's why this job is such a good fit for me. Plus, I have a second cousin on my father's side also named Sonny, but he is a male, so it's Sonny with an "O" but that helps too."

"Hi...Roger, right? No second cousin I'm afraid, but I did remember," I said.

"I am so glad you made it back today. I have a workroom in the back with a big table. I have pulled several boxes that have a lot of documents...all Hotel Montague related items from the Fifties. I was so excited to have someone in here wanting to do some research. We don't get much of that. People are always ready to move on to the latest and greatest, they never want to look over their shoulder.

"I have spent a lot of time putting this collection together. I do have something I think you will love. There were some sales brochures that were produced for the hotel. More of a book than a brochure really. It is in color and it has great pictures of all the rooms and grounds. The place was fantastic in its heyday."

"Thanks so much for doing this. I can't wait to get started," I said.

We went into the back room. The picture book was on the big table as well as several boxes, just as he had promised. I felt slightly uncomfortable being alone with him in the workroom, but I was so excited to see what was in the boxes. I was holding the handle of the suitcase a little too tight.

"Well...have at it. Whatever you need, just let me know. There's a coffee pot back here too...over by that sink. I just made a fresh pot. I will be out front setting up some new displays. Junkanoo is coming up, you know. We always get a big crowd for that. Lots of people in the streets with the parades and parties. They usually leave me quite a mess out in front of the building but at least it brings in a crowd...that and the free champagne. I would like to look through that suitcase before you leave the Island. Thanks for bringing it," he said as he left the workroom. I was alone and glad for it. He seemed scattered.

I sat down and grabbed the Hotel brochure, pondering what a Junkanoo was. I should ask him about that when he comes back. I was excited. Most of my photos were in black and white. The brochure was color. The front cover showed an overall view of the hotel looking at it from the beach. It was tropical pink just like the hotel tower I was staying at. It had a grand staircase up to the main entrance right in the middle with a wing on each side. There were the tennis courts on the right. A street separated it from the beach. I recognized it as Bay Street, from my mis-adventure the day before. The small details made the hotel beautiful. Ornate white moldings and a seashell motif along the cornice in three-dimensional relief in the plaster. The columns adorned with starfish at the top. Everything had a nautical theme to it.

The first few pages were all exterior shots. There was the large dock jutting out from the beach that was in line with the grand staircase. There was an aerial view that looked down on the entire hotel property, it revealed a rooftop pool. That was new. I had not noticed that in the photos that I had.

The interior photos started with a large, inviting lobby decorated with palm trees and tropical themes. There was a room labeled as the Jungle Room which I recognized from my great uncle's photos as well. There had been lots of parties, buffets and even a game of Bingo in that room. There were pictures of a bar. The Hibiscus Lounge it was labeled. Tall glass walls behind the bar in the lounge looked into the water of the rooftop swimming pool. A beautiful lady swam underwater in the pool, wearing a mermaid tail and a sea-shelled bikini top. She smiled and waved at the photographer as she held her breath. Her auburn locks fanned out and her head was surrounded by a halo of bubbles.

The brochure included pictures of the typical hotel room, which were basically the same as what you find in any hotel throughout the world, and then there were photos of the glamorous suites that adorned the top floors. The color images showed off their gold-leafed opulence. I couldn't help wondering if I was looking at one of the rooms where Murray had been found dead. His body badly charred beyond recognition. 78 degrees and sunny. Just another day in paradise.

I flipped through the rest of the pages. On the inside of the back cover, I found a smiling G. Walter Fender alongside a special written invitation that bore his signature. They had included a photocopy of his actual signature. I recognized it from the many letters I had seen. He was listed as the General Manager and Vice-President of the Montague Hotel. He looked so handsome in his cream-colored suit and slicked back jet-black hair. I found it hard to believe that I was related to him. I felt a sense of pride and unity, but the voice in my head rebuked me, telling me that I would never be on his level.

The Historical Society really had a remarkable collection of records and letters from the Montague Hotel. Roger had many of the same press releases that I had in the suitcase. The documents I was going through were in much better condition than the jumbled mess I had found in Walter's suitcase. Things were in chronological order, for the most part, as well.

I found myself once again marveling at Walter's life. He was in so many of the photos. It was his job to make sure that everyone was having the time of their life while in paradise, and I guessed that he was very good at it. He smiled at me from a photo, in a bathrobe with a painted-on mustache and uni-brow, pulling out a bingo ball from the cage. There he was dressed as a cowboy with a toy gun and a cigarette hanging off his bottom lip. And another image showed him hamming it up on the dancefloor in the Jungle Room.

There were some file folders full of business letters and accounting records. Those were not so interesting, but I flipped through them as well. Hours went by. Roger poked his head through the door to check on me a couple of times, but he mostly left me to my own devices. I wouldn't say I learned anything new or earth-shattering, but I was back in the Fifties, partying with the rich and famous and loving it. A world of celebrities that was a million miles away from my reality. It was always a fun trip.

A folder caught my attention in the business documents. It was labeled G. Walter Fender. I pulled it free and opened it up. It contained several letters. I grabbed the first letter in the file and began to read it. It was on a lawyer's letterhead. A law firm out of Miami. It was from one of the lawyer's that was listed on the letterhead. He was an investor in the hotel, apparently. They had sent someone down to the hotel for a weekend to check on things. It appeared stories were getting around about the staff of the Montague Hotel and the books were not matching up. My great uncle was the focus of the letter since he was running the place.

I had never bothered to give much thought to why Walter would leave the hotel, but this letter seemed to give some explanations. Fast living would always catch up with you in the end. I just wanted Walter's good times.

The letters were a disappointment and I decided that I could not end the day on that sour note. I went back to the photos and hotel brochures; back to the good stuff. I stumbled across a newspaper clipping. It showed the same photo of the mermaid in the bar pool

that was in the brochure. The caption said, Angela Merriweather –
Montague Hotel Mermaid. It was the woman that my Uncle had
written the letter to. They had worked together at the hotel, so he
obviously knew her from there. Was it more serious than that? Was
she one of many that had succumbed to his charms?

I heard the door opening again and I hurriedly slipped the old
clipping into my pocket. I had found her, and I didn't want to lose
her. I had identified the woman I came to find, at least what she
looked like. I promised myself that I would return the clipping. I
stretched and arched my back. I needed to get up and move around.
Roger walked in and asked how I was doing. I told him I was done
for the day and I thanked him many times. I asked if I could help
clean up.

"No...no need for that. I am sorry for not being more helpful
to you. Is it alright if I keep the suitcase for a while and go through
it? I promise it will be in good hands. We have a top of the line
security system in this building, believe it or not, although who
would want to steal ancient photos and newspaper clippings of
people they never heard of?"

"Of course, no problem. That's why I brought it," I agreed. "I
will be back later this week...maybe do some more research? This
has been a wonderful opportunity for me. Thank you so much. I
promise I will be back with a coffee and a bagel for you next time,"
I said with a smile. "Oh, and by the way...what is a Junkanoo?
Seems I am learning some new vocabulary on this Island."

"Yes, of course, it's the Island version of Carnival, like in Brazil,
or Mardi Gras in New Orleans. It goes back to the time when slaves
worked on plantations around here. There are still a few crumbling
plantations left on the Island. Junkanoo was the three days off they
were allowed each year for celebration, like Boxing Day. There are
actually a few different versions of the story, but it grew from there.
Oh, ...look at me going on again. I give you a simple goodbye and
you are welcome back any time."

He escorted me back to the front of the museum. I was a little nervous about leaving the suitcase, but he had been so free with the museum archives that I felt obliged. I had grown attached to that old suitcase in such a short time. Like a drowning man clinging to a lifesaver. I walked out into the afternoon light. He waved goodbye and shut the door.

🌴 🌴 🌴

I stretched again and looked around. No Charles in sight. I had kind of been hoping to run into him again. This area near the tourist market seemed to be his hangout. I guessed he had moved on to bigger and better business opportunities. I knew I should have given him a ten-dollar bill instead of the five. Oh, well. It was time to head back to my hotel. I could grab some early dinner and maybe take a dip in the pool, or even better, I could soak in the hot tub while drinking some fruity cocktail.

I crossed the familiar bridge to the resort. I parked my little moped out front and walked inside. I decided to check in at the front desk. I had not heard anything from back home since I arrived. Of course, I had not called home either, but it would cheer me up to get word from David or Mom and Dad. It was not busy at all, so I went straight up to the counter.

"Hi, I'm staying in room 902. Have I had any messages, I've been out all day?"

"Oh…no messages, but your husband just checked in, ma'am."

"What? But I'm not married," I said with confusion.

"Oh, dear. That is a problem."

The front desk attendant called over a bellhop to escort me up to the room. He looked to be twelve years old in his maroon monkey suit and cap. He couldn't have weighed more than ninety pounds soaking wet. Charles was bigger than this kid. The desk clerk said she would have security meet us upstairs. I hoped security had a weight requirement.

67

We took an elevator up to the ninth floor. My heart was pounding, and I felt shaky. The elevator ride seemed to last forever. I looked over at the bellhop and thought he looked worse than I felt. There was sweat dripping down his forehead. We stepped out of the elevator at last and headed down to the room, I was in the lead.

We rounded a corner of the winding hallway and ran into a very large man, coming out of my room. He had on dark clothes and a short, white military-style buzzcut. He was just putting his aviator sunglasses back on with a thickly muscled arm. It would have taken four of the bellhops to equal one of him.

The bellhop and I froze as he turned to look at us. He slid the sunglasses up on his nose as he considered his next move. His square jaw set and his eyes grew wider. He knew instantly that he had been made. He turned and ran for the exit stairwell in the opposite direction of where we were standing. Thank God, I thought silently to myself. I heard a loud thud behind me and I turned to see the bellhop unconscious on the floor. Great!

I walked over to my door slowly, hoping the man had been alone. The door was still open, and I looked in. My room was trashed. My clothes and the rest of my belongings were scattered all over. The drawers were all pulled out. Even the Gideon bible had been thrown down on the floor. I thought for sure he must have had the wrong room. I had nothing of value. It did not look like anything was missing. My extra credit card and passport were in the room safe, which looked to be unharmed.

A tap on my shoulder made me jump a foot in the air. It was a hotel security guard. He was a good-sized guy in a dark uniform. Too bad he wasn't around two minutes earlier. He had the bellhop with him. He must have slapped him back to his senses; there was a large red handprint on his left cheek. The guard led the bellhop to a chair in my room and dropped him on to it. The guard asked me a bunch of questions and then looked around briefly. I don't think he was too concerned since nothing appeared to be missing and no one was hurt.

He said they would file a report and that maintenance would be by to give me a new key and swap out the lock. I wondered if there was a limit to how many times they would do that before they started charging me; it was the second time they were changing my lock in three days' time.

"I would like a new room, please. I don't want this guy coming back."

"Sorry lady, the hotel is full. Actor's convention." With that, he grabbed the bellhop again and dragged him off down the hall.

I walked around my room looking at all my stuff. I noticed the guy had even pulled down one of the curtains. I would have to point that out, so the hotel management didn't think I did it. So much for closing the curtains so I could sleep in a little longer.

I jumped even higher when I was tapped on my shoulder a second time. I had not shut the door when the security guard left.

"Hello, Queenie. Not much into housekeeping are you…or was it a rough night with Brooks?"

I spun around and found myself face to face with Carter Davis. He was carrying a large paper-wrapped object. I was instantly surprised and suspicious. I didn't think he would be foolhardy enough to have someone trash my room and then show up immediately afterward, but I had seen him following Brooks down the beach last night. Besides, I didn't like his comment either. He must have seen the anger in my face because he quickly backed off. I did manage to keep my tears at bay at least. I hoped he couldn't see my panic.

"Hey, …what's wrong? What happened?"

"My room was just ransacked. I don't know who the guy was," I said truthfully. "I mean I didn't recognize the guy. I don't think this was random though because he specifically targeted my room. He got a key from the front desk under false pretenses. He said he was my husband and he was checking in, but he didn't take anything as far as I can tell."

"Wait a minute…you saw who did this to your room? What did he look like?"

"Big…white hair…crew cut and dark clothes. He looked like he might be in the military or maybe retired military…and really big, did I mention that he was extremely large?"

"I see," he said in response to my description. "Wow, that is quite a story. Can I at least help you with clean-up or something?"

"No…no, but thanks." The thought of him looking through my stuff was unnerving even though it was already spread out all over for him to see. I kicked some underwear and a bra under the bed. I let out a nervous laugh and he looked at me curiously.

"Well I was actually stopping by to deliver this," he said holding out the package.

"Okay, thanks," I said absently taking the package and setting it down on the table.

"Are you hungry? I know a great place not too far away."

That caught me off guard. I was hungry, but I did not want him to know that.

"Thanks for the invite but I have some plans already."

"Meeting up with Brooks?"

"No, but that is not really any of your business, is it?"

"Don't take it the wrong way, please. I have known him for so many years. We were good friends in our younger days, but I learned the hard way that he looks out for number one…always. I would hate to see you get taken advantage of."

"That's funny coming from you because Brooks warned me to watch out for you as well. So, which one of you should I believe? Besides, you already warned me on the yacht."

"You really should take this seriously. For starters, his name is not even Brooks Laughton, he made that up," he said as his tone became harsher. He adjusted his jacket. There was lots of bad blood between these two.

"Many Hollywood actors change their names – big deal."

"True, but he is not who you think he is, trust me. Come on Queenie, let's not be so serious. How about that dinner? My treat."

"Thanks again for the offer, but I'm really not up for it tonight plus I need to straighten out this mess and talk to the hotel management about a new key. I wish I could change rooms, but they said they're full."

"Okay," he said as he kissed me on the cheek and wrapped a finger in my curls. He lingered a little too long and made me feel uncomfortable. He was good at that. I was glad the door to my room was still wide open.

"Don't forget you are modeling for me tomorrow, Queenie. Get some rest. I don't want any bags under those eyes."

With that, he was gone. I had forgotten about the photo shoot I had agreed to. That thought made me laugh and cringe at the same time. Me doing a photo shoot. How did I even get hooked up with these two; Brooks and Carter? Or whatever Brooks real name was. I had some fun and it had been a real boost to my ego, but they were both getting in my way all the time. I needed to focus on Walter and Angela.

I straightened things out with the hotel and got a new room key. Then I ordered up some dinner from one of the hotel restaurants. I was feeling better after that. I decided I still wanted to get in the hot tub, so I undressed and put on my swimsuit and threw on my cover up. I remembered the news clipping in my pocket, found it and threw it on the table, on top of Carter's package. Angela smiled up at me; daring me to find her. I promised myself I would return it to the Historical Society. I wasn't sure why I even took it in the first place. I guess I just wanted to hang onto this tangible proof that Angela existed.

🌴 🌴 🌴

I went downstairs and out of the hotel, heading to the pool area which felt like a real tropical oasis with its lagoon, big boulders and palm trees. Tourists stretched out on loungers, enjoying the view. There were several pools and hot tubs. The pool area was between the hotel and the beach and encircled by low stone walls. There were still some people down at the beach. Some were coming over to the pool area as the sun was beginning to sink in the orange and pink streaked sky. I imagined Walter sitting on a lounger looking out at a sky just like the one I was looking at. The beauty of this place must have had a tight grip on him. I bet he was sad to leave.

I grabbed a towel and made my way to one of the unoccupied hot tubs. My scabbed-up knee stung as I lowered myself into the bubbling waters, but it was healing. The sun was waning further as the electric lights of the pool area were coming up. There was tropical reggae music playing softly over the speakers. A waiter came over to the hot tub and took my drink order. I decided to go fruity and tropical. He was back in an instant with the drink.

The warm water soothed me, I was enjoying some people watching when I spotted Carter sitting at a table with a drink and a cigar. Damn it. I didn't think he had seen me yet, he was on the other side of a large swimming pool, away from me. Maybe he was spying on Brooks or some other old high school chum. So much for relaxing. I didn't know how I got into the hot tub without him seeing me or how I would get back out.

He did appear to be watching someone, but I couldn't tell who and I didn't recognize anyone. I sank down as low as possible in the hot tub, trying to not be seen. After about ten minutes he got up and walked over to one of the other hot tubs on his side of the main pool. There was Brooks, soaking with two babes. I had missed him. He had an arm on each girl and they were all laughing. Carter said something to them and Brooks' expression changed to one of exasperation. I couldn't hear anything they were saying, but the body language and gestures were clear.

After a couple minutes of back and forth, Brooks climbed out of the hot tub and casually wrapped himself in a robe. He walked over to Carter and they were nose to nose in a heated discussion. I wished

I was closer to hear what they were saying. Suddenly Carter gave Brooks a shove and he stumbled backwards. The two babes jumped out of the pool and quickly got between the two men. They moved like they were twins, in unison, but they didn't look alike. The only thing they had in common was their bleached blonde hair.

Things quickly deflated, and Brooks gathered himself once again. A few more words were spoken but in what appeared to be a much calmer tone. Brooks had his arms back around the girls and was smiling again. Carter still had that set look on his face, but after a few more minutes he stormed off and Brooks and his friends got back into the hot tub.

I was off the hook. Neither one had seen me. What was the deal with these two? They had such a short fuse for each other. The waters ran deep, and I was genuinely afraid of getting to the bottom of that stirred up, muddy river. I wish I could figure out who was the good guy in all of it. It was usually painfully obvious in my spy books. This real-life rivalry escaped me.

I needed to stay away from them both, but I knew that I wouldn't. I knew I would be falling all over myself if I ran into Brooks again. No matter how many women I saw him with. I could not deny my attraction to him. It was like watching an accident occur and I just could not turn away from it.

I ordered another fruity drink and sipped it in peace. The pool area was slowly filling up with people and I decided it was time to head up to my room. I grabbed a six-pack from the lobby store to stock my room fridge. I was hesitant to open the door to my room, but it was as I left it this time. I put the chain on the door, and then I jumped into the shower and dressed for bed. I grabbed a beer and sat on the balcony for a while, staring out to the moonlit ocean. The longer I was on the Island, the more I seemed to drink.

My mind floated off to thoughts of family, as it had done a lot lately. I was lucky to have escaped my biological family if truth be told. But now that I knew who they really were, was I bound to end up like them? Uncle Walter seemed to be a shining star with his celebrities and parties…at least for a little while but his lifestyle caught up with him in the end too. More like a comet that blazed a quick burn through the sky only to plummet and smolder into the atmosphere. It swallowed him whole. Was my family fate inescapable, adoption or not?

I finished my beer and headed back inside. I closed the glass doors and turned toward bed but then I remembered the package that Carter had brought me. I went over to the table where it lay and ripped off the brown paper wrapping after I set the news clipping aside that was laying on top. It was a large picture in a frame.

There was a post-it on the glass that said: *For Queenie, Merry Christmas.* It was a picture of me from the Yacht. I had a leg up on the yacht railing and my dress rippled out in the breeze. My bandaged knee was successfully hidden from view behind the other leg. My face was turned away from the camera and covered by my hair that was blown by the wind. The sky was an explosion of sunset behind me. Wow, Carter was a great photographer. It was pure art. The voice in my head said *good thing your face was covered up.*

I walked over to the bed and collapsed onto it. My last thoughts before drifting off to sleep were that I sure hoped no one tried to get into my room again while I was sleeping and maybe Carter and Brooks weren't quite as bad as they sometimes seemed. I couldn't resist the feelings I had no matter how hard I tried to push them away. Maybe I was reading more into things, but I was too tired to worry for long.

BROOKS
December 22, 1988

I was in the ocean near a rocky shore and waves were crashing down. I could hear people yelling, but I couldn't make out what they were saying. A blanket in the water had wrapped itself around me. I grasped at it but all it did was drag me downward. I tried to swim toward shore, but it never got any closer. The blanket wrapped itself tighter around me, like a serpent. Like a living being that wanted to keep me under the waves forever. Rain poured down from the dark gray sky. I heard an unfamiliar woman's voice call my name and that was the moment that I woke.

I sat up in bed immediately. I was grateful that Bobby had not visited my dreams, but I was still shaken. Sweat covered me, but I felt chilled at the same time. My curtains were wide open again and still broken. I got up and walked out onto the balcony in just the boxer shorts and tank top I had slept in. The world was quiet. No cars or horns or people chatting too loudly yet. I had no idea what time it was, but it was early.

I looked out at the ocean and I noticed a lone figure on the beach. He wore running shorts and sneakers but nothing else. He ran at full speed, parallel with the ocean. It surprised me, how fast he ran. He never looked in my direction. He was focused. I wondered if Carter was out there somewhere watching Brooks like I was. I could not look away. I hoped I would run into Brooks again, maybe get invited to another party. I knew it was wrong, but I felt such a strong pull toward him and his lifestyle. *But what would you have to offer someone like that,* Ivey asked?

I couldn't make a case for myself with her. She was right. I lay on the bed, wide awake then, with no chance of falling back to sleep. I decided to get my day started. I looked at the photo of myself on the table, the one that Carter had taken. Maybe I would see how else Carter could surprise me today. Maybe I could learn more about Brooks by talking to Carter at my photo shoot. First, I would return to the Historical Society for a couple of hours. Carter's studio was close by the museum I discovered when I looked up his address on the phone book map.

I was dressed and ready to go. I had thrown on shorts and a T-shirt since I didn't really have any supermodel clothes. I put my hair up in a ponytail. I wasn't sure how early Roger showed up, but I would take a chance. I grabbed my bag and made sure I had all I needed for the day. Then I went downstairs and grabbed a couple of coffees and breakfast for myself and Roger. I exited the oversized, glass doors of the lobby and found my moped waiting with a new helmet. I was trying to figure out how to keep the coffee from spilling when I heard a familiar voice.

"Hey ma'am, you need my help today?"

It was Charles in his faded T-shirt, tennis shoes without laces and Yankees cap. This was perfect. He could take me sight-seeing later this afternoon. Wait a minute…how did he find me? How did he know where I was staying at? The kid was good.

"Hi, Charles. How are you? I missed you yesterday."

"Yeah…my parents made me spend time with my grandmother, she is here visiting from Cat Island, and she said she would meet you. I told her about us going to the Montague Hotel and all the Obeah stuff there. It's dark magic. Voodoo stuff. She believes in it, but my parents don't like her doing her magic. So, she does it when they're not around. She's teaching me. You must come and meet her today, okay? Before she leaves."

"That is awfully kind of you to do that. You have been a great help to me. Can you meet me at three o'clock down at the tourist market? We can talk to your grandmother and do some sightseeing after that. I need to take care of a few things first, this morning."

"Yes ma'am, no problem. How much did you say you are paying today?"

"I didn't but trust me it will be worth your while," I said with a smile. "Charles, have you had breakfast? You're old enough to drink coffee, right?"

He grabbed a cup and a bag from me and took off running before I could change my mind on the coffee. He yelled "see you at three," over his shoulder as he ran off. I hollered after him to see if he needed a ride, but he was already gone.

I went back into the hotel for a replacement breakfast. I got everything situated on the bike and then took off. I was lucky, Roger was there early. He greeted me at the door, and he was very excited. I delivered the breakfast to him. He said thanks and set it aside distractedly. I could tell he was eager to talk.

"Come back to the workroom with me. Thank you so much for letting me go through the suitcase. You provided me with some amazing historical documents for a history buff such as myself. I found a few things that we don't have. Just brilliant, truly."

We walked to the back. The suitcase contents were spread all over the big work table. He went piece by piece explaining each one to me. He took a break after an hour or so to grab the now cold coffee and breakfast I had brought him. Then he started back up. I was his captivated audience. I traveled back in time with him, into Walter's world once again. I wanted to stay there forever.

"Now this is one of the most relevant items in the suitcase...historically speaking, that is. Here are your Uncle and others greeting the English Governor of the Island, and his wife. I found records of several charity balls and parties they sponsored. Fundraisers for the Tuberculosis Ward and the Children's Fund among others. They did a lot of good work for the people of this Island."

"Who are the others in the photo?"

"Hotel staff and owners including the Island's most infamous victim of scandal…one Arthur Murray originally from Canada. That's him right there," he said pointing to the photo.

"Wait a minute…Arthur Murray? He's the Murray that was killed at the hotel back in the Fifties?" This could not be a coincidence. This had to be the Arthur that was mentioned in Walter's letter to Angela.

"Yes. Arthur Milton Murray."

Arthur was right next to Walter who was shaking hands with the Governor. Arthur had his hand casually resting on Walter's shoulder in a gesture of familiarity as he waited for his turn to shake the Governor's hand. I looked a little closer at him. Arthur was tall and skinny, with a receding hairline and pencil-thin mustache.

"There are some items that I would like to copy if that's okay with you. May I hang on to the suitcase for a few more days? One other thing – I know a chap, he does all my reproductions, he can put that 8mm reel of film onto a video cassette. I am assuming you don't have an old projector lying about to watch it on. Not too many of them still around. Everyone has moved on to video cassette recorders, and such. I once had a laser disc machine but those never really did catch on, did they? Anyway…I would love to see what is on the film if you don't mind."

"Sure, I would be honored if some of these things ended up on display here. The movie idea sounds good too. I hadn't really thought about doing anything with the film."

"Now, on a final note, I wanted to show you one last collection from your suitcase. I organized and tried to group things together the best I could. There was a group of photos that I found particularly fun. See all these images? They are from the Hobby Horse Race Track, another bygone piece of Island history.

"People came from all over the world to race here back in the day, including the mafia and other unscrupulous types. At least those were the rumors back then. Some say Arthur Milton Murray's death was due to his ties to the Mafia, among other theories. These photos are all from the day that Better Off Dead won the championship race for the season. Nineteen fifty-five, I believe. Better Off Dead was owned by the hotel…or rather some of the owners of the hotel."

I flipped through the photos. I had gone through them all before but now I looked with renewed interest. There was Walter, handing out a little trophy to the jockey. The jockey was a local child, barely older than my friend Charles. There was a photo finish shot of the horses crossing the line. There was Walter presenting a much larger trophy to the owner's, including Arthur Murray. There was a photo of a beautiful woman filling little paper cups with champagne in the Winner's Circle. It was my mermaid – Angela Merriweather.

"Roger, do you know this woman? Can you tell me anything about her?"

"Oh yes. She was a real beauty and quite an enigma here on the Island. Everyone thought she was destined for fame and fortune. Her name was Angela Merriweather and she worked at the hotel with your uncle. She helped with special events and publicity for the hotel. She was your uncle's *Girl Friday* back in the day. She did everything at the hotel," he said, pausing to push the glasses up on his nose.

"Worked her way up. She even swam in the swimming pool dressed as a mermaid on occasion. She was well known for her temper as well. She was a fiery red-head, you know. There were lots of rumors about that temper. It was surprising that she remained employed there, if even half the rumors were true. No one really enjoyed working with her either, from what I have heard.

"She had many admirers due to her looks, but she never married. She had an illegitimate child, which was really frowned upon back in those days, and she became a recluse of sorts after that. There were so many rumors about who the father was, but no one knew for sure.

"She stayed with the hotel until the very end, when it was torn down. She resorted to cleaning rooms in her later years, just to make ends meet. She never did make it off the Island. She died relatively young, cancer, I think. Very sad. She was a smashing beauty."

"That is so interesting. I came to this Island with a letter for her from my uncle. It had never been mailed and it was dated around the time of his death in nineteen sixty. None of it matters anymore now. I lost the letter and they are both dead."

"What did the letter say?" he asked.

"I wish I still had it…it was an apology of sorts but for what I am not sure."

I looked at my watch then and realized I was running late for my modeling gig. I had a lot to think about, thanks to Roger. I did enjoy walking through Walter's world with him. His knowledge of the Island and everything on it was formidable. He mesmerized me with the history of the Island.

Maybe others would not be as interested as I was, but it had become my obsession since that very first night I opened the suitcase back at my parent's house in Buffalo, Wyoming. It was strange, but I felt like there was something I was missing in all this if I could just connect the dots.

"Thank you so much, Roger. I have to run, but please keep the suitcase till you're done with it. I will be back again. You have been so helpful."

"Thank you, Sunny. Be sure to come down for Junkanoo. We always stay open late; besides, this is one of the best places to watch the festivities. You will have a great view through the front windows. We're a little higher than street level, so you really get a good vantage point from in here. We serve champagne. Free champagne."

"Thanks, I might just take you up on that. I will still be on the Island then."

I hurried off to my moped and made the short ride over to Carter's studio. I was late. Maybe he would just say to forget the whole thing if he was mad at me, besides, I think he was more interested in getting under Brooks' skin than taking my picture. I was no model. *You can say that again,* my inner voice said in a disdainful tone.

I found the place easily. It was a nondescript brick building. I walked in through the glass storefront doors. Carter stood inside, staring at a blank wall. He had on old jeans and a white T-shirt. A toolbox laid open at his feet. He didn't hear me come in. Maybe I shouldn't have come. I stood there saying nothing and thinking about leaving. Then the door banged shut behind me and he turned to look at me. Sweat dripped off his brow. He gave me a modest smile, but it was something on that dark and brooding face.

"Well look what the cat dragged in. I wasn't sure if you would show up," he said.

His words made me feel bad for thinking of skipping out.

"I would never think of standing you up," I said with a big smile as I lied through my teeth. "Besides, I had to thank you in person for the portrait you dropped off yesterday. I loved it. You can make anything look good. I had to come back for more."

"You are too modest, Queenie, but I am glad you came. Let me call my crew and then we can head out."

"Oh…head out to where?"

"I have some great sites in mind for your photo shoot, you will love them."

"Okay, but I have to meet someone at three."

Carter made some phone calls and then I helped him for a while in the studio, handing him tools and holding pictures for him. He was taking pictures down, not putting them up, as I had originally thought.

"So why are you taking all these down?" I asked.

"I'm making room for your exhibit."

"Oh, really? I didn't take you seriously when you said that on the yacht. Maybe I do need to rethink this whole photo shoot," I said.

"Of course, I was serious. You can see the photos first if you want? We'll have an invite-only opening before Junkanoo. The invites were already sent a while ago, actually. Before I even knew what or who I would photograph. I promise you will love it."

I was going to protest but his crew showed up. He introduced me to them. They both looked like they had just graduated from high school.

"Sunny, this is Jenna, my stylist and this is James, my assistant. Jenna has some outfits picked out for you. Let's load up and head to the beach. You can change in the van."

We took two vehicles. His crew rode in the van and Carter and I took his car. I climbed into the modest little car with the open sunroof. We wound our way to a little beach off the beaten path. We made small talk along the way. I wanted to ask questions about his past and Brooks, but I wasn't sure how to approach it. I ran out of time when we arrived at our destination.

I climbed into the back of the van with Jenna once we stopped. I liked her bubbly personality and short blonde pixie cut. She wore trendy clothes and accessories; the opposite of myself. Carter would be better off photographing her, she was beautiful. She handed me a tuxedo jacket and a bikini bottom and said I should put it on and roll up the sleeves.

"Where is the rest of it?" I asked.

She laughed, "you know, Carter usually only shoots people for *The Tabloid*, not his studio. You should be honored. He is a remarkable photographer. He doesn't float me too many jobs, but I make sure my calendar is always open when he does."

"How long have you known him?"

"Years," she said.

I found that hard to believe since she looked so young.

"He is a kind and generous man. A real good guy...He even let me stay in the spare room over his studio during a rough patch. It was a bad breakup with my jerk of an ex."

I had immodestly slipped on the jacket and bottom in front of her and then she wrestled with my thick unruly hair. She brushed it out and sprayed a lot of hairspray on it. The fumes were overpowering in the back of the van. She rolled down a window. She deftly applied makeup to my face after my hair was done.

"Were you born on the Island too?"

"Yeah...lived here my whole life."

"Do you know Brooks Laughton?"

"I know of him...who doesn't on this Island. I would love to do his hair and makeup. He would never forget it," she said haughtily.

"He does like blondes I've heard. So, what's the deal with him and Carter?"

"You mean the whole love-hate relationship thing? I don't know all the details. They used to be tight, but they had a falling out over a girl they were both into. It's always a girl or a guy, isn't it...that gets between the best of friends? They talk tough, but they can never seem to stay completely away from each other... at least when Brooks is back on the Island that is. The girl that came between them left the Island. Neither of them ended up with her. From what I heard there was more than one gal that came between those two.

"I don't know about Brooks, except for what shows up in the tabloids, but I don't recall Carter dating anyone seriously since I have known him. It has been a few years anyway. Come on...you are ready for your close up," Jenna said.

We left the van and walked over to the beach where Carter and his assistant, James, were waiting. James moved some equipment around in the sand. The sun reflected off his slick, broad-shouldered torso; he had removed his shirt. I averted my eyes. The last thing I needed was to get tangled up with another guy on Euphoria.

Duran Duran sang out from a portable radio. The song was called *My Chauffeur* and the name seemed to have nothing to do with the lyrics of the song. It wasn't one of their big hits but something about that song always brought back summer memories from earlier days. It was on my summer favorites mixtape that I made in high school. That and *The Boys of Summer* by Don Henley. Another summertime favorite.

"Lovely," Carter said as he spun me around. He was all business now like he had been on the yacht when he was taking my picture. He propped and posed me and clicked away. I gained a new respect for supermodels. The stamina and muscle strength required to hold all the poses was surprising and painful. I was going to need that hot tub again and maybe a good massage.

I chuckled quietly to myself. Here I was thinking of modeling, yachts and hot tubs. How had my reality changed so much in a matter of days? I needed a reality check. *Bingo*, Ivey said, sarcastically.

We loaded up and headed to the next location when we were done. Back in the car with Carter, I was trying to come up with a good way to bring Brooks into the conversation when Carter did it for me.

"So, did you have a good time with Brooks last night?" he asked rather brashly and something about his accusatory tone really got to me. He didn't have a right to talk to me like that. I didn't like being stuck in the middle between these two men that I barely knew. And besides, I knew he had seen Brooks with the other women at the pool yesterday evening, but I played along anyway.

"Oh yes…let's see…we started with a super expensive dinner. Hundreds of dollars. Then we went dancing…then we went to a party at some millionaire's house that Brooks knew. Then I drank so much that I don't even remember how I got home," I said sounding a little crazy in my own ears, but I didn't care. Ivey just rolled her eyes in my mind.

"Impossible. I know all of Brooks millionaire friends and none of them invited me to any party last night. Trust me, I am always on the guest list."

"Okay, you figured me out," I said laughing a little at his joke. "But what is the deal with you two? And honestly, I have not hung out with Brooks or talked to him since the yacht party, where I met you."

"Brooks is a real playboy. I hate to see anything bad happen to you. You seem nice, Queenie," he said avoiding my question.

"Really? Because this feels more like you keeping tabs on him, rather than watching out for me."

"Ahhh...now you have figured me out. Old habits die hard, I guess. I can't help myself." I didn't really understand what he was talking about.

"What happened between you two?" I asked.

"Let's just say that we grew up together, so we know everything about each other...the good and the bad. We are tied together forever whether we like it or not. In other words, he knows my secrets, most of them, so either I keep tabs on him when he is on the Island, or I kill him."

He stopped the car and turned off the engine. We were at our next location. I was glad. I didn't like the tone our conversation had taken. I knew he was joking about that last part but something about his tone made me edgy. Maybe Brooks was right. Maybe Carter held on to some twisted jealousy and that was why he was interested in me, because Brooks had shown an interest in me. I didn't like where that thought could lead either, but truth be told I was only on this photo shoot with hopes of learning more about Brooks. I was using Carter just like he was probably using me to get at Brooks.

A few location and costume changes later and we were ready to wrap things up. Carter had to help me up after the last shot. I was on some rocks and my muscles were aching. I was glad to be done with this. Jenna had brought a bikini for the last session and I was feeling extra insecure. I never owned a bikini and I would not have chosen to wear one, but I had come along this far, and I wanted to finish this off.

I brushed the sand off my body and then I grabbed a cover-up. I needed some more sunscreen, I was starting to turn pink. Carter walked back over to me with his camera in his hands. Jenna and James were back at the van.

"You know, Queenie, Brooks doesn't really like you. He doesn't like anyone, except for himself. You are a prop to him. He uses everyone he meets, myself included. I learned that lesson long ago."

Click-click-click.

He put the camera right up to my face and took a close-up.

"You are not even his type. What was it about you that caught his eye? Maybe he just felt sorry for the lonely tourist on vacation all alone, or maybe he wanted a break from the Hollywood gold diggers. I really don't get it. He never does anything for anyone else…never. He must have some ulterior motives, why else would he hang out with you?"

Click-click-click.

"Are you rich? Maybe you're the millionaire friend? Do you have Hollywood connections that he could use to his advantage? Why is he hanging out with you?"

Click-click-click.

"You need to stay away from him," he finally finished with.

"Why are you doing this?" I cried, completely ashamed.

Tears dripped down my face and I didn't wait for his answer. How could he be so mean? I didn't comprehend what had just happened. He turned on me so fast. He was an asshole just like Brooks had said. I ran away from him and over to the van.

I brushed past Jenna looking down at the ground to hide my tears of shame. I climbed into the van and slammed the door shut. I was the biggest fool in the world. I was just a game to be played by both of them. I was one big joke to them. That inner voice of mine was belly laughing at me now. She loved it. *You deserve it...thinking you are a model,* she said.

I wiped my face and put myself back together as best I could. I found my clothes and changed. I was going to make a quick exit. Maybe I could find a cab back to my moped. I didn't care if I had to walk. There was no way in hell that I was getting back into Carter's car to let him humiliate me again. I opened the back of the van and hopped down and there was my knight in shining armor, Charles, on my white moped. I had never been happier to see anyone in my life.

"Charles...what are you doing here? How did you find me? How did you hotwire the moped?"

"I got you covered, ma'am. Come on, we must go. My grandmother is waiting for us."

"One minute, Charles."

I waved and thanked Jenna and James. They looked at me funny. I didn't think they had heard anything that Carter had said to me, so they were probably wondering what was wrong with me and my tear streaked face. Or maybe it was the fact that a thirteen-year-old boy had shown up on a moped to pick me up.

I marched over to Carter.

"You are a complete asshole," I said quietly too his face. I was surprised by my own calmness. I don't think Jenna or James heard that one either.

Carter looked shocked and I was glad for it. Then I stormed off and hopped onto the back of the moped, behind Charles. I wrapped my arms around him too tightly. Gravel sprayed all over as he left the beach parking area. He drove a lot faster than I would have but I didn't care. I had no idea what had just happened. I was tired of the games. This was not what I came to Euphoria for. I needed to refocus. Another tear tried to slip down my cheek, but the wind pushed it back toward my ear.

Charles was driving us down some roads I had not traveled before. We came to a stop in front of a sunny little cabin. The yellow paint was starting to peel, but the place looked homey even though it was small. A Christmas wreath hung on the door. I climbed off the bike first and then Charles did the same. I turned my back to him as I dried my face on the bottom of my T-shirt.

"Are you okay? You don't look so good," he asked pointing his withered hand at my face.

"Yeah...yes. I'm fine."

"Well, this is my house. My mom and dad are at work, but my grandmother is here visiting. She came over from Cat Island like I said. She took the mail boat over. It's the only way to get back and forth. She wants to meet with you because I told her about the Obeah stuff we saw at the old hotel. Come on in."

I followed him up to the little porch and into the house. It smelled good inside, like home cooked meals and laundry soap. I asked if I could use the bathroom first. When I entered it and turned on the light, I found myself confronted by a stranger in a mask of streaky eye makeup over red-rimmed eyes, looking out at me from the mirror.

I looked a mess. No wonder Jenna and James had looked at me funny when I left the beach. I turned on the sink and washed up as best I could with a bar of soap I found on the sink. The cold water felt refreshing on my face. Then I went back out into the hallway.

"Okay, Charles, let's meet your grandmother. Thanks for doing this."

"Sure, this way," he said as he grabbed my hand with his good one.

We walked through the little living room to the back of the house and into the kitchen. It was clean and quaint with bright yellow wallpaper on the walls. His grandmother was a large woman with a kind, soft face. Her shocking white hair was a stark contrast to her dark skin. It glowed pure white like my grandmother's, but without the silver tone.

She was sitting at the little wood table in the kitchen wearing a yellow and orange flowery dress. She overflowed the rickety chair that she sat on. Some bottles with lit candles stuck in them were spread out on the table. She had been waiting for us.

"Hello dere," she said in her thick accent. She had a warm, friendly smile.

"Hi…I'm Sunny. Charles' friend. Thanks for seeing me."

"I'm Janine. Charles tol' me all about you. You been good to him. What is troublin' you, child? You los' someone, ain't ya?"

"Yes…my grandmother passed away…how did you know that?"

"Why did you come here den? Was she from here?"

"Yes…I mean no. Her brother was from here…I mean her brother lived here for several years. I think this was his favorite place of all the places he lived. I don't know how to explain it, but I just feel connected to him and this place. I wanted to come see this Island for myself. He died before I was even born."

She laughed but she was looking into my eyes so hard that it made me squirm in my chair and look away.

"Why else you here?"

"Well…there was a letter…I found a letter in my great uncle's stuff that had never been sent. It was addressed to a lady on this Island. I thought maybe I could find her and give it to her. Unfortunately, I lost the letter," I said, glancing at Charles.

"Dey do have mailboxes," she said laughing. She gave Charles a knowing look.

"I know…I just wanted to make sure it was delivered, personally. It doesn't matter now though…I found out she is deceased anyway."

"Dat's it?" she asked skeptically.

"I guess the other part of it is that I wanted to learn more about my Uncle. He seemed to live such a glamorous existence on this Island."

"All da white folks does."

"I'm sorry. It's been one dead end after another anyway. I haven't really learned much of anything since I have been here to tell you the truth, except that everyone and everything that I was looking for is gone. All gone."

Janine grabbed a cup and shook it. Some contents rattled about inside as she swirled the cup, then she dumped the contents on the table. It looked like some old bones and a couple of coins.

"Obeah takes no sides. It can be done for good or bad. Jus' like people chooses to do good...or do bad...but most are a mixture. Remember...that the past wants to fade and be forgotten. You spend too much time chasin' it and you be forgotten too."

She leaned across the table and grabbed me with rough scratchy hands. She was pulling me towards her and looking at me with those penetrating eyes.

"You should go home. Dere is nothing here for you anymore. You botherin' da sperrids. Quit stirring up the shadows from da past. You never know which ones will come a callin'. Da good or da bad or somewhere in between. An let da child go too. He needs his rest. You keep draggin' him around wit' you. Let him go."

Her words chilled me. I thought I understood, but how could she know such things? I could not let it go. I had to press her further. She knew the answers I sought, but she was keeping them to herself.

"Okay, okay...but do you know something about the old hotel? The Montague Hotel that was torn down? Charles took me there and something strange happened while I was there. It felt like I was not alone."

"Un huh. Dey watchin now. You stirred dem up. Let dem go back to rest. Leave. And I don't want Charles pulled into it. I got a feelin' dat you not one to take good advice – am I right?" she said with a grin, but her eyes were not smiling.

"Wait...who's watching?"

"Sperrids."

"Are they trying to hurt me?" I asked alarmed.

"I'm a not sure." She stood up surprisingly fast and left the room. I glanced over at Charles who stood quietly in the corner. He looked scared. I did feel bad for getting him involved. His grandmother would probably be mad at him. She took all this Obeah stuff very seriously, but I was disappointed to hear the things she had told me. Things that didn't quite connect in my mind. She came back into the room and laid some items down gently on the table.

"Take dese. Dey will provide protection, but I am not sure if da protection you need is magical or not. Now Charles, you best take her and go. Your ma and pa be home soon. Dey don't like me doing my magic in da house."

I grabbed the trinkets. A necklace with a raw, uncut moonstone charm and a small packet of some herbs and powder.

"Wait, what do I do with this stuff?" I asked.

"Keep da charm wit' you at all times. Dat stuff is some tea I made. Drink it tonight. It's good for the soul an' indigestion too. Now shoo!"

Charles ran over to her and hugged her and then we exited the house together. I looked at my watch. It was getting late. We would only have time for one excursion today. I felt guilty even asking Charles to go with me after talking to his grandmother, but I needed his help to find the place. I didn't think there would be any danger in it.

"Thank you, Charles. Your grandmother is a very smart lady. Would you have time to take me to one more place? That's all we have time for today," I said. I did not want to be anywhere unknown after dark. I also didn't want to completely abandon him. I would try to be more careful and respect his grandmother's wishes to keep him safe.

"Sure, ma'am. Where do you want to go?"

"Have you heard of the Hobby Horse Racetrack? Do you know where it is?"

"Yeah…I know where it is, at least what's left of it. For a tourist you sure like to visit some strange places, you know that?" I laughed as we climbed back on to the bike. This time I was driving the moped. Charles pressed on the appropriate shoulder when I needed to turn. The racetrack was in the opposite direction of my hotel but not too far. There was still plenty of daylight left when we got there.

The Racetrack property had a tall chain-link fence all the way around it. There were weeds and garbage everywhere. The covered bleachers, a few scattered buildings and the oval track could still be seen. Someone had cut the chain that held the gate closed so we had easy access.

We walked through the gate and then spread out to explore the property. I was pretty sure that we had found another dead end. I had no idea what I thought to find at this place, but I wanted to see everything, and follow all possible paths. That's what all the good private investigators would do. *Now you are lumping yourself in with your detectives from your books? You are delusional,* Ivey hissed at me, but I pretended not to hear her.

The whole place was dilapidated and overgrown. I kept looking up, afraid that something was going to fall in on me wherever I went. It looked like squatters had been hanging out to do their drugs, or at least get a good night's sleep out of the rain. It smelled bad, a mixture of urine and garbage. I hoped we didn't run into any of the illegal occupants.

There was nothing here and I was feeling bad for bringing Charles to this dump. Just another dead end. I wanted to get him away from the racetrack. I gave up my search. I was tired, and I wanted to head back to the hotel.

I walked around again and checked the buildings, looking for Charles. I found him and told him I was ready to go. He had managed to find some loose change on the ground in a corner of one of the buildings and a couple of trinkets that he could sell down at the tourist market. He was proud of his discoveries.

He was showing me his treasures as we headed back the way we had come. That was when I heard a noise. I looked across the racetrack towards the gate and I saw someone walking. He was watching us. Once he realized that we had seen him he took off running. I recognized the white-haired crew cut and sunglasses, I had seen this man before exiting my hotel room. This time he had a camera as well. I took off after him knowing I would never catch up, but maybe I could get his license plate.

"Hey!" Charles yelled after me.

I was out of breath by the time I got to the gate. I stepped through and out onto the gravel road, but he was gone. A cloud of dust drifted toward me. That was all that was left from his exit. I didn't even see his car when I looked down the road, only more dust. Charles popped up beside me.

"Who was that?"

"That was the man who broke into my hotel room and I think he's been following me. This is insane. Come on Charles. I need to get you out of here. Where should I drop you off at?"

"Home," he said sounding confused, but he didn't ask any more questions.

I gave Charles a twenty and thanked him for his help when I dropped him off. His grandmother was in the front window watching us. She had something in her hand and was waving it around as she crossed herself like a catholic priest. She was right about everything. I waved goodbye to them. She did not wave back. Then I was alone with my thoughts as I headed back to my hotel.

🌴 🌴 🌴

My trip seemed more bizarre every day. Why would anyone care what I was up to on the Island of Euphoria? I doubted anyone on this Island even knew or remembered who my great uncle was, besides Roger that is. Why would someone be following me? Maybe I should listen to Charles' grandmother and forget about all this. I had fun listening to Roger at the museum, but the past was long gone, and I should let it go. It was just a make-believe world for me anyway; a way to escape.

It was never a tangible connection to my family no matter how much I wanted it to be. I should face the facts. I feared starting my life. I just graduated college and now I was expected to settle down with my job and marriage. That's just what people do. But how could I do all that when I felt like my whole life growing up had been a pretense?

Now that I had spent time with my biological grandmother, I was only just beginning to figure out who I really was. I had to start that process all over again. This detour was a way for me to avoid the inevitable at least for a little while longer as I internalized things.

I didn't want to hear it, but I needed to start being honest with myself. I needed to admit that there was some unfinished business from my past too, business that I was trying desperately to avoid. Business that had been dredged up by all these thoughts of family and time spent with my grandmother. Business that had to do with Bobby.

I reached the bridge to the resort property as the sky was darkening. There was a cop car leaving the resort as I crossed the bridge and when I pulled up to the hotel, I saw a few more police vehicles parked down near the beach. There were cops walking around on the sand, near the rocky shoreline where the bonfires had been the other night.

I parked and left the bike for the valet with the replacement helmet on the seat. As I was walking to the lobby doors, I felt a hand on the back of my left elbow. I was already on edge and I spun around fast. There was Brooks, standing in the shadows. Darkness was rising, electric lights were coming to life on the hotel property, casting their yellow hue on him. I smiled, in spite of myself. But after my day with Carter, I wasn't in the mood for Brooks right at that moment. I needed to be alone with my thoughts.

"Hey, Sunny. Where have you been hiding?"

"Hi. I was just out seeing some sights. What's going on with all the cops around here?" I asked, trying to change the subject.

"I don't really know. They just showed up about an hour ago. Can you come over here?" he motioned to a spot away from the lobby doors and further in to the shadows of the greenery.

"Are we hiding from the cops?" I asked jokingly.

"No, of course not. There've been some paparazzi around here today. Not sure where they are from, but I am trying to stay out of their way and out of their lenses," he said, sounding on edge. I knew the feeling. I wanted to avoid being the target of any lenses for the rest of my trip and maybe for life.

"Was it Carter?"

"No, not him. I didn't recognize them, but Carter is going to be damn jealous. They have been following me all day. They probably took some good photos too. I think they came down from the mainland when they heard about the convention. Now, the real reason I have been waiting here is that I was hoping to run into you. How about dinner and drinks?" he said turning the charm on and physically pulling me towards him with those big warm hands.

"Oh…I don't know. It has been a long day. I don't think I could handle the Hollywood types tonight, sorry. I could use a shower and a change of clothes, though."

"No Hollywood types tonight, I promise. You forget that I grew up here and I know how to get away from the Hollywood types. Besides, you would be considered overdressed for the place I have in mind. I know all kinds of places on this Island. Besides that, I want to hear about today's sleuthing Ms. Marple," he said with his customary wink.

The charm was coming at me in full force and I found it hard to resist. He looked good in his shorts and T-shirt. I hadn't seen him so casual before. Even his hair was tousled, in a good way. Dark locks fell across his forehead and into his eyes. I did need some dinner, so what the hell I thought, wondering if I would regret the decision later.

"Okay. Let me go change and…"

"No! Eyes everywhere…have to go now. Meet me down at the bridge behind the Seahorse Tower. Bring the scooter."

He kissed my cheek and disappeared. I stood there for a minute, frozen in place. I wasn't sure whether I should laugh or run. I decided to just go with it. I walked over to the bike and got back on it. I hoped the dinner would be worth it because I was starving. I rode around the resort property heading back to the bridge which I had just crossed.

I turned right before entering the bridge and rode into the back-parking area for the Seahorse Tower. Each building on the property had an ocean-themed name to it. Brooks was hanging out by a dumpster enclosure. Either he knew a good shortcut, or he had run all the way over here.

I pulled up and hopped off the bike. He jumped on and then I climbed on behind him. He peeled out and I had to grab on tightly to keep from falling off. He felt warm as I pressed up against him. I really didn't mind having to hang on tight. He drove faster than Charles had, and I felt a rush of adrenaline. It was obvious that he knew his way around town as he weaved in and out of traffic effortlessly. The temperature dropped a little. I felt goosebumps crop up on my arms as we drove along. I didn't have a jacket.

The city had a different vibe at night. The sounds and smells were unfamiliar to me and there wasn't that visible connection to the sea. The locals took over at night. The Island felt authentic and wild. People were out and about in the streets and I could hear Caribbean steel drum music. I couldn't see where it was coming from.

We pulled up to a little diner and parked. Brooks held the keys out to me. We went inside and found a booth. He was right, I was overdressed for the restaurant but the smells from the kitchen were good ones. A couple of guys gave him a quick greeting and a hi-five. He did have connections.

"I just want a good old greasy American cheeseburger and a beer. I get tired of all the canapés and the French cuisine that I can't pronounce…and the champagne…they always have champagne at all the parties. Sometimes I just crave a beer," he said.

"Ditto," I said, as my stomach started to growl. Good thing the restaurant was noisy, so Brooks couldn't hear it, but my cheeks flushed anyway at my embarrassment.

The waitress was a beautiful, dark-skinned girl. She was quick to take our order and she came back shortly with the beers. She gave Brooks her full attention; leaving me to feel like chopped liver.

"That is an unusual necklace that you have on," Brooks said as he reached across the table to touch the pendant that hung around my neck. He jerked his hand back with an expletive.

"Damn thing shocked me," he said as he nursed the finger.

"Sorry. I forgot I was even wearing it. A friend gave it to me today."

"Really? Well you are a fast one, aren't you? Only on the Island a few days and already receiving gifts of jewelry?" I felt my cheeks grow redder as he teased me.

"It was from the grandmother of a friend, actually. It's supposed to be a protection charm…you know…the kind that wards off evil. Funny…I didn't feel anything, but I see that it must be working," I said, as Brooks laughed.

"Be careful about buying into all the local voodoo. They are just using it to part the tourists from their hard-earned cash. So…tell me about the detective work today. Was it a good day?"

"Yes and no. I met with Roger at the Historical Society. He went through many of the items from Walter's suitcase with me. He knows so much about the history of this Island. I felt like he was giving me a guided tour of 1950's Bahamas. It was exciting for me because of my uncle, but probably a big bore for anyone else. You know…come to think of it…I have never seen anyone inside of the Historical Society except for Roger, and one guy who made a fast exit out the back door. That explains a lot."

"Wait a minute. You never told me you had the suitcase here with you. Where is it now? I would like to get a good look at it, and its contents."

"Well, Roger still has it, for now."

"Let me know when you get it back. I must get a look at it. Any other big revelations from the suitcase?"

"Not really but then again I don't know what I am looking for exactly. I did learn more about the woman that my great uncle had written the letter to. The letter that was stolen by the kids."

"Really? What did you find out? Inquiring minds want to know."

"Well...I saw pictures of Angela and she was beautiful. She worked with my uncle at the hotel and did all sorts of jobs there including swimming in the glass-walled rooftop pool as a mermaid, she even wore a fake fish tail. Everyone thought she was really going places, but she ran into some hard times, I guess. I still have no idea what my uncle's apology letter was about. I may never know."

"Interesting, but I was hoping you would uncover a buried mystery or even better, a buried treasure. Maybe drug smuggling or a good gangster connection? No such luck, huh?"

"Well...there was some horse racing involved. The hotel owners had a racehorse that won the Island championship one year. There were pictures of my uncle, Angela and Arthur Murray celebrating the win. Arthur Murray was one of the hotel owners."

"You are going to have to dig deeper than that to come up with my next blockbuster I'm afraid. We need some sex and maybe a death or two...but it's a good start."

"Well Arthur Murray was killed, and the crime was never solved. I think his name was mentioned in the letter."

"Really? Now you are on to something. Was it the mob? A jilted ex-lover? Or maybe the jockey from the horse race?" he said dramatically tapping his temple with a finger.

Just then our food showed up. Brooks ordered another round of drinks for us. We dined in silence. I admired how he ate voraciously, not caring who was watching him. Of course, he was used to being watched.

I self-consciously wiped my face after every bite of my cheeseburger that was too tall to fit in my mouth. I must have missed a spot because Brooks leaned across the table with a napkin to wipe some catchup from my chin. He could make me feel like a shy little school girl so easily and I loved it. He knew it too. My inner voice said I was a fool, but I didn't care. I was the one eating dinner with a movie star.

We finished up our meal and he went to the counter to pay the bill. We left the bike parked in front of the diner and he lead me down the street by the hand. I so liked the feel of his hand wrapped around mine. We strolled along, through the vibrant streets. Music and laughter surrounded us. We bought some fresh fruit from a street vendor for dessert. People were hanging out and having fun. I wiped at the pineapple juice running down my chin.

We found a little hole-in-the wall bar that Brooks knew. The whole side of the building had several garage doors that opened to a vacant lot that was enclosed by a block wall and had lights strung across it overhead. There was a DJ playing loud music.

We went right up to the bar and did a shot of some Bahamian rum, then we got a couple of beers and wandered out through an open garage door. He pulled me smiling into the crowd of tightly packed dancers. People were greeting him as we spun around the dance floor. They were buying beers for us too. Lots of people knew him even here.

We had to find an empty table to set the bottles down. The music switched to a slow song and he pulled me towards him and put his head down on my shoulder. His arms around me felt electric, but then the dance music was back too soon, and we were dancing with everyone around us again. I wanted this night to keep going.

Brooks had danced his way across the floor from me. I felt hands on my back from behind. I turned around and I was dancing with a guy who had drunk one too many beers. He was friendly and just having a good time. I didn't mind. But when his hands slid down my back a little too low, Brooks was instantly there pushing his way in between us. They were shouting and gesturing at each other. I wondered how they could hear each other because I couldn't understand anything they were saying over the pounding music.

The DJ turned on a mic and told them to take it outside. Brooks grabbed the guy and dragged him over by the bar and out of the back door. A few others followed them. Friends of the drunk guy I guessed. This was not good. I pushed my way through the crowd and followed after them. Only the screen door was closed when I got to the back of the building. I looked out through the screen and saw Brooks pummeling the drunk down on the ground. The guys that had followed them outside were circled around and looking at each other nervously.

I knew they were about ready to join in on the fight, which was pretty one-sided. They were not going to let their friend take a beating for much longer. I had to do something.

I ran outside yelling "POLICE" at the top of my lungs. They all froze and then the friends scooped up their bleeding buddy and dragged him off down the alley. Brooks did not look happy. He walked over to the back wall of the bar and kicked a garbage can, then he glared at me. I could see he was drunk.

"What the hell are you doing? I totally had that guy. I did not like the way he was putting his hands all over you. I would have kicked his ass," he said as he turned back to the garbage can and kicked it again. His anger was directed at me and it scared me. I thought I was doing him a favor. Maybe he didn't realize that the others were getting ready to join in on the fight.

"I'm sorry. I thought his friends were going to jump you."

"I could have taken them too!" he said irritably.

"You're bleeding," I said softly, walking over to him. I found a tissue in my bag and wiped off his cheek. I wasn't sure if it was his blood or the other guys, but I didn't see any wounds. He looked down at me and his eyes softened then.

I stood there looking up at him, feeling like that silly schoolgirl again. I pushed him back against the graffitied block wall. I reached my hands up around his head and I pulled his mouth down to mine. I couldn't help myself and I was just drunk enough to not care. Then I slid my hands under his shirt. His skin felt warm and slick. I could tell he was surprised but he started to kiss me back. The kiss grew deeper. Suddenly he pushed me back and broke it off.

"You really should not be alone with me in a dark alley...you know that," he said breathily with his hands on my waist. I smiled and then tried to kiss him again.

"We can't do this...I'm sorry," he said softly. "Let's go back to the restaurant and get some coffee. Come on."

I let him grab my hand and lead me back through the bar and out the front door. There were a lot fewer people in the streets than there had been earlier. We headed down the block, to the restaurant where our evening had started. I was in shock. How could I have been such a fool? I really thought he was into me, but I was wrong again. I felt humiliated for throwing myself at him the way I did and the self-righteous voice in my head was not helping.

We went back into the diner and sat down. I wasn't sure what to do next, but I wanted to get out of there fast and head back to my quiet hotel room. He ordered two coffees as if nothing had happened between us. My shame was turning slowly to anger. More games. What else could I expect from him or Carter for that matter? Our coffee came with some cream and sugar on the side. The dark-haired waitress that had served us earlier was back. Brooks thanked her with a wink. I would have been jealous if she was a blonde.

"So...you never finished telling me about your day. Any other news? I really want to get a look at some of your photos one of these days, since you brought the suitcase with you," he said as he drank some coffee.

I laughed; unbelievable. All the drinks had made me feeling less inhibited. That was not good. I couldn't hold my tongue anymore.

101

"Wow! You are something, aren't you? Well, I met up with your good friend Carter after I left the Historical Society. He is almost as big a jerk as you are. Then my buddy Charles showed up to save the day. Then I had my fortune told and then I caught someone spying on me at the old racetrack, the same guy that broke into my hotel room.

"There is your synopsis. Now if you will forgive me, I am done with this day and I am done with you. Thanks, and goodbye," I said, as I stood up and dug into my purse. I was not going to let him pay for my coffee that I didn't drink. I wouldn't give him the satisfaction. He grabbed my wrist and pulled me back down to my chair.

"Damn it…what do you mean, spying on you? Someone broke into your hotel room? What happened?" Brooks asked. He seemed truly flustered and I was glad. But then I remembered that he was a professional actor.

I stood back up, staring down at him. I dropped some cash on the table without taking my eyes off him.

"Goodnight Mr. Laughton, or whatever your real name is."

I ran out of the restaurant and climbed onto the little moped. Brooks had followed me out, but he didn't say anything or try to stop me. He probably had a hot blonde waiting for him around the corner.

I put my helmet on and squealed the tires as best I could for effect. I shouldn't have driven the bike after all I had to drink, but then Brooks' rejection had sobered me up fast. Besides, I was tired of being the good girl. I could see him standing on the sidewalk with a dark frown in my diminutive handlebar mirror. I watched him grow smaller in it as I drove off. I was hoping he was the confused one this time. I told my inner voice to shut up before she even had a chance to get started.

102

The streets were quiet as I made my way back to the hotel. I thought about David for the first time since I arrived on Euphoria. I was ready to betray him tonight with Brooks. He would have never known. He was trusting and naïve to a fault. He was never cynical like I was. I was surprised by how easy it had been to kiss Brooks without even thinking of David. It had felt good. What was this Island doing to me? What were Brooks and Carter turning me into? I tried to blame everyone but myself.

I pulled up to the front entry of my hotel and parked the bike in its usual spot. I unloaded and headed to the elevators and up to my room. The clock on the bedside table said 3:30 AM. I wasn't sure what time it would be back home; my head was too groggy to do the math. I decided to give David a call on the hotel phone. It would probably cost an arm and a leg, but I didn't care. I wanted to hear his voice.

"Hello?"

"Hi David, it's Sunny."

"Hey, how are you doing? What time is it?"

"Really late…early morning actually."

"What are you doing up?"

"I…was out at the bar actually. I…ah…met some tourists and I was hanging out with them. Tourists from Minnesota," I said lying through my teeth and not sure why I had landed on that story for a cover-up.

"Oh. Really? Sounds like fun," he said distractedly.

"How is everything back home?"

"Good. I helped your dad redo a bathroom yesterday for their neighbor. Thank god I am not a plumber!"

"Mrs. Jenkins?"

"Yeah. Everything okay? You sound…strange."

"Yeah, great…just tired," I said, carefully. I didn't want to let my emotions come through in my voice. I wished I could tell him everything but then I would have to explain all the time I had

103

been spending with Brooks. He would not like it. He would not understand, even if he said he did.

"Well, I have to go. I have a meeting in the morning, and I want to be rested up. Glad you called. Talk to you soon, okay? Bye."

"Okay…Bye."

Click.

I was alone again. I laid down and tried to sleep. I tossed and turned full of confusion. David had seemed so cold. I hoped I was wrong. It is easy to read things into a phone conversation when you can't see a person face to face. He had been sleeping, but still, something seemed different. I had spent so many hours with him on a phone when I was away at college. I had grown good at reading into his words.

You screw up everything, she told me angrily; that cruel voice inside. *Why can't you just be happy?* The dark sky was beginning to lighten with a pink tinge when I finally drifted off.

CARTER
December 23, 1988

I t was past noon when I woke up. Bobby's contorted face had come into my dreams again. He woke me with a start. Half the day was wasted, and I felt awful. It seemed that the day was beyond salvaging before it started. A Bloody Mary sounded good. I heard those were good for a hangover and good for forgetting.

I took a long steamy shower and found some semi-clean shorts and a T-shirt to throw over my swimsuit. I needed to find a laundromat. I put my hair up in a bun, I grabbed my bag and threw in my camera. I was taking a day off. I had nothing planned and I was going to wander the Island by myself. I didn't want to talk to anyone.

I made my way to the elevator and down to the lobby. When I walked outside, I found Charles sitting on my moped with the helmet on. He quickly jumped off when he saw me. He turned and looked at one of the valets and said "See!" with a flourish and bow.

"Hey, Charles. Have you been here long?"

"No, not really."

"Still on holiday break from school?"

"Yes, ma'am."

"I don't know if I would make the best company today. I had a rough night and I didn't get much sleep."

"Well, I know where they make the best coffee on the Island. It might be worth your while to keep me around today. You can make another donation to my college fund too."

"Okay. Are you hungry? One's man lunch is another man's breakfast after all, and I am intrigued by the coffee. Lead the way."

I let Charles drive the moped. As we drove off, I noticed that a rocky part of the beach had some yellow crime scene tape around it. I made a mental note to ask someone at the hotel about it. Must have something to do with all the cops that were around yesterday.

The warm sun felt hot on my shoulders and back. The breeze blew through my hair and caressed my face as we drove along. I chuckled to myself when Charles parked the moped in front of the same diner that Brooks and I had been at the night before. Must be a popular local spot for sure. The sunlight baked off the silver panels of the façade.

"Best coffee in town, huh?"

"Yes, ma'am."

"And how are the bacon and eggs?"

"First class, just wait."

We walked in and walked down the narrow row of booths. Charles was dragging his good hand along the edges of the tables. One table still had dishes on it and some cash. He paused at that table and then turned back to look at me. Our eyes locked a moment and then he proceeded to an open booth and plopped down.

Charles was right about the coffee and breakfast. I had never taken a sip of the coffee the night before, I was too distracted. Charles had a cheeseburger and coke after which he let out one of his world-famous burps. He looked around proudly to see if anyone was paying attention. He made me feel like a silly school kid and not the shy flustered girl that Brooks turned me into. Charles was my co-conspirator.

"That was good," I said as I unbuttoned the top button of my jean shorts. Good thing my T-shirt hung down low enough to cover the top of them. I looked over and noticed Charles playing with a necklace that hung around his neck.

"What's that," I asked, motioning to the trinket.

106

"Oh, it's my charm that my grandma gave me. She was pretty upset after talking to you. She didn't believe me when I said I was going to stay away from you, so she said I needed a protection charm too. Like the one she gave you. This one is black onyx, she said it protects against evil spirits. The one she gave you, moonstone, is special protection for travelers."

"You sure know your stuff. I think your grandmother is rubbing off on you," I said as I played with the moonstone around my neck.

"Yeah, I like to help her and learn about her magic. I believe in it even if my parents don't. Make sure you keep the necklace and stone with you all the time, okay?"

"I promise. So, Charles, where do the real tourists go when they come to this Island?"

"Oh, lots of places. There's the Cloisters, the forts, the lighthouse, the museums and of course the beaches. The pirate museum is my favorite."

"Well if you want to make some big bucks today, I would like to start at the pirate museum with you as my guide...I want to see your top three tourist sites and then maybe a beach? Were there really pirates around here?"

"Yes, ma'am. They all stopped here back then. Henry Morgan, Blackbeard, Calico Jack; all of them. They would build fake lighthouses to trick the Spanish ships into the barrier reefs, so they would wreck. They say there is treasure buried around here too. I have been trying to get my friends to help me look for it, but they think the tourists are an easier way to get rich...like you," he said and then looked down at his shoes intently. I think he truly felt bad about how we met, at least I hoped he did. I didn't want him going back to those ways.

We made it to the pirate museum, but we spent so much time there that we decided to save the other sites for another day and just head to a beach. Charles said he had a special beach that he wanted to take me to, so I let him drive the moped again. He pulled into a small parking lot littered with broken glass. It glittered like crystals in the bright afternoon sunlight. We unloaded. I had a towel and a couple of bottles of soda that I grabbed from the storage pouch of the moped. We walked along a gravel trail amongst some boulders and tall grass, down to the beach.

It was perfect and so serene. The beach was made of pink sand that dazzled against sparkling pale aqua waters. There were not that many swimmers left in the slowly fading light of the sun. We laid out the towel I brought. I hadn't thought to ask if Charles had brought a swimsuit, but he said he was always ready for swimming and he swam in the shorts he had on. I let him dunk me a few times before I finally reciprocated.

We splashed around, jumping the waves as they came in to lick the shore. It took me back to my childhood when we went to Atlantic City for a summer vacation. I would jump as the waves came in. It felt like they lifted me ten feet off the sandy bottom of the shore back then. I used to call them Jell-Os.

I hadn't thought about that trip in a long time. It was a trip that I had taken with my biological mother in better days. I had to be less than four years old on that trip. The clarity of it surprised me, but I thought it better not to dwell on those days. A lot of memories had tried to push forward since I landed on Euphoria. They were getting harder to block.

After a couple of hours, we were sitting side by side on the towel drip drying in the late afternoon sun. I felt a crusty coating of salt on my skin as I dried. I dug in my bag and found some lotion to slather on. I asked Charles if he needed some, but he said no. He was rubbing his bad hand.

"Is it hurting?" I asked.

"Naw, not much."

"What happened? How did it get that way?"

"I was just born with it, I guess. That's what my mom said."

"I'm sorry. I don't mean to pry."

"It's okay. I like you. You're my friend now. I don't mind talking about it to you. Some of the kids at school are not so nice. They tease me about it. I guess that's why I like the kids down at the tourist market. They don't tease me about this hand. They never say anything bad to me. That's why I go along with what they do. They accept me."

"You are a good kid, you know that? I'd like to have a chat with those kids at your school. But don't let them ruin our day. It's been terrific. They can only hurt you if you allow it. And don't go back to those old ways, okay? I couldn't stand the thought of it. It's not who you are," I said with a tug on his baseball cap.

"Okay," he said with a smile.

"So, what else do you like to do for fun?"

"My friends and I like to cliff dive."

"Sounds dangerous."

"No, not really. You just have to do it right. Euphoria is the best place in the Bahamas for cliff jumping."

"Doesn't it scare you though?" I asked.

"Well, you have to do it right, get a good run and jump out away from the rocks. You need to reach the deeper water, so you don't hit bottom. And when you're in the air you should point your toes and squeeze your arms tight. If you jump from a really big cliff, you can get bad bruises if you don't. My friend had his arms straight out sideways once and the bottoms of his arms turned black and blue."

"Thanks for the pointers but I will leave the flying to the birds. Hey, what's that dark spot out in the ocean?"

"That's called a blue hole."

"And what exactly is a blue hole?"

It's a cave under the water. The water is deep there, so it looks darker. There's a whole bunch of underground caves on the Island too. I always wondered if they were all connected. I know some of them are. My friends and I like to explore them but my mom doesn't like me doing it. Tourists like to scuba dive in the blue holes. I heard it's amazing...the fish that you see down there."

"Scuba diving sounds fun. Well, just be careful...when you are doing the dangerous stuff...and you should always wear your

WALTER'S SUITCASE

109

protection charm." I felt silly saying it out loud, but I believed it would help in some strange way. At least cliff diving and cave spelunking were better hobbies than tourist robbing.

We sat in silence and watched the sun drop lower and lower in the sky until it hovered just above the azul water. Then we reluctantly packed up and climbed back on to the bike.

I asked him where he wanted me to drop him off and he said the tourist market. He was hoping to catch up with his friends down there. This time I was driving. He helped me find the way. We managed to cruise by a few of the attractions we had missed exploring due to time. We were back at the tourist market all too soon. He jumped off the bike and I handed him a couple of twenty dollar bills as he handed me the helmet.

"Thanks, Charles. I had a great day today."

"Thank you, ma'am," he said, smiling big with the cash in hand. "I will be in touch."

He was off running and stuffing the cash into his pocket. I put the helmet on and throttled the bike, heading back toward my hotel. I pulled up out front and headed inside with my stuff. I wanted to take a shower and then find something for dinner. I was famished.

🌴 🌴 🌴

I turned off the shower and I stepped out to grab a robe when I heard a knock on the door. I called out "just a minute" as I wrapped myself in the robe. I looked through the peephole and I wished I hadn't said anything. It was Carter. He stood in the hallway in jeans and a white T-shirt holding something round in his hand. It was too late, so I opened the door a crack with the angriest look I could muster.

"Yes?" I said with an icy expectancy that surprised me.

"Hi Sunny. I see you're still upset with me. I wanted to apologize. You know...for being an asshole yesterday at the beach."

"You certainly were. Apology noted, now I have someplace to be, so goodbye," I said as I pushed the door closed.

"Wait, that's not the only thing," he said as he knocked at the door a second time.

"What is it?" I said as I reopened the door.

"I wanted to ask you where you got this roll of film from," he said holding out the small metal canister with the 8mm roll of film that I had given to Roger at the Historical Society.

"Where did I get it from? Where did you get it from? I gave that to a friend."

"Yes, Roger. I do reproductions for him. Another side business of mine. He gave me this to transfer to a video cassette."

"Oh," I said feeling a little confused and not wanting to explain anything to him.

"Where did you get this film from?" he persisted.

"Why are you asking?"

"I was curious as to why you have an old movie of Brooks' mother?"

"What?"

"This film has images of Brooks' mother on it."

"Really? But that's crazy…but I mean I guess it could be possible. He's from here, right."

"Where did you get this?" he said holding up the canister to my face.

"That was in my great uncle's belongings, in an old suitcase that I inherited. He lived on this Island at one time and worked at the Montague Hotel for about eight years back in the Fifties. Wait…what else does the movie show?"

"I didn't watch the whole thing, I was so shocked to see her. It was film of a party. Does Brooks know about this?"

"No, wait a minute," I said as a realization came to me. I hurried over to the dresser, grabbing the little news clipping that I had pocketed at the Historical Society. I walked over to Carter and held it out for him to see.

"Is this Brooks' mother?"

"Yeah. Where did you get that?"

"Look, it's not important," I said, not wanting to explain my theft.

"Well, why don't you come with me and we will watch the whole thing together. I have a film projector at my place."

"Okay, okay, but give me a few minutes first? I need to get dressed."

"Sure. I'll be down in the piano bar." With that, he exited, and I slammed the door shut.

I plopped down onto the bed after he left not believing what had just happened. My mind was racing. I really wanted to see what was on that film. I would worry about being mad at Carter later. I figured I better hurry up and finish getting ready. I was walking to the bathroom when the phone rang. I walked back to the little table between the beds and picked it up.

"Hello?"

"Hi. It's David. How are you doing?"

"Good, thanks." I was glad he called but I was distracted. Feeling better today?"

Yeah. How are you doing?" I asked feeling like something was out of sync but not sure what. "Is everything okay? Are mom and dad okay?"

"Yeah, nothing to worry about. Everyone is fine but there is something I wanted to talk to you about. There is no good way to say this. I think it's time for you and me to take a break."

"What...wow. Really? Are you saying what I think you are saying?"

"Yes. I am sorry to do this to you now, but I don't want to hold you back anymore and I met someone that I would like to ask out. I didn't want to be one of those guys that sneaks around on you. If we're really honest, things haven't progressed for us in all these years that we've been together. Maybe it's been easier to keep hanging on to this since we were always in different towns. I know you may need some time with this. I just hope you'll still consider me a friend."

"Wow. This is a lot to dump on me over the phone…and with everything going on…and Christmas coming up," I said trying not to let the emotion that overwhelmed me creep into my voice.

"Yeah, I know…"

"I guess I do need some time to come to terms with this. Consider us over, you have my blessing to pursue other interests if that is what you were looking for. How could I stop you? Friendship might not be so easy though, I'm afraid. Hey…I have to go now. This is costing you an arm and a leg. Besides, I was heading out to meet up with some friends I met. Might be a late night. Talk to you later," I said, trying to lighten the mood so he wouldn't hear the sadness in my voice.

"Goodbye Sunny."

"Bye," I choked out. I hung up the phone in shock. I had not expected this, but could I blame him? He was right. His timing really sucked though. He could have waited until I got home.

Maybe I pushed him too far with my late-night call and partying story. I wiped at a stray tear on my cheek. I needed a drink and I needed to see what was on my great uncle's roll of film. I would push this conversation to the back of my brain and deal with it later. I had to. It was too painful and raw to think about. I was afraid of losing it it I dwelled on David's call. *He really deserves better than you, just like Brooks,* Ivey said in a sympathetic tone. I wished she was real, so I could slap her.

I grabbed a beer from the fridge and then I hurried into the bathroom and splashed some cold water on my face several times. I opened the beer and guzzled half of it down in one drink. Then I applied some make-up and brushed out my hair. I twisted it into a loose bun and then I finished the beer. I thought about grabbing another one, but Carter was probably wondering what had happened to me. I put on a sundress and a sweater and then I took a last look in the mirror, hating myself. I grabbed my bag and exited the room.

I walked into the piano bar off the lobby, it was dark and smoky. Carter was sitting at the bar, but he was not alone. I was surprised to see Brooks standing next to him. They were deep in conversation. Carter was holding up the film canister. Brooks had two girls with him, his usual arm candy in skimpy dresses. Both blondes of course, but not the two from the hot tub. They stood there waiting on him.

Brooks was wearing a dark suit. He was too damned attractive for his own good. I didn't want any of them to see me, so I hurried over to the opposite side of the bar and sat down in a booth where I could watch them. They both looked around nervously, or maybe that was just my overactive imagination kicking in. I needed to cut back on those crime novels.

Carter looked at his watch and then Brooks and his friends started moving toward the door. One of the blondes had grabbed Brooks by the hand and was pulling him and smiling. Once they were gone, I waited a few extra minutes, and then I made my way over to where Carter was sitting. The little canister of film was on the bar next to him.

"Hey, Queenie. I was just thinking about coming to find you," he said looking up at me intently. Had he seen me come in? Did he know I saw him talking to Brooks? "Is everything okay? You look like you are wound very tightly," he said.

"Yeah, I'm fine. I could use a Kalik Crisp though," I said as I flagged down the bartender. "And a shot. You need anything?"

"Why not. I'll have another beer too."

I slammed down a shot of some rum and then I sipped at my beer while munching on peanuts that were in a bowl on the bar. Carter and I both sat in silence nursing our drinks. I didn't know what was eating at him, but I was lost in my own world anyway.

He stood up and threw down some cash on the bar when he was done. Then he grabbed the roll of film and he turned to me and held out a hand.

"We better get a move on. It's getting late. Are you hungry? We can grab some Chinese take-out on the way."

"Sounds good," I said. I was feeling comfortably numb. He drove which I was glad for. He could be okay company when he wanted to, but I had not forgotten the Carter on the beach who had taunted me.

🌴 🌴 🌴

We pulled up to his house as the glowing orb of the sun clung to the edge of the sea, ready to slip away for the night. It was a sweet, pale blue cottage with white trim. It lacked Christmas decorations like his neighbors had on either side of him. The cottage sat on a gentle hill, a block off the beach.

The waning sun reflected off the glass of the picture window at the front of the house. A couple loungers on the wrap around porch made good use of the view. I inhaled the salty air. My sundress clung to my sticky skin, with no breeze to cool it. Carter was carrying a couple of bags of take-out and a twelve pack of beer, so I helped him unlock the door.

The masculine interior was an unexpected contrast to the outside. Bare wood ceilings exposed the structure of the house. A loft area sat above what had to be his home studio. It was full of equipment and computers. Photographic artwork adorned the walls. Seascapes and marine life. He had a good eye. The furniture consisted of oversized, brown leather pieces and dark wood.

"Nice place," I said.

"Yeah. It was my parent's place. I've been remodeling it for years since my parents...moved up to Florida...and left it to me," he said as he wandered around, opening windows for the breeze that wasn't there.

We sat down on barstools at the kitchen counter and ate quickly. I think we were both anxious to watch the tape. I helped him clean up and put the leftovers in the fridge and then he motioned me to follow him to the back workroom under the loft. He had an old-fashioned projector and portable screen set up. He pulled up two office chairs for us to sit on and then he grabbed us each a beer. He loaded the film and started the projector.

"Sorry I don't have any popcorn," he said.

I smiled. He could be laid back when Brooks wasn't around, or the topic of conversation. The movie started. Black and white images flickered on the screen. There was no sound, but I was instantly swept away to the Bahamas of the Fifties. Walter's world came to life in a way I had not experienced it before.

It started with footage of the visit from the Governor of the Island to the Hotel. English royalty that I had seen many photos of. The Governor and his wife were attending a party in the famous Jungle Room at the hotel. The party guests were dressed in tuxedos and shimmery evening gowns. They entered the room, ready to see and be seen. They shook hands and kissed cheeks as they greeted each other.

A band appeared on stage and began to play. People floated onto the dance floor and began to dance. Even though the film had no sound, I could hear the music and laughter in my mind. The unseen photographer stood in the middle of the dance floor, panning around to capture various couples. They all smiled at the camera person and tipped glasses, as they swirled around. A lady walked up on to the stage and the camera followed her as she grabbed a microphone to make an announcement. Carter paused the film. He turned to look at me.

"That's Brooks' mom. The lady from your newspaper clipping."

"Yes. I was trying to find her, but I found out she was dead. I didn't know she was Brooks' mother, though, until you told me," I said.

"Her name is Angela Merriweather. Why were you looking for her? Did you know her?"

"No...I don't really," I said. Then I proceeded to tell him a brief version of the story of the suitcase and my trip to the Island.

"Angela's been long gone I'm afraid. She was a wonderful lady with a quick temper. Better than Brooks ever deserved. I don't blame her for that temper, having to raise a kid like him. Did you tell him about any of this?"

"I did, but the strange thing is that he never told me who she was to him. I lost the damn letter my first day on the Island, thanks to some young thieves, so I will never get to pass it on to anyone now. Another long story. Brooks kept asking me if I had learned anything new every time I saw him, but he was the one that could have helped piece things together for me. Strange, very strange…"

I really was a fool. I could see it plain as day and I didn't want to share my epiphany. Brooks was never interested in me at all. Or in making a movie about my adventures. He was only interested in why I was on this Island and what I would turn up about his mom. His invitations were all pretense to keep tabs on me, and I stupidly threw myself at him. He never wanted to spend time with me.

But why? Was he hoping to learn something new about his mother? Or was he trying to hide something? The latter I guessed. Why else would he be so secretive? I didn't want to pursue this any further. Let sleeping dogs lie. Charles grandmother was right. I was in over my head and I had no idea what I had really stumbled into. And just how did Carter play into all this? I looked over at him. He was staring at me intently, watching my inner thoughts and emotions play out across my face, I feared. I must have been an open book to him.

"Can we watch the rest?" I asked, not liking the way he was looking at me. It was a look I had seen many times before. He had little use for smiling it seemed.

He turned the film back on. Angela finished her speech and exited the stage with a bow and a big smile. She was beautiful in her silvery evening gown, with her dark, flowing hair. I knew it was a smoldering, auburn color, but it looked jet black in the old movie images. My grandmother's hair had been more of a fiery copper hue. The color of a mint penny that I had seen in photos, but never in real life. I only knew the silver-white of her senior years.

The camera was back to weaving through the dance floor, amongst the party-goers. People went in and out of focus. I didn't recognize many of them, but they had the look of importance, even if they were from a now forgotten era. Fame and fashion moved so fast.

The camera found Angela again on the dance floor. She was dancing with Arthur Murray. I recognized him from my photos. They looked like happy drunks, dancing cheek to cheek in a dramatic tango. The camera blurred out of focus and spun around, then there was Walter smiling silly and dancing cheek to cheek with them, holding the camera out at arm's length. Angela was in between the two men.

Tears came to my eyes when I saw Walter. I didn't know if Carter had recognized the two men, but I kept silent. Then Walter pulled away from the other two and broke into a goofy Charleston while still holding the camera above his head and filming down on himself. A smile came to my face as the tears threatened to spill from my eyes.

I looked over at Carter, but he was still watching the movie. The dance floor was suddenly gone, and the scene changed to a luxury hotel room. I was pretty sure it was one of the Montague Hotel suites that were at the top of the hotel. The camera circled the room very slowly and stopped at the oversized windows to look out to the ocean beyond. There were several people in the room including Angela Merriweather.

She was sitting on someone's lap, but he had his back to the camera. One cuff-linked wrist draped across her shoulders. They were all drinking champagne and smoking cigarettes; a haze hung across the room. People were talking back to the camera as it moved in on each of them in turn. Words uttered that would never be heard again except for that first time by the cameraman.

A woman in an evening gown walked up to the camera and grabbed it. She turned it on the cameraman. It was Walter again. He was playing bashful, with his head down, giving the camera a sideways glance and batting his eyes. Suddenly, he beat his chest and blew a kiss to the camera and danced around.

A chimpanzee sat on the couch wearing a white bow tie and tuxedo jacket. Walter walked over to the chimp and bowed. Then he grabbed its hand and kissed it. He tried to give it a lit cigarette, but the chimp threw it across the room. Several people ran over to stomp out the burning butt.

Walter walked back over to the camera until his grinning face filled the screen. He reached out to grab the camera and then the film was done. It had unwound from one reel to the other and the loose end of it was spinning around noisily.

Carter stood up and stretched, then flipped the projector off. He whipped off his white T-shirt and started to fan himself with it. He stood with his bare back to me for a moment, as he fanned himself, deep in thought.

"Damn, it's hot and muggy tonight. Must be something moving in," he said as he turned back toward me. "Hey...what's the matter?"

I turned and wiped my eyes. I did not want him to see me crying. Watching Walter on the film had stirred things up for me again. I would never know any of my family. Just faces in a photo or an image on a screen. That was all that was left to me. I still had my drugged-up mother, but she was a joke. She was a real mess. She was the only other one left. That hurt most of all and I tried to keep the hurtful thoughts at bay. I tried to stop feeling sorry for myself.

I needed to leave. I had seen the film and I just needed to get back to my hotel room where I could deal with my emotions, in private. But Carter came over to me and pulled me up out of the chair, dropping his T-shirt on the floor. He gently grabbed my chin and pulled my face toward him.

"What's wrong Queenie?"

"I'm sorry. I am a world-class sap," I said. I didn't need Ivey to tell me that. "I have been on a roller coaster since I came to this Island. It's just that the cameraman, from the movie, he was my

119

great uncle. My grandmothers' brother, Walter. Sorry for overreacting. I never even met him."

"It's okay. I get it. So, you ended up on this Island to deliver a letter to a lady that you never met, from a relative that you never knew. That is quite the story. Keep talking," he said as he put an arm around me and rubbed the back of my sundress.

"Wow! We could be here all night if I told you the whole story. Brooks told me that he wanted the rights to my story for his next blockbuster. That was probably just a lie...like everything else. It has been a lot to deal with, that's for sure."

"Tell me. I want to hear about how you got here."

"Well...it all started with a Christmas card from my biological grandmother almost two years ago, I guess if you want to go all the way back. I always knew I was adopted but I couldn't believe that she had tracked me down after all that time. She had been looking for many years. My mother had put me up for adoption without even telling her. I was four years old then. How horrible is that?" I asked, knowing a question like that didn't require an answer.

"My first trip to New Jersey was great. That's where she lived, not far from New York City. Nana was already ninety-one years old then. I was lucky she was still around. She lived in a tiny apartment and I slept on the spare bed in her room. We went by train into New York City and did the typical tourist things. Museums, tours, the Statue of Liberty, and lots of good restaurants and wine. Nana liked her wine I found out quickly."

"Don't we all?" Carter broke in, taking another swig of his beer.

I smiled at him, wondering why I was pouring my heart out to this stranger. Maybe it was all the alcohol. Maybe it was the fact that it had always been easier for me to be open to strangers, instead of those who were close to me. People who I loved. Strangers would come and go, taking my secrets with them. Loved ones would stick around and remind me of the things I didn't want to think about. *But maybe David wouldn't have dumped you if you had been more forthcoming with him,* Ivey chimed in, with her fake sympathy.

"We talked quite a bit that first visit, but it all seemed sort of superficial. There were a lot of silent moments too as if just being together was enough for her. Explanations were not needed or wanted. That would come later, I hoped, but I was not going to push it even though I knew that I may not get much more time with her. Looking back, I wish I had pushed harder," I said, pausing for a moment as my thoughts drifted backwards.

"And?" Carter said, turning that single word into a question.

"Well, it's funny how fate or destiny or whatever you want to call it, sometimes plays out. I guess I was just meant to be with her in those last couple years of her life. I'm grateful for that. I decided to move out to New Jersey and start college again. I had dropped out right before I reconnected with her.

"Anyway, I found out some things that I wished I hadn't. My grandmother and grandfather only had one child, my mother. She was in and out of institutions for a while. Then she bounced around between a bunch of loser boyfriends, my Dad included. No one knows who or where he is. My grandmother was always there to bail her daughter out, even though she was battling her own demons. She put her life on hold to be there for my mother. Look, the stories go on and on…I don't mean to bore you with all this."

"No, no, please, I want to hear it," he said, encouraging me.

"Okay…well, I just wasn't that good at dealing with this family I didn't know. Too many memories were coming back to me, things I had pushed aside. I could have handled it much better. I should have done more, but I felt guilty. I was starting to see the life my grandmother had led more clearly, and it saddened me. What right did I have to stop her from drinking at her age? I just did the best I could to keep her safe from herself when she was really out of it."

I realized I was telling Carter things that I hadn't shared with anyone. I needed to push these thoughts back where they belonged. Lock them away before more escaped. They weren't thoughts I cared to dwell on. Besides, I never fully understood what was at the root of my grandmother's drinking.

"Anyway, My grandmother did live long enough to see me graduate from college, she was a big part of helping me to accomplish that goal by letting me live with her and helping me financially. The graduation was a happy time for both of us. My adopted family was there too. It was so nice to have them all together for that one time. I like to think that maybe I did her some good as well in her final years, but I just don't know."

"I bet she was truly grateful to have you with her," he said.

"I like to think so. Sometimes I think it would be nice to unknow some of these things. Addictions and mental illness can be hereditary. These thoughts have given me some sleepless nights."

"Anyone who learned these awful things about their family would have every right to be concerned. I think you were lucky to get away. You know, to be adopted."

"I hope you're right. Sometimes I wonder if I'm doomed to make their mistakes over again."

"You are stronger than you give yourself credit for. I can see that, and I have known you less than a week. Well...I was going to offer you another beer, but maybe that's not the best idea after your story. I'm not sure..."

Instead of moving, he pulled me into a hug, and we stood there embracing. His bare skin against me smelled of soap and perspiration. His skin was damp with it. I noticed a subtle change in the way he was rubbing my back and how he was leaning into me. Then he reached up and caressed my cheek.

NO.

This was not what I wanted, even though I did feel my body reacting to him. My head and my heart were not in it. I pulled away from him gently, pushing him with my hands. He got the message. This was all wrong.

I stupidly wondered to myself what if this was Brooks? Would I stop him? Even after all I had learned? What a mess. Things were so jumbled in my brain. All the beer wasn't helping. How could I still like Brooks knowing that he had been lying to me and using me?

Plus, he had a different girl on his arm every time I saw him. He made no secret of that.

Carter walked off to the kitchen and came back with a couple more beers. He silently led me out to the front porch and we sat on the loungers and drank our beers in silence. He had put his shirt back on. The moonlight glittered off the black ocean surface before us. The stifling night air pushed in on me from all sides. I felt like I was spinning as I reclined on the lounger. I had drank too much.

I did feel bad for rejecting Carter as Brooks had rejected me. Carter pulled out a couple of Marlboros' from a pack that was laying on the little table between us. He lit them both and handed one to me. I took it, the cigarette smoke smelled good. I took a couple of deep puffs and felt a soothing rush as I coughed a little. I wanted to get up and ask him to take me back to the Hotel. *No, you don't, you like the attention and, besides, Carter makes you feel closer to Brooks.* Ivey was getting louder and louder since I came to Euphoria. I hated her and her twisted logic.

"Thanks for…everything," I said with a yawn. "Thanks for listening is what I really mean."

"Sure," he answered.

"So, what's the real deal with you and Brooks?"

"I guess I have always been in his shadow, even though I'm a couple years older than him. I graduated in '75 and he graduated two years later. We just seemed to gravitate towards each other in school and all the activities. We were best friends, but he always had to be better at everything we did. Football, basketball and then girls. It got old.

"I was in love with someone once and he made sure that ended badly. You don't want to hear this garbage. I made a promise to myself a long time ago that he would never do it to me again. That I would never let him make me angry like that. I was glad when he left Euphoria, but I make it my business to know whenever he comes back to the Island."

123

More of his same vague rhetoric. What else did I expect from him? Even after I had been so open. I should have known better. I was feeling groggy. I put out the cigarette in the black plastic ashtray on the table and thought to myself that I should really be leaving. But I was too drunk to follow through with my plan, and my head was swimming. Instead, I fell asleep on the lounger to the sound of the ocean waves caressing the sandy shore.

EXHIBIT
December 24, 1988

I woke with a start. I was still at Carter's. Why the hell had I let myself get so drunk last night? I smelled bacon and freshly brewed coffee. My stomach growled. I was on the couch with a blanket. He was working away in the kitchen and a little TV on the counter was broadcasting the morning news. His hair was still damp from his morning shower.

I stretched and arched my back. It felt good. My head felt fuzzy from the night before. I was mad at myself for staying over, and for dumping so many personal things on him. He must have heard me moving around.

"Good morning Sunny. Did you sleep okay? I hope the couch was comfortable. I thought putting you in my bed might be…awkward."

"Yeah. Thanks."

"I was just making some breakfast. Are you hungry?"

"Yes. Can I use your bathroom?"

He showed me where the bathroom was and gave me a fresh towel and washcloth. I jumped in the shower just to wake myself up a little. I would have to put my same clothes back on. After cleaning up I headed into the kitchen and sat down on a barstool at the counter as he cooked. I looked at the TV and there was a news reporter in front of my hotel talking into a mic. I reached over and turned up the volume with curiosity.

"…her body was found in a secluded area of the beach in front of the Island's most prestigious resort complex two days ago. Foul play is suspected. Police are still investigating. Her identity has not yet been released," the announcer said.

Carter clicked off the TV.

"Oh my gosh. Wait, turn that back on. Does that kind of thing happen a lot around here?"

"Not really," he said as he turned the TV back on. It was too late; the news reporter had moved on to the weather. Storms were in the forecast.

"That explains all the cop cars and crime scene tape that I saw at the hotel yesterday. I never would have guessed...,"

An icy chill went up and down my spine. I was shocked and not sure what to say or do. I had been so wrapped up in the past, but here was a gut punch from the present. This had nothing to do with me, but it put me on edge. A girl murdered at the hotel where I was staying...

"It's a real shame, but I guess there is good and evil in all of us. Might be scary to see the on-going struggle of right and wrong...love and hate...that occurs on a daily basis. Luckily the sane ones keep it in check, and there are a lot more of them around. It balances things out," Carter said.

"Now that is deep. I need coffee before I can process a thought like that; besides, you are not the first one to tell me something like that since I have arrived on this Island."

"I think your boy Brooks falls into the minority," he said in a warning tone.

I gave him my best don't-go-there glance. I did not like where this conversation was headed. I had not forgiven Carter or Brooks, yet.

"You know his real name is Samuel. Samuel Merriweather. Just in case you were curious. Here you go, coffee and breakfast as promised." I was glad he let it go and moved on to breakfast. He was a good cook and the coffee burned the back of my throat as I drank it down. We ate in silence as I dwelled on the thought of someone being murdered at the same hotel I was staying at. It did not sit well with me and I found my appetite fading as I pushed the food around on my plate.

"I have to head into the studio. Can I drop you off at your hotel?"

"That would be great, and do me a favor? When you transfer that film for Roger Hodair...would you make a copy for me too."

"Sure, planned on it."

"Thanks."

I helped him clean up breakfast and then he drove me back to the hotel.

"Hey, Queenie...don't forget the opening at the studio tonight. You're my guest of honor. Starts at eight. Dress like a princess. Oh, and Queenie – be careful, okay?"

"You developed all the photos already? That was fast."

"What can I say? I am that good, and you inspired me. Besides, I don't sleep much, and I was under the gun to get something finished for tonight. Your photos turned out great."

"Well, I am still furious with you, you know. Don't think you are off the hook so easy."

"See you at eight sharp."

I smiled and waved as he drove off. I didn't know what I was going to do for the rest of the day, but now I needed to worry about finding a dress. Would it be bad to wear the yacht party dress that Brooks had bought me? Probably. I would have to visit Karen at the dress store. Maybe they have a clearance rack.

🌴 🌴 🌴

I was standing at the elevator doors waiting when I felt a warm hand on the small of my back. I turned around and there was Brooks smiling down at me, with the charm turned all the way up. I wasn't too keen on talking to him. I gave him a cold smile and said, "Hi."

"Hi Sunny. What have you been up to?"

"Nothing much," I said, guessing that he had probably just watched Carter drop me off outside, but I wasn't going to explain anything.

"Uncover anything new since last we met?" he said dramatically, but I wasn't biting.

"No, not really. Nothing important," I said.

I guessed he could see the conversation was going nowhere and his tone changed. "Is something wrong? Is this about the other night at the bar?" he asked.

I just laughed. His ego was big, and of course, it was about the other night at the bar and so much more. I would not admit it, though.

The elevator doors opened with a ding and we both stepped in and turned around to stand side by side. When the doors closed, he turned to glare at me. He was angry. I moved a step away from him.

"Just because people watch me in a couple of movies, they think they know me," he snarled. "Guys think I'm their best friend and women think I'm their boyfriend. That's quite ridiculous, really. They don't know me; you don't know me. I'm not public property. I'm not a piece of meat."

"Guess I'm off the hook then, since I've never seen any of your movies," I said, as I laughed again. I couldn't help it; I was angry with him and wanting to make him feel bad.

I wondered if his mom felt that same internal conflict that he did, as she swam and posed in the Montague Hotel swimming pool, playing the mermaid for bar patrons. Wanting fame, wanting to be known and celebrated, but hating the invasion of privacy that it brought with it.

I felt bad for laughing at him when I saw the effect my words were having on him. No need to anger him. I knew what his temper was like. I was being careless, but it was too late to undo what had been done.

He pushed the alarm button and caused the elevator to stop with a jerk; then he backed me up to the wall with a shove. He reached his arms down around my thighs and lifted me off the floor of the elevator cab. I was trying to grab onto something afraid I was going to fall and the only thing I could latch onto was him.

"Is this what you want?" he said kissing me hard. "Should we go to my room or do it right here in the elevator?"

He started kissing down my neck and then pulled on the front of my sundress as his kisses moved lower. I was panicking and trying to push him away. I couldn't even put thoughts to words. All I could come up with was a weak 'no'. I said it over and over again as the tears started falling. One of his hands started to pull up my skirt and the shock turned to anger. This was not what I wanted at all.

I arched my back and pushed off with my elbows and hands as hard as I could from the wall of the elevator. The surprise caught him off balance we both tumbled to the floor. I jumped up and pushed the button to get the elevator moving again. I turned back to him, he was still on the floor. I walked toward him and reached down to slap his face, hard.

"What the hell is your problem? You have some issues, don't you," I shouted at him. My hands were clenched and shaking; my breath came out in ragged bursts. The elevator stopped, and the doors slid open. I stepped out backwards, crashing into a couple that was waiting. I reached an arm back in, to keep the doors from closing. Brooks was still on the floor, rubbing the cheek I had just slapped.

"You are an asshole. A word I have been throwing around a lot lately. You are so full of yourself you Hollywood phony. Oh, and by the way, I did uncover some things - why didn't you tell me that Angela was your mother, Samuel? That's just the tip of the iceberg, Samuel. I have been finding out about all kinds of things that I am sure you would be interested in keeping secret."

He was glaring at me and his anger changed to cold surprise as the doors slid shut.

"Stay away from me Samuel," I shouted at the closed doors.

The couple had moved over to wait for a different elevator. I ran to my room, fumbling to get the room key to work. It took a few tries and then I crashed through to safety. I made sure the door was locked and bolted with my shaky hands as the tears started back up. I walked into the bathroom and threw up into the hotel toilet as violent sobs racked me.

I was so scared. I was mad at myself for the inflammatory comments I had made. I should not have pushed Brooks like I did, not a good idea. I had no inkling of what else he was capable of, but he had a short fuse. That I knew for a fact. I had seen it in the alley behind the bar the other night. Ivey said nothing, but in my mind, I knew she was shaking her head at me. I felt ashamed, like it was my fault that Brooks had attacked me. I knew that was crazy.

I wished I could call David but there was no way I could explain all this, plus he probably wouldn't want to hear it. It would be a confirmation for him that he had done the right thing by dumping me.

🌴 🌴 🌴

I knew I wouldn't be able to rest or even watch the television, and I didn't want to be alone with my thoughts. I threw on my swimsuit and a cover-up and headed downstairs to the pool, where I would be surrounded by other people, not all alone. I was nervous about getting back into the elevator, but I made it to the lobby safely. When I was down in the lobby, I decided to make a detour into the dress shop. Karen was working so I went right over to her.

"Hi Karen, I'm Sunny, remember? I was wondering if you could help me find a dress for tonight."

She looked at me funny and then the light bulb came on.

"Oh yes. I remember you. One of Brooks' girls. What are you looking for?"

"Umm…a cocktail dress, I guess. Kind of like the last one…only how about black this time. The last one was white," I said, gritting my teeth at the thought of being called Brooks' girl, but I did my best to ignore the comment.

She grabbed a few garments off the racks and took me back to a dressing room.

"Try these and let me know what you like."

Luckily, she had remembered the size, so I didn't have to embarrass myself again. I tried on all three. I decided on the least revealing dress. They were all beautiful. It felt good to distract myself from thoughts of Brooks in the elevator. My hands weren't shaking anymore.

Karen said she would have it delivered to my room. I didn't ask about the price and she never brought it up. I was sure I would be regretting it later when I got the bill. I thanked her for her help.

I was on the way out to the pool when I decided to detour to the spa and see if I could get in for a massage. I had never had one before. They had an opening that gave me time for a swim and a soak in the hot tub first. And a good stiff drink of something. I booked it thinking I would regret that expense later, along with the dress.

After swimming and the massage, I was back in my room where I crashed hard. I took a two-hour nap. The pool and massage had relaxed me enough for that at least, along with a couple of beers. I wondered what Charles had been up to. I hoped he wasn't out conning any tourists and I hoped I would see him tomorrow, but it was too late for today.

I stood staring at the beautiful black cocktail dress that Karen had helped me pick out. It was time to get ready for the exhibit. I would make a quick appearance and leave. Maybe go for a drink in the piano bar later.

After the way I had screwed so many things up on this trip, I just needed to get my head straight. I felt like I couldn't skip the opening though, and besides it might be good to see Jenna and talk to a female for a change. Maybe I could make amends for leaving the beach so abruptly with Charles after the photo shoot. Anything would be better than sitting in my lonely hotel room by myself all night. Besides, I would take any ego boost I could get after my run-in with Brooks in the elevator.

I put on my new dress along with some makeup. I decided to put my hair up in a sloppy bun to keep it off my shoulders. I stood in front of the mirror looking at myself. My week in the sun had given me some color on my normally pale skin. Even my sandy brown hair seemed to be touched with a few golden streaks. Paradise was looking good on me I realized with a smile. At least something was going my way, even if it was the superficial.

I grabbed a beer out of the room fridge and drank it down. I let out a burp that Charles would have been proud of. I was gathering some things and putting them into my little bag and thinking maybe I should wipe off just a little of the eye makeup, when the phone rang.

"Hello?"

"Hi, Ms. McQueen? This is the front desk. Your car is here."

"Oh…okay. I guess I will be right down. Thanks."

I didn't order a cab. I was a little nervous, but I headed downstairs. I was planning to take the moped to Carter's studio so I could leave whenever I wanted to. I stopped at the lobby desk and they said my car was out front. I walked out of the lobby doors and there sat a sleek, black limousine parked under the porte-cochere. The driver stood by the back door of the car, waiting for me. I walked over to him.

"Hello…but I didn't order a limo…"

Hello, Ms. McQueen. Carter Davis sent me to pick you up for the opening. Let me get the door miss."

I shrugged my shoulders, but I motioned for him to open the door. Maybe this opening was a bigger deal than I thought, but how could that be when it was just pictures of me? Oh well, I could play along. The chauffeur opened the door and I climbed in as modestly as possible in the little black dress.

The interior of the limo smelled of leather and spilt booze. Lights twinkled at the ceiling. The big sunroof was partially open. A bottle of champagne chilled in a silver bucket and the mini-bar and fridge were well stocked. I found a Kalik Crisp that was ice cold.

The limo pulled up in front of Carter's studio. The driver came to the back and opened the door for me. I felt self-conscious as I stepped out, pulling my dress down. There were lots of people and waiters with trays wandering around outside, in front of the studio. I didn't see anyone I knew. I wondered if Brooks would show up. I hoped not. I made my way inside.

I spotted Carter surrounded by a crowd. He cleaned up good. The dark tuxedo fit him like a glove. He wasn't wearing a tie. A couple of the top buttons on his shirt were opened. His brown, wavy hair was combed back. He was smiling with a wine glass in his hand and chatting away. He looked so at ease, which seemed out of character for him. I felt like I was on the outside looking in again. He saw me and smiled and waved me over. Jenna and James were with him.

Carter introduced me around and kissed my cheek. Jenna gave me a hug. Just like that I was part of the group and talking away. Carter grabbed me a glass of champagne when the waiter went by and then he pulled me aside.

"Queenie…I want you to look at your photos, really look at them. I have already sold half the images. I owe that to you and I wanted to say sorry again for what I did at the beach. I hope you will forgive me after you see the photos."

He kissed my cheek again and walked back over to his friends. I turned and looked for the first time at the photos adorning the walls. They were not portraits of a person, they were artwork that captured the interplay of light and dark on the human form. They were in black and white, unlike the photo on the yacht, and my face was turned away or obscured by the focus of the camera or covered by my hair. I was okay with that. I didn't want to be recognized and become the center of attention. I walked my way through the partitions of the studio, winding around to the back.

I stopped and listened to the praise-filled critiques of some of the party-goers. It made me proud of Carter and my anger at him subsided a little. I saw the sold tags on many of the framed pieces. I was surprised by how many people were there. Carter must have a big following on the Island.

As I walked around the last partition at the back of the studio I was shocked to run into my own face. There was a five-foot-tall color photo, made up of smaller images pieced together like a puzzle. It had been strategically placed behind a couple of partitions so that it wouldn't be visible from the rest of the studio. It was only stumbled upon when you reached the back of the gallery, and it was the only image in color.

It was one of the photos he had taken after he insulted me on the beach. My face filled the entire wall. Tears and mascara stained my cheeks. I had come face to face with my ugly and sad inner self. Carter had brought her out and captured her for all to see, like a sideshow freak.

I panicked. I looked around. No one else was looking at the photo. I had to get away from that image. It was too real. I felt humiliated. I was at the back of the studio and I saw the door into Carter's office. I ran to the room and slammed the door behind me. More stupid tears came to my eyes and I was breathing too fast. He had tricked me into exposing myself for the sake of selling his art. I was so tired and confused. It seemed I had no control over my emotions ever since I landed on this Island.

🌴 🌴 🌴

I heard some noise and realized I was not alone in the office. A twenty-something guy was sitting in a chair at the desk. He ran a hand through his curly, dark hair that hadn't been brushed in a while.

His white shirt was unbuttoned half-way down his chest, exposing some hair and a gold marine-link chain. He stared up at me with a questioning glance. The Marlboro Man was riding off into the sunset on the little TV that sat on the desk. I wanted to go with him. The scenery on the little black and white TV reminded me of Wyoming.

"Hello," he said after I had turned to look at him.

"Hello. Who are you?" I asked wiping at my eyes. My face was probably a mess again. I grabbed a tissue from the box on the desk.

"I'm Jenna's friend...boyfriend...I mean ex. My name is Carlos. Nice to meet you," he said, standing to shake my hand.

"Oh. She mentioned you. I didn't realize you were still...friends. My name's Sunny."

I saw a small fridge and walked over to it, hoping there was a beer inside. I was in luck. I set my empty champagne glass down on the desk, opened a beer, and then sat down in a chair. The news had come on and they were talking about the body that was found in front of my hotel.

The reporter said the body remained unidentified and they were asking for the communities help in identifying the victim. The news showed an artist's rendering of her face, void of all expression in an unnatural way. I didn't know her name, but I knew someone who did. It was the Bikini Blonde that I had seen with Brooks.

This was crazy. What was going on? What had I gotten myself into? I felt fear in the pit of my stomach and that was starting to become a far too familiar feeling since I had arrived on the Island. That along with confusion.

"That is such a shame. Beautiful girl too. What a waste. Hey, you want a hit? This is some good shit," Carlos said.

I realized he was smoking a joint and he had the window opened to air out the office. I wondered if it was why Jenna had left him.

"Does Carter know you are in here."

"Sure. He doesn't care."

"Really?"

"Oh yeah. Come on, hit this. You won't be sorry."

I let him hand it to me and I put it to my mouth. I hadn't smoked pot before. I was numb and not really thinking about what I was doing. My brain was a scrambled mess. I inhaled it and held it in like I had seen in some movies. I coughed a couple of times and then I handed it back to him.

I felt calmer after a few minutes and I was grateful. I put out my hand for another puff. He handed it over and this time I took two drags and then passed it back. I sunk down into the chair trying to get my thoughts straight as I adjusted my dress. My head was spinning. Carlos munched noisily on a bag of chips.

Could Brooks have had something to do with Bikini Blonde's death? I had seen him with her more than once and Brooks certainly had proven how angry he could get in a short amount of time. But I just couldn't bring myself to believe that he would kill someone, even though I knew what a jerk he was.

The office door banged open and Carter came in. Carlos casually threw his joint out the open window, but it was too late, Carter had seen it.

"What the hell is going on in here?"

"Nothing Boss. Just came back here for a quick smoke," Carlos said.

"Smoke of what? That's not tobacco, Carlos. What did I tell you about using my office? I don't know why Jenna even invited you. Get out of here before I throw you out."

"Nice to meet you, Sunny," Carlos said as he stood up.

Carlos casually strolled out as Carter glared at him. Once Carlos was out of the room, Carter turned his gaze on me.

"Were you smoking pot with him?"

"No...no," I said, but saw that he didn't believe me. This night was going downhill fast. What was I doing? This wasn't me. I wondered if Walter had ever dabbled in drugs, or did he just stick with good ol' alcohol?

"What were you doing?" Carter asked while running a hand through his hair.

"I just came in to…sit down for a minute…I didn't know anyone was in here…I saw my pictures and then I saw the girl on the news. The dead girl. I've seen her before…a couple of times, but I don't know her name. I can't deal with all this," I said, as I started crying.

I hated my tears that were betraying me in front of Carter, once again. Why couldn't I get my damn emotions under control anymore? Fear mixed with the confusion in my head and the pot was not helping one bit. I couldn't keep it together.

"Sorry, Queenie. I'm sorry if the photos upset you. I saw the news earlier too, about the dead girl. She looks familiar," he said as he came over to me and wrapped his arms around me. I leaned my head on his shoulder. My fear overtook my anger towards him. I let him comfort me.

"Hey, I have to get back out to the guests. I just came in here to grab some keys. We close in half an hour. Come and have a glass of champagne with me. It will take your mind off…things."

"Okay, I guess," I said regaining some composure.

"Besides, your boyfriend just showed up."

"Who…Brooks?" I asked.

"Yeah."

"No, NO! I'll just hang out in here for a little bit if that is okay. You go. I'll be fine."

"What's wrong? I thought you would want to see him."

"Let's just say we had a falling out. Trust me – I don't think he wants to see me right now either. I'm surprised he even came. He must not have known that the photos were of me."

"Well, he would never miss a party. Are you on the outs?"

"Yes. Hey, Carter?"

"Yes?"

"Last night, I saw you talking to Brooks in the piano bar, before we went to your house."

"Oh," he said cautiously.

"What were you talking about?" I asked.

"Not much really. He said hello and he asked about the film when he saw it on the bar. I just told him I was transferring it for a client. He doesn't know what was on it or who it was for."

"That's it?"

"Yeah…that's it. Am I on your suspect list now too?" he said.

"No, of course not," I replied.

"Good. Now care to tell me what the falling out was about?"

"Well, it's stupid, really."

"What happened?"

"He just…he tried to force himself on me…in the elevator at my hotel…I slapped him," was all I could get out before the tears started back up.

"God damn it," he said angrily. "That just confirms it all for me. He is one arrogant bastard. Don't worry, he will get what is coming to him. I promise you that."

"It's ok, really," I said as I grabbed a tissue. He sounded so angry, it scared me. "It's done. I'm done with him, I promise you that. Just forget about it, okay?"

"All right, for now. I won't make a scene here, but this isn't the end of it. You stay here. I will let you know when he's gone. If you are truly over him, that might be the best news I have heard all week."

"Carter…there is something else too. That girl on the news, that was murdered, I saw her with Brooks…a couple of times," I said.

"Damn it. This just keeps getting worse. Look, I really think you should call the police. Tell them about the girl and how Brooks attacked you. Don't let him get away with it. If he physically tried to hurt you, then maybe he had something to do with what happened to that girl too. He's dangerous. You should see that by now."

"I don't know. I'm just not sure…I can't imagine him being involved with a murder, no matter what else he has done," I said.

"Well, at the least, you could call it in anonymously…to the cops. Let them know they should ask Brooks about the girl. If they talk to Brooks maybe he can tell them who she is, if nothing else. She deserves that, doesn't she? Her family deserves that."

"Yes, of course. You're right," I said, wiping at my eyes again.

"Use that phone on my desk there. There's a phone book beside it. You'll feel better about all this if you help the police figure out who she is."

"Thank you, Carter. I'll call right now. It's the right thing to do. The police will sort it out. But I will only tell them about the girl, for now, okay?"

Why was I trying to stupidly protect Brooks?

"All right, but don't take too long thinking it over. I think the police need to know everything. Look…I promised Jenna and James a ride in the limo after the show. We'll drop you off at your hotel. You might want to, ah…clean up your face a bit," he said as he left the office.

I sat back down in the chair watching the little TV and wishing Carlos was still in the office with his smokes. I grabbed another beer from the fridge as I gathered my nerve. I picked up the phone book and found the number for the Island police, and then I made a phone call. They took my anonymous tip without pushing me too hard for my name. Carter was right, I felt better.

I cleaned up my face and then I decided to snoop around a little since I was stuck in the office until the party was over. Maybe I could find a pack of regular cigarettes at least. I needed something. I was feeling shaky. I opened the desk drawer but all I found were some newspaper clippings about Brooks current visit to the Island, a broken cross necklace and some keys. The prodigal son had returned, and the Island still loved him.

I was on my third beer when Jenna popped into the office. She smiled at me and kicked off her high heels. She plopped down into the desk chair that Carlos had been sitting in and she put her feet up on the desk. Her smooth, tan legs laid across all the papers on the desk.

"You want a beer?" I asked, hoping she couldn't see that I had been crying.

"Sounds good."

I grabbed one out of the mini-fridge and handed it over.

"Your pictures were terrific. I think Carter was really surprised by the success of the show. He usually does beach scenes and wildlife, but this was a huge hit for him tonight. He will probably sell even more when Junkanoo gets going."

"Thanks. I must admit, it is a little disconcerting to see all these images of myself up on the walls. I don't like being the focus of everyone's attention. I think you would make a great model for him. You are so beautiful." *Much more so than you,* my inner voice agreed.

"You are sweet. Thanks."

"I met your ex tonight," I said, hoping I sounded casual.

"Oh, Carlos? I invited him. I just feel sorry for him. He has some issues. Carter can't stand him though."

"I noticed."

"Damn it – men. What happened?"

"Carter found him here in the office smoking."

"Damn Carlos. I told him to lay off that stuff. Some things will never change," she knew without me even saying it. She knew what he had been smoking.

"So, what's up with you and Carter? I can tell he's interested," she said, changing the subject.

"I don't know," I said honestly. I did feel some affection for him when he wasn't pissing me off. But it had been overshadowed by my attraction to Brooks. Now I didn't know what I wanted. My thoughts turned to David and I pushed them away with another beer. I didn't want to think about him or Bikini Blonde. I just wanted to forget.

"Brooks Laughton showed up at the last minute. God, that guy is gorgeous. I was surprised to see him here."

"That is surprising," I said.

Carter and his assistant James entered the office then and both grabbed a beer. I hoped they didn't notice how many were missing from the mini-fridge.

"That was a great opening. I could not have done it without all of you. Thank you," Carter said. "Now how about that limo ride?"

We all piled into the limo, laughing. After all the beers and the pot, I was not so worried about my little black dress when I climbed in the second time. Carter talked to the driver and gave him directions. He opened the iced bottle of champagne and Jenna poured us all a glass. She turned up the radio and sang along with the song as she draped an arm around James. She was so carefree and confident; I wished I was more like her.

Jenna began to kiss James. I hadn't realized they were together. She really had moved on from Carlos. I felt awkward watching them. I turned to look at Carter sitting beside me. He was watching for my reaction to them. I felt even more uncomfortable.

A different song came on and Jenna jumped up to pop her head out of the open sunroof and sing along with Joan Jett and the Blackhearts. She was dancing. James grabbed her bare legs to keep her steady. He had a big smile on his face. The limo pulled up in front of an apartment building. It was Jenna and James' stop. As they were climbing out, Jenna leaned over to kiss my cheek and whisper in my ear.

"He really is a good guy if you give him a chance," she said.

I smiled into her face as she held mine in her hands and looked into my eyes. She had such a sweet and lovable heart. She surprised me with a peck on my lips and then she giggled. The limo door slammed shut after they were out. I realized I had never mentioned the photo shoot at the beach, but it didn't seem to matter. I had meant to apologize for my abrupt departure that day on the beach.

Carter hollered to the driver that the next stop was my hotel then he moved to one of the side seats. He grabbed my left foot and undid my sandal. Then he started to massage my foot.

"Foot massage Ms. McQueen?"

"That feels good. Thank you."

"It's the least I can do. Thank you for tonight."

"I would say you're welcome but...I'm still mad at you. I was not very comfortable with that last photo either. The one at the back that was in color."

"Touché. If it makes you feel any better, that one is not for sale. So, tell me, are you really done with Brooks?" he said, quickly changing the subject.

"Yes. You were right about him."

"Sorry, but I can't say that I am sad about it. You deserve better."

"Are you better?"

"No, not really," he said, without a trace of a smile.

"Well, Jenna thinks highly of you and put in a good word."

"So I heard. She is sweet. I have always had a soft spot for that one."

"Have you two ever dated?"

No...we've always been more like brother and sister than anything else. I'm an only child though...like Brooks. Besides, I am interested in someone else," he said, meaningfully.

"Oh," I responded with, feeling my cheeks burn.

"Yes. You make me feel things that I haven't felt in a very long time. If you have truly moved on from Brooks, there might be a chance for us. At least a chance to try and see what happens. I haven't done anything like this in such a long time. Sorry, if I am doing it all wrong. I think I could learn to put an end to the things that I have been hanging on to...give myself a fresh start...give myself a chance at normal."

He put my left foot down and grabbed the right one. He took that shoe off and began to massage it. I didn't know what to say or do. I had been making a mess of everything since I started this trip. David had dumped me, and Brooks had attacked me; did I really want to jump back in with Carter? He hadn't treated me so good either.

I couldn't help it. He seemed so sad and vulnerable in that moment and I was so drunk and stoned. I climbed over to him spilling some champagne as I went. I put my lips to his and kissed him gently as I wrapped my arms around him and held him. I wanted to heal him with everything in me even though I knew it was all wrong. A big mistake...

The limo had reached my hotel. Carter pulled me away from his lips and looked at me. He was playing with my protection charm that hung around my neck. The one that Charles' grandmother had given me.

"Your stop. Take some time. Think about this," he said. "This is new territory for both of us."

"Okay. I will."

"Goodnight Queenie."

"Goodnight, Carter."

I climbed back out of the limo barefoot, with my sandals in my hand. I watched after the limo as it drove off. I waved at the impenetrable jet-black windows and wondered what the hell I had just done.

BAD DAY
December 25, 1988

I woke up thinking my trip is half over and I need an aspirin, lots of aspirin. I found some water and the pain reliever, then I decided to head down to the pool for a swim and a soak in the hot tub. I had slept in again and it would be lunch time soon, but my stomach felt queasy. The days were blending together, and they seemed to consist of more and more night, and a lot less day.

After the pool, I showered and did some laundry and then I hopped on the moped in clean shorts, tank top and ponytail. I drove around the Island of Euphoria for a couple of hours, discovering new streets. I rode along, past the beaches of pristine sands, stopping to take in the view every now and then. I wound my way along narrow mountain roads of lush vegetation, thinking of everything and nothing.

I found a roadside café and ordered a late lunch of salad and tea to go, then I found a nearby beach and sat down to eat. The seagulls circled around, wondering if they would be lucky enough to snag a dropped bite.

My week on the Island had been a roller coaster ride. Improving my drinking skills; that was all I had seemed to accomplish. I was getting damn good at it too. I could keep up with Walter, I thought, proudly and repulsed all at the same time. I tried to reason with myself. It's okay to cut loose occasionally, right? I was on vacation. But, was that all it was or did this go deeper?

Would I even be asking these questions if I had not learned anything about my biological family? Or if this trip had not turned into such a mess? How could I even think about a relationship with anyone when I was so torn up inside? Bikini Blonde tried to creep into my mind, but I shoved her away. I didn't want to dwell on her murder either. I had given the cops all the information that I had about her. It was in their hands to sort out, including Brooks involvement. I finished my food and found a garbage can, then I got back on the moped, driving aimlessly.

I found myself back at the tourist market. I wanted to stop and walk around, maybe do a little shopping to distract myself from thinking too much. But I found the streets empty. Everyone had closed-up shop and disappeared. Cars passed by where the market vendors had sat, selling their wares.

I cruised the streets around the market area, hoping to run into Charles. I knew I should stay away from Charles, let him be a normal kid. Like his grandmother had asked me to do. I had no luck finding him either.

I drove along down the narrow, busy streets of the Island, heading back toward my hotel. The breeze tickled my face with strands of my hair. I checked the rear-view mirror on my left handlebar remembering the night I watched Brooks grow smaller in it. The night I had kissed him behind the bar. But then thoughts of his attack in the elevator crept in.

Something in the mirror caught my eye as I was speeding along. Two vehicles behind me I saw a white-haired crew cut with sunglasses in a small pick-up. I was being followed by the man who had broken into my hotel room and spied on me at the race track.

I immediately turned a hard, sharp left at the next intersection. I was no stunt driver on my little moped, but I managed to piss off the guy in the silver sedan that I turned directly in front of. He laid on the horn as I buzzed by. My move slowed down the truck a little, but I could still see him behind me, so that meant he could see me as well. I turned left again and then right. The right was at a stop light which happened to change immediately after I went through the intersection. The truck was stopped behind me.

I drove part way down the block and turned right again, into an alley. There was a large dumpster in the alley and I parked behind it, so it would block me from the street I had just left. I turned off the bike and sat silently, watching through the crack between the wall and dumpster.

I waited and watched for what seemed like forever. I was sweating and my whole body felt tense. I saw the truck out in the street. He passed by without a glance in my direction. I lost him.

I realized I had been holding my breath. I exhaled and took in a deep breath of the stale alley air, it smelled of rotted food and garbage. I waited a few more seconds and then started the bike back up and exited the alley, back on to the street where the truck had just passed.

I saw the truck, one block ahead of me now. I gunned the moped and decided to follow. I did my best to stay behind vehicles, so crew cut wouldn't see me. I followed him for several blocks, trying to keep him in my sights without being seen. It looked easier in the movies.

He finally pulled over and hopped out of the truck. Then he walked into a brick office building without so much as a glance back in my direction. I parked about half a block back on the opposite side of the street behind a large truck. I sat there for a moment trying to decide what to do. I shut off the bike and decided to walk over to the building he had entered. I wished I still had the mace Dad had given me, but it had been stolen along with everything else that had been in my purse on my first day on the Island.

I entered the building through the glass door, into a small lobby area with some seating and a coffee table full of old magazines. The floor mat had bunched up between the door and frame so that the door had not shut all the way.

A gangly plant, overgrown in its pot, sat in the corner of the lobby by the window. Off the lobby, ran a long corridor with many doors. A row of locked mailboxes lined one wall of the lobby. I walked over to the mailboxes and saw that they were labeled with business names.

Attorney, realtor, accountant – I didn't think any of those were right. I couldn't picture crew cut as an attorney or realtor. I wouldn't buy a house from him. I kept looking. Island Security and Investigative Services Suite 108 – that had potential. I remembered the matchbook I had found in Brooks jacket pocket on the night of the yacht party – had it been the same name? I couldn't remember for sure.

I walked down the hallway and found the door. I could see Crew Cut sitting at a desk through the glass. I had to know why he was following me. I opened the door. He turned to look at me and his expression changed quickly to one of surprise. He stood up and knocked over a cup of stale coffee on his desk. It fell to the floor.

"Damn it!" he exclaimed. "What the hell are you doing here and how did you get in?" he asked as he searched around for something to clean up the mess with.

"Why are you following me?" I asked back.

"What are you talking about?"

"I've seen you, you know…many times, actually. You're not a very good private investigator, are you? Not with as easily as I spotted you. You were in my hotel room, at the race track and following me down the street not more than five minutes ago. I was able to lose you, easy. Why are you following me?"

"Look lady…I don't know what you are talking about. And unless you are looking to hire me, I am going to ask you to leave now. I have somewhere to be."

"Come on, you just walked in. Tell me the truth…who hired you to spy on me and why? Was it Brooks? Brooks Laughton?"

He burst out laughing as he found some paper towels and wiped at his desk and picked the coffee cup off the floor. It's contents leaving a brown stain in the orange shag carpet.

"You think Brooks Laughton, the famous movie star, is checking up on you? HA! That's a good one and besides, he likes blondes.

You're crazy lady and I don't know what you are talking about. Now I really have to get going, so don't let the door hit you on the way out."

"But I saw a matchbook with your company name in Brooks jacket," I said.

"I give out business advertising to lots of people…so what?"

I was confused. I turned around thinking this is getting nowhere. Maybe I should go. I walked over to the door and then turned back. Crew cut was watching me warily.

"Carter Davis? Did Carter Davis hire you?" I asked. I thought I saw a flicker of something. I could see it in his reaction. Maybe he just knew the name or maybe Carter had hired him.

"Christ, lady. It's Christmas day. What the hell are we doing here? I just stopped in the office to grab a couple presents I was hiding here. What is your problem?"

"Well, thanks for nothing…and stop following me," I said as I walked out and slammed the door. What the hell was I doing? I had forgotten Christmas. What was wrong with me? No wonder the tourist market was gone and there was no Charles in sight. All the sane people were celebrating Christmas. I still had time to call my family back home at least.

So maybe Crew Cut had not been following me today, but this still made little sense. He had been in my room. Was Carter having me watched? Carter was there at the hotel right after Crew Cut had been in my room too, acting innocent when maybe he knew exactly what had happened. But why would Carter be keeping tabs on me? Or did I misinterpret the detective's reaction? I had been hoping to find answers but once again all I was left with was a big fat nothing. And on top of that, I was feeling stupid for forgetting all about Christmas.

I exited the building and walked over to the moped. I made my way to the location of the tourist market, figuring it would be easier to get back to the hotel once I got there. I pulled up alongside an open space of curb and just stopped. The engine idled for a couple of minutes before I even thought to turn it off.

I heard laughter and looked around to see some tanned tourists walking hand in hand down the street. They were enjoying their vacation and I was jealous. It was time to see about an earlier flight off this damned Island I told myself. *That is the first smart thing you have said all week,* my inner voice agreed.

Movement across the street caught my eye. I looked up and saw Roger waving at me through the big window of the Historical Society. He was waving me over. I was surprised to see him there on Christmas, but maybe this was the perfect opportunity to see about retrieving the suitcase since I had decided to leave.

"Hello, Roger. Merry Christmas and all that jazz."

"Uh…yes. Merry Christmas to you too."

"I'm surprised to see you here on Christmas, I didn't think the museum would be open," I said.

"Well, I just stopped in for a bit, but holidays can be a busy time on the Island. Anyway, I have no one to celebrate with since I am a confirmed bachelor. And I am afraid my parents are both gone now as well. My mum died eight years back and my father has been gone for ten now."

"I am sorry to hear it," I said, looking down at my toes.

"No worries. They have been gone for so long now. I am glad to see you, though. I have something I think you might be interested in seeing. Now I warn you, it is not for the faint of heart. They are very graphic images. I forgot I even had the photos, but you got my wheels turning. Maybe you and I can solve the crime. The biggest whodunnit of the Island's history. You can be Watson to my Sherlock Holmes. Maybe there was something the detectives missed."

"Look, I was just wondering about retrieving my suitcase…I'm not following you…"

"First things first, love. I have in my possession the crime scene photos from the murder of one Arthur Milton Murray. I bet you would like to get a gander at those, eh?"

I was shocked and not sure what to say. I wasn't too crazy about looking at the photos, truth be told, but I thought I would humor him since it was Christmas and he was alone. Hell, I was alone as well, and he seemed so pleased with his find. We made our way back to the workroom and he produced an old box of 8x10 photos. He pulled them out one by one and we looked at them together, in somber silence.

The police had photographed every angle of the room where Arthur Murray had died; and his body, or at least what was left of it. Thankfully the photos were all black and white. The photos sickened me. I was repulsed but I couldn't look away.

The charred remains of the body laid wrapped in a bundle of blackened cloth. It had been wrapped up in the curtains and tied up before being set on fire as Roger had previously told me. A blackened arm had escaped the wrappings. I tried to distract myself by taking a mental inventory of items in the room, so I wouldn't look at any one thing for too long.

The arm that had escaped it's wrapping…that was what had bothered me most…a flash of an image came to mind. It popped like a camera flash, leaving a white-hot spot in my brain. I pushed the thought away fast.

Roger said that the fire sprinklers had activated. They saved the room and hotel from major damage. There were a couple suitcases on the bed and clothes hanging in the closet. Some shoes on the floor. A watch and miniature seashell cufflinks on the bedside table. The bed was messed up like someone had sat on it, and there was a giant stuffed teddy bear on it. It had a big bow around its neck. It looked like the kind of thing you would win at a carnival.

Shattered booze bottles littered the floor, cleared from the empty bar cart I guessed. A metal ice bucket full of water sat on the table in the room, with a pearl-handled ice pick lying next to it. The ice had all melted by the time the photo had been taken. A couple of half-filled rocks glasses sat on the coffee table, along with an ashtray full of cigarette butts.

The suite was just like the one in the 8mm video that I had watched at Carter's. Maybe even the exact same room. It was one of the suites at the top of the old Montague Hotel. Roger had a copy of the autopsy report as well, but there was nothing new in it, at least nothing I couldn't already see from the photos. They couldn't determine much due to the condition of the body.

I didn't like the feeling I had, looking at the photos and documents. I felt like a stranger at a funeral. I wanted to leave, get away from the nightmare images. I wanted to cling to my version of Walter's world, not this grim reality.

"Wow. Interesting stuff, Mr. Hodair, but I really should be going now. Thanks for showing me. Oh, and are you done with the suitcase? I might be leaving a little earlier than I thought. Some things have come up back home. Family matters," I lied. Not sure why I felt the need to lie to Roger, but it sounded more convincing in my ears.

"No, actually, Carter still has some of the items. But I should have it tomorrow. Would that be soon enough?"

"Sure. Did Carter make a copy of the movie for me?"

"Yes, he copied it on to a video cassette for both of us. I watched it several times. I would love to have that playing on a loop in the museum. Such a wonderful glimpse of the glamorous life here on the Island back then."

And such a contrast to the crime scene photos I had just looked at. I followed him out to the museum. He seemed a little bit disappointed by my reaction to the photos. Maybe he had thought I would vomit or at least become woozy and pass out. He had lost that conspiratorial tone he had when I first entered the Historical Society.

"Well, Sunny, will you come back tomorrow night then? I promise to have your suitcase ready to go. Junkanoo starts. The parade passes right by here. This really is one of the best places to watch the festivities. I will have champagne, and not the one-off brand either. Only the finest from France," he said as he leaned in a little too close and put a hand on my shoulder. What was it with the men on this Island? *Don't flatter yourself,* my inner demon said.

"I guess it's a deal then," I said, smiling.

Roger and I said our goodbyes. I left the museum and found my scooter. I followed the familiar road back to my hotel. I had made up my mind one hundred percent by the time I reached the lobby doors. I was done. I was leaving as soon as possible. This adventure was over for me.

Maybe I had learned some things about Walter and my biological family. Maybe the most important thing I had learned was that my real family and real life was back in the sleepy little mid-west town where I had grown up. Why couldn't I be happy with that? Maybe I had accomplished what I had set out to do without realizing it.

Arthur Murray had died long ago and now an innocent girl was dead as well. Somehow, I had enmeshed myself into something that I did not understand ever since the first day I came to this Island. It seemed to be all connected, but the harder I looked the further out of focus everything went. A girl had been killed at my hotel and I hadn't allowed myself to think too hard about that. This was all real and not just some made up story like my detective novels.

Along with that, I was tired of the drama with Brooks and Carter. Why did I even want to get tangled up with either of them in the first place? I regretted kissing Carter. I felt embarrassed by my back and forth behavior. I couldn't even bear to think of what Brooks had done to me. I felt a pang of ridiculous guilt for it, that I could not shake. I was done with the cat-and-mouse games I promised myself.

I dropped off the scooter out front and headed into the hi-rise hotel. I spent a couple of hours talking to hotel staff, and on the phone with the airline company. I breathed a sigh of relief when I was able to move up my flight for an earlier date. I felt calmer then. Only two days left on the Island instead of another week. I would make sure to avoid Brooks and Carter for the next two days and then I would be gone. All I had to do was pick up my suitcase tomorrow from Roger. I did hope to see Charles before I left. I wanted to say goodbye to him at least.

🌴 🌴 🌴

After a late supper in my room, I called my folks and wished them a Merry Christmas. They didn't want me racking up a large phone bill, so the conversation was thankfully short. I laid on the bed and watched the television for a couple of hours after that.

The phone rang but I did not answer it. There was a knock on the door a little while later, but I didn't answer that either. I just laid there, immobile on the bed, and whoever it was left. It was getting late. I realized I had not even had one beer yet. That thought cheered me a little, so I decided I should celebrate with a drink in the piano bar downstairs. My mini-fridge was empty, and I couldn't sleep, so why not? Besides, it was Christmas. I could quit drinking when I got home.

I entered the bar and it was quiet except for the soft tinkle of the piano keys. I was glad to find the place open on a holiday. I found a table and ordered a beer when the bartender came over. I sat in silence with my thoughts and my beer. I motioned for a second beer when the first was gone. The bartender obliged.

The piano player had started a new song. "Me and Bobby McGee". I know it was written as an ode to a lost lover, written by Kris Kristofferson I think, but for me it was different. It reminded me of my Bobby…and the thoughts I always tried to suppress.

153

I made sure to push him away whenever he tried to creep in. He could only successfully reach me in dreams. I barely even knew him. He was just an image in my head. An image of a baby under a sheet in a police man's arms. My mom's ugly sobs in the background. I will never forget that look on the police man's face as he carefully cradled Bobby and carried him away. One little baby arm had fallen free of the sheet and was hanging there lifeless...like Arthur's in the crime scene photos.

That was the Bad Day and it would never be forgiven. That was the hole in my chest that I tried to keep far from my thoughts all these years. I should have been too young to remember or understand but instead, it was burned into my memory like a cauterized wound that wouldn't heal. Thinking of it knocked the breath out of me. I was always so careful to keep the image tucked away. I was more like my grandmother than I realized, keeping the painful memories at bay. I began to sing along softly with the piano as I tried to put the thoughts back in their box.

"Nice. You have a nice voice," someone behind me said as he put a hand on my shoulder.

I turned to look, it was Carlos, Jenna's ex. He sat in the booth behind me, wearing a red and white Santa hat, as well as a goofy grin.

"Hi, Carlos."

"Hi Sunny. Can I join you?"

"Sure."

"Hey, sorry for the drama at Carter's," he said, as he plopped down across from me.

"No worries, really."

"I meant what I said. You have a nice singing voice."

"Thanks. I am not much of a singer though, really...but that song always reminds me of...someone. I don't usually sing in public. I save it for the shower. Janice Joplin sang it so much better. I thought I was the only one in here besides the workers."

"Well, you should sing in public more often."

"Thanks. So, what are you doing here on Christmas day?"

"I used to work here. So now I stop in sometimes. The bartender knows me. He gives me free drinks. Better than hanging out alone in my apartment on Christmas. I don't have any family on the Island. Lucky a lot of places stay open for the tourists."

"Well, let me buy you a beer or something."

"Naww…you want to go down to the beach for a smoke?" Carlos asked.

"Why? We can smoke in here…oh…I get it. What the hell. Okay."

I paid my tab and we grabbed a six-pack to go. We walked outside into the crisp night air. Carlos said he wanted to swing by the parking lot to get something out of his car. We made our way to his old AMC Matador. He opened the back door and grabbed a guitar case off the seat. Then we headed off down a gravel path toward the moonlit beach.

It was a noiseless night, and the ocean was still. I didn't see anyone around. We found a cozy spot near the rocks and sat down. It was close enough to the resort property to get some light from one of the street lamps but hidden enough to remain out of direct view. I opened a couple of beers and handed one to Carlos.

"So, do you want to make out or something?" he asked.

"No, not really."

"Okay."

He set his beer down on a flat rock and opened the guitar case. It was worn brown leather, just like Walter's suitcase. He grabbed a little baggie and opened it. He had some pre-rolled joints in it. That was what I wanted, not Carlos. He lit one up and took a long drag and then he handed it to me. We smoked silently as we watched the endless ocean in front of us. I could get anywhere from there. My mind felt clear. I could even reach my sleepy Midwest town that I called home.

After Carlos stomped out the butt end of the smoke on a nearby rock, he grabbed the guitar from the case and began to strum it. He twisted a couple of the pegs for some fine tuning. He started playing

"Me and Bobby McGee". He was singing the words and I joined my voice to his. He had a nice voice. So much nicer than mine. I thought I could see a glimmer of the appeal that Carlos might have had to someone like Jenna.

We finished the song and Carlos smoked a second joint without any help from me. Then he began to strum the guitar again, this time playing a Christmas carol.

"So why is that song so special to you," Carlos asked me when he had finished singing his song. He kept strumming at the guitar as he asked.

"I lost a Bobby too, I guess. He was my brother."

"That's sad. What happened," he asked as he continued to play.

"I haven't ever talked to anyone about it before."

Ivey was telling me to shut up. She said I had no right to talk about Bobby. But there I was again, thinking of giving my most personal stories to a stranger, in my haze of drugs and alcohol.

"You can tell me."

"No…not here. Not now…"

"Go on. It's okay. I want to hear about it," he said, still strumming the guitar.

"Well, alright, I guess…I was only four when it happened, so I shouldn't remember much of it, but I do. It was the Bad Day. That's what Mom had called it afterward. How she referred to it. The worst of all possible days. Bobby was just a baby. So little and tiny and innocent. My mom did not deserve him. He was only my half-brother but that never mattered to me. I didn't understand what that even meant back then. I loved him more than anything the first time I saw him in the hospital. It's funny…I was so little but, yet I can see it all so clearly. I wonder if these thoughts are truly memories of things that happened…or some story created by my mind. I should not have crystal clear memories from so long ago…you know what I mean?"

DONT, Ivey screamed. But I couldn't hold it back any longer.

"I know what you mean," he said as he lit another smoke and handed it to me. The acrid smoke stung my nostrils.

"Bobby was my doll…my toy right from the very start. Mom never objected. She was too busy getting drunk or high or whatever she did. She had a different boyfriend every week. She was much too busy to worry about me and Bobby. She didn't even have a job that I can remember. It was all okay with me. Bobby was mine and I took care of him the best that I could. Changing his diapers and scavenging food for him. Better to focus on his sweet little face and not the depravity that was our daily life back then."

STOP! Ivey yelled, but I couldn't push it back any longer. The memory had been trying to escape for so long. The dam had finally broken.

"The Bad Day started good. Mom was awake early and in a respectable mood. She had a new boyfriend. She was happy. She had even showered and put on a pretty dress. She had her hair up and some makeup on. She was beautiful that morning. She made us pancakes for breakfast as she sang softly and danced around the kitchen. I figured she would be leaving us again to spend time with her new boyfriend. She only got dressed up pretty when she was leaving. I never knew when she would be back once she left. Sometimes it was hours, occasionally it was days. When it was too long, and the food was running low I would walk across the hall and knock on the door.

"There was a nice old lady who lived across from us, and she never turned us down when we needed something. She always had some bread or milk for us. Even fresh fruit on occasion. What must she have thought of our sorry excuse for a mother? She never said anything though. She was always so sweet and kind even though I knew she didn't have much more to live on than we did," I said, pausing to think.

I hadn't thought of that lady in years. The tears started up then. Carlos was still playing the guitar. His eyes were closed, and he was reclining against some rocks. I didn't know if he was still listening, but I had to finish the story now that I had started it. If I could pull it all out, then maybe I could toss it aside for good. Throw away the pain. How had I been able to keep it down for so long? I pulled up the bottom of my shirt and ran it across my face. I was a real mess. *NO MORE!* Ivey was screaming. Carlos started to snore, but I didn't care. I was telling the story for myself anyway, not for him.

"Around lunchtime, the phone rang, and it was my grandmother. I could only hear what Mom was saying but it was obvious that they were having a disagreement about something. I didn't hear all the words. Mom finally slammed the phone down without even saying goodbye. I never knew what the fight was about. It was one of many.

"Looking back on it I think that maybe my grandmother felt guilt for the Bad Day. Maybe that was why she locked it all away too and spent the rest of her years trying to forget and trying to make it up to my mother. Maybe that was why she was always there to bail her out. I think they would both be shocked to know how much I remembered from that day. That time period. None of us had dared to look back or share it with each other. But a four-year-old should not have those kinds of memories.

"Anyway...the call had set mom off. She took a few beers into her room and shut the door. She came out a couple of hours later when the phone rang again. I wasn't sure who she was talking too. That call ended as badly as the first. Mom went to the Kitchen and grabbed the big bottle with the amber liquid off the top of the fridge. She took it to her bedroom. She hadn't bothered to grab a glass. Bobby and I stayed quiet. We knew better than to say anything when she was like that. We played with our toys in the tiny living room of our apartment.

"I heard her snoring after a while. That made me feel a sense of relief. She couldn't turn her anger on us at least. I put some cold hot dogs on to pieces of bread for Bobby and me. We were out of ketchup, but hot dogs were Bobby's favorite. It was getting late and we were hungry. After we ate, I could hear the water running in the bathroom we all shared. She was taking a bath. It was dark out then. "I decided that I should get Bobby ready for bed. He seemed restless and he felt warm to the touch when I tried to pick him up. He squirmed out of my arms and threw himself down on the green shag carpet. He was whimpering and saying 'tummy'. I didn't know what to do. I went to the bathroom and knocked on the door. There was no answer.

"Bobby was crying louder. I twisted the glass knob that looked like a big diamond and opened the door a little, so I could peak in. Mom was in the tub with her head back and snoring softly. Bubbles covered her body. I called out for her as quiet as I could. I needed to wake her, but I was scared of what would happen when I did. She bolted up angrily looking around. I tried to tell her about Bobby, but she only yelled at me and told me to get out."

NO! Ivey screamed. I never realized how much Ivey sounded like me.

"I shut the door and ran back to Bobby. I picked him up and cradled him in my arms. He seemed okay with that. It comforted him. I heard the water draining out of the tub. Mom stumbled out in her thread-bare bathrobe. She stumbled into the kitchen banging around and knocking things over. I heard a glass shatter on the floor. I sat quietly on the couch with Bobby in my arms. I caressed his little cheek. His eyes were almost closed.

"Mom went back into the bathroom and began to fill the tub again. I could smell the fresh bubble bath soap that Bobby and I used. She came out to the living room and pulled Bobby from my lap. He protested and began to cry. She tried to soothe him, but I couldn't understand anything she was saying because the words were all slurred together. His cries grew louder as she took him into the bathroom and then shut the door. I tried to sit and patiently wait for them in the living room, but I dozed off on the couch after a while to the sound of Bobby's cries."

no...

"I was startled awake by loud yelling from the bathroom. This time it was not Bobby. This time it was mom shrieking. I ran to the bathroom and opened the door. They were both on the floor naked in a puddle of water. Bobby looked blue and he wasn't moving. Mom had him in her arms and she was rocking back and forth. Her face was red and ugly; wet with a mixture of tears and bathwater.

"I ran out of our apartment and across the hall to the little old lady that lived there. I don't even remember her name. Maybe I never knew it. She followed me back to our apartment and saw everything. With one swift glance, she saw it all. She grabbed the phone off the table and dialed the police emergency number. She talked to them briefly and then hung up. She looked at me and started to cry. She put her arms around me and pulled me close, holding on so tightly. I began to cry too.

"The policeman came and left with Bobby's little body. Mom never even looked at me or said anything to me. She went back into her room after the police left. Our neighbor gently guided me to her apartment and made a bed for me on her couch with some scratchy old blankets that smelled like bleach.

"A month later I was moving halfway across the country to be with my adopted family. I never saw my grandmother before I left either. Mom hadn't talked to her after the bad phone call, I guess. I wonder when my grandmother even found out about Bobby...or me leaving."

That was it. I had the story out of me. Tears were pouring down my face and I shivered uncontrollably even though it wasn't cold out. I looked over at Carlos. He was still asleep or passed out. His arms were wrapped protectively around the guitar.

My grandmother was not the only one who had carried around grief and pain all these years. I realized that I needed to stop blaming myself. There was nothing I could have done about any of it. I was only a small child. I did the best I could, and I loved Bobby with all my might. He and I had both escaped from our sad excuse of a mother, each in our own way.

I had not been able to process it all when I was young. I didn't know how to grieve then. I locked it away for all these years. Maybe now that I had relived it, I could finally allow myself to move on from it. Maybe this was the real reason I had ended up on Euphoria. Fate or destiny or whatever one called it; it had brought me here to find peace. Not just for Walter or my family, but for myself.

I promised myself I would never live a life of secrets as they had. I would be different than all of them. All my biological family. I would be more open and honest with the ones that I loved. I would stop burying the past.

I had to admit one other thing to myself as well. I had been the one to push David away because I had always held him at arm's length. I never let him in. He had tried. I could see that plainly now. It was all my fault. It was over, but I promised myself that I would be different if I got another chance.

Ivey had tried to stop me from letting go of the past, but she had failed. She was done. She left, taking my guilt with her. Like that, she was gone forever once I admitted the truth to myself. Once I stopped hating myself and let go of that mutated portion of my inner psyche by reliving the Bad Day. I was ready to go home and move on.

I stumbled back to the hotel, leaving Carlos to sleep it off on the beach. I swatted at a lone firefly that buzzed my face, not sure if it was real or imagined in my intoxicated state. It was early morning and there weren't many people around inside the hotel when I entered. I walked into my room and flopped face first on to the bed, physically and emotionally drained after finally confronting my past.

JUNKANOO
December 26, 1988

The TV was on when I woke up. I didn't remember turning it on. Gray light tried to creep in around the edges of the closed curtains that had finally been fixed by the hotel staff. I felt refreshed. I felt renewed. This would be my last full day on the Island. It was bittersweet in mornings dim light, but it had to be this way. I should try to find Charles and tell him goodbye, and I still needed to pick up the suitcase.

I ordered up a small breakfast and coffee and then I found my way down to the beach. There were few people around and the sky looked hazy and overcast. The heavy air pressed against me, filled with moisture. My hair frizzed out of control. I heard people in the lobby talking about incoming storms as I passed by, heading back up to my room. I would take the hotel shuttle to the tourist market instead of the scooter just in case it rained I thought to myself.

I made it back to my room without any run-ins. I took a steamy, hot shower. I decided to wear a sundress that I had bought at the tourist market; and of course, my signature ponytail with a touch of makeup. I would bring a sweater too, just in case.

The sky had not cleared, in fact, it looked to be darkening. Maybe I could pick up an umbrella in the lobby on my way out. I was feeling calm and relaxed after my lazy morning. My night on the beach with Carlos seemed like a dream that I had years ago. It was fading fast and calmness had settled over me.

Once I was ready, I boarded a shuttle bus out front of the hotel that took me over the bridge and back to the tourist market. I had my pick of seats on the empty bus that mirrored the city streets. I saw some barricades and remembered Junkanoo was starting. I exited the bus where the tourist market should be, but only saw barricades. I walked around some of the side streets hoping to catch sight of Charles but no luck. He was nowhere to be seen.

I kept on walking until I found a corner diner. I had a late lunch all alone. I was hoping to buy Charles a sandwich and soda today. Then I could hear one of his world-famous burps one last time, but it was not meant to be. He had always seemed to be around when I needed him before, but not today.

As it got closer to the start of Junkanoo, it was as if someone had opened a door or flipped a switch. People slowly filtered out into the streets, milling about. I could see them going by, through the greasy diner windows. They moved around in costumes and masks. I could hear music now too. It felt later in the day than it should have, due to the dark skies.

I paid my tab and went back into the street. The gray clouds overhead churned. People pushed past me as I stood there thinking about my next move. I would have to give up on Charles. I didn't want to show up at his house, it would be an intrusion. Besides, he and his family were probably busy with Junkanoo themselves. It was a big holiday on the Island.

I made up my mind to head back to the tourist market area. I would stop in at the Historical Society and get my suitcase and then I would go back to the hotel. It was sure to be quiet back there with all the revelry going on in the city streets. I didn't want any more parties or glamour. I wanted to go home. I felt lost now that I had given up on my search, and so much more. It seemed I had no reason left to be on the Island.

The sidewalks started filling up faster and it was getting harder to move. Music and laughter grew louder. The sound of rhythmic drums was a deep thumping that I could feel in my chest. It took me much longer to get back to the tourist market than it had taken to get to the diner. Costumed marchers and bands were in the streets, parading along.

Roger Hodair greeted me with a glass of champagne and a smile when I entered the museum. There were more people inside than I had ever seen before. It was still calmer and quieter inside, making it a nice respite from the busy streets.

"I was hoping to see you tonight," he said in his slurred English accent as he put an arm around my shoulder. He had been drinking and he was overly friendly again. "I have something for you, my dear."

He motioned for me to follow him back to his office. He walked in and grabbed the suitcase, holding it tight against his chest and staring back at me. I stopped in the doorway, propping the door open. When he realized that I was not going to enter he came back over to where I had stopped.

"Sunny McQueen, I would like to thank you on behalf of the Island Historical Society and myself. It has been a remarkable trip through a golden era with you. I enjoyed visiting places and times long forgotten," he said with a wink and a smile. When he winked, both eyes closed, and his nose wrinkled up.

"It was my pleasure Mr. Hodair," I said, with a tired smile.

"Please stay and enjoy the festivities," he said, as he thrust the suitcase into my hands and waltzed past me to join the other guests in the museum.

I followed him lugging the suitcase. I made my way up front, so I could watch the street scene through the large picture windows. Tables and chairs had been set up near them. I found an empty spot and set the suitcase down by my feet.

It felt good to have the suitcase back in my possession but there was a finality to it also. I would be leaving the Island tomorrow. The suitcase would probably end up in the back of a closet at my apartment, just the way I had found it at my grandmother's. The adventure would be done. Real life would start again. It made me want to grab a glass of champagne for myself, but I resisted the urge.

I watched the revelers outside. Things were really heating up and the volume was increasing. The parading crowds swiveled and danced past the window, body to body in their colorful costumes and masks. I was not in the mood for any of it. I decided to slip out the door and make my way back to the hotel, besides it was getting late. Roger was busy with his guests. It looked like he had spilled some champagne on the front of his jacket and down his shirt. He would never miss me.

🌴 🌴 🌴

I picked up the suitcase and headed out into the thick, night air pushing my way through the crowd. Rain threatened to start falling at any moment. Luckily, I was on the right side of the street because I don't think I would have been able to cross the parade path. I walked along, as the wind began to stir. A raindrop hit my cheek and the breeze lifted stray tendrils of hair off my neck. I tried not to bump people with the suitcase as I made my way through the throngs. I walked along as fast as I could manage.

Suddenly, I felt a hand wrap around my upper left arm as something hard was pressed into my back. The person behind me leaned into me and brushed against my ear. They whispered in a low growl for me to keep walking. I didn't recognize the male voice.

We walked on for blocks in the crowds of party-goers. All those people around me and I still felt helpless. I tried to turn and look but the hand tightened on my arm. I didn't know for sure what was pressing into my back, but I guessed it might be a gun.

The suitcase hung heavy in my hand, but when I tried to shift it to my other side, the grip on my arm became painful. My fingers were tingling with the weight of it. I did my best to avoid hitting people with the case as we passed, but I did get a few dirty looks along the way.

As we walked by some glass storefront windows, I was able to look off to my right side and catch a quick glimpse of my captor but unfortunately, he was in full costume, with a mask and cape. The mask was that of some Fifties movie monster. He fit in perfectly with the rest of the mob that surrounded us.

We walked on, following the parade. After twenty minutes or so, and a few more raindrops, the wind really picked up. People were having trouble controlling their costumes and I felt like a pinball in a machine, bouncing from one person to the next.

He shoved me down a side alley. There were still plenty of people around, but it was a relief to have a little more room to maneuver, even though my left arm was aching due to the weight of the suitcase that hung from it. I tried to switch hands again but was stopped once more by another squeeze of my arm.

A man in a tuxedo and small velvet eye mask stepped in front of me and I almost ran into him. I recognized him immediately. I wanted to throw my arms around him and thank him for saving me. It was Carter. He must have seen that I was being forced along against my will, but something seemed all wrong.

I looked up into his eyes and I could see that he seemed upset. I did not understand. He looked from me to my captor and then back again. His reaction didn't fit the situation. Didn't he see what was happening? Why would he be looking at me angrily?

"Hello Queenie," he mouthed. I could hardly hear him over the sounds of the parade and wind that whipped my dress back and forth against my legs, now that we were not moving forward. I didn't know what to do. I felt paralyzed with fear. My captor tightened his grip on me once again. I couldn't move or speak. I feared for myself, but also for Carter. What if the man behind me did have a gun? If I tried to alert Carter, we might both be shot.

Carter reached a hand up and gently placed it under my chin. His gaze softened, and there seemed to be a sadness in his eyes. I foolishly wanted to protect him the same way I had wanted too in the limousine. Why would I ever have wanted Brooks more than Carter? There was something so lost and innocent in those eyes that stared down into mine at that moment. What had I done to hurt him? Why didn't he understand what was happening to me?

He let his hand drop from my face. I could see him hardening again as the anger came back. All traces of kindness had left his eyes. "I really thought we had a chance, Queenie. I will make it painless for you though, I promise," he said as his cold gaze froze me in place.

Carter abruptly turned and disappeared into the crowd. My chance at escape, slowly disappearing with him down the alley, and there was nothing I could do about it. I stood immobile and confused. My captor pushed me onward again, deeper into the alley and away from the crowd, into the darkness. We reached a block wall and some dumpsters, he was pulling on my arm and motioning for me to stop. He turned me around to face him and then let go of my arm. The hood of his cape was up over the hideous mask he wore. I couldn't see a gun, but I knew it hid somewhere under the shadows of his cloak.

"Suitcase," he said, in a loud gruff voice as he reached a hand toward me. I finally switched it to my other hand and away from him, as I shook out my sore arm.

He moved at me menacingly and quickly reached around me to get a hand on the suitcase. We both pulled and struggled. The handle of the old suitcase was so small that neither of us had a good grip on it. We both lost our hold at the same instant and stumbled apart.

The suitcase flew up in the air and came down with a loud crash between us. The latches popped up when it hit the ground and papers and photos went flying. Tears welled up in my eyes when I saw everything scattered. I dove for the ground, trying to grab the contents and keep them protected from the raindrops that had now become a steady sprinkle. The wind blew papers up against the block wall.

My suspicions were confirmed when the man finally raised the gun up from under his dark cape and pointed it at me.

"Put everything back," he barked angrily. But couldn't he see that I was already doing that? I scampered around the back of the alley down on my hands and knees. Scrounging to get every last piece. I didn't care that my hands and knees were beginning to bleed from being cut up by the alley floor and its contents.

I grabbed and stuffed as fast as I could, not caring if things were torn or folded over as I went. I could not stop until everything was back in the suitcase, just like I could not stop the tears from falling down my cheeks again in my panic.

As I worked, I noticed a tear in the suitcase lining. An envelope that must have been hidden in the lining was now poking out through the tear. I positioned myself between the suitcase and my captor, so he wouldn't see me remove it, and I slide it down the sleeve of my sweater. I prayed the darkness would hide my actions. He yelled for me to hurry.

I had everything picked up by the time the hard rain started. I re-latched the suitcase and fell on top of it, still crying. The envelope was on the inside of my arm and I squeezed it against my body, hoping to keep it dry. The rain had soaked me to the bone in a matter of seconds. The man grabbed my wrist and jerked me upward off the ground.

"Come with me," he barked.

I had made him angry, but I didn't care. The thought of losing the contents of the suitcase had taken all the shock out of me. I was not scared for myself anymore. The suitcase was what mattered. It had to be protected, that was the only thought my brain could process.

He grabbed me by the arm again and pulled me, but this time he walked side by side with me as he dragged me along. We headed back the way we had come but halfway down the alley he turned us, and we squeezed through a narrow void between two buildings that I had not noticed before. I had to hold the suitcase out in front of me.

Then we were back out on the street, but the crowds were fading fast. A quietness had settled along the parade route, only the beat of the raindrops on the cold concrete was left. A few stragglers remained, too drunk or distracted to notice the blood that the raindrops washed off my hands and knees. The pinkish-red water ran down my legs and dripped from my fingertips.

We walked another block and then came upon a non-descript rental car, with local license plates. He put a key in the trunk lock and opened it. The gun was visible again. He motioned for me to put the suitcase in the trunk. I did, begrudgingly. Then he opened the passenger door and motioned me inside. I bent down to climb in; squeezing the envelope tight against my body. Then everything went black.

WALTER'S CONFESSION
Day Unknown

I was dreaming again. I knew it, but I couldn't escape the dream. I climbed upward. On and on I went. Step after step. I kept moving, afraid to stop. And then nothing as I crumpled to the ground.

Nothingness. For how long, I didn't know.

I stood on a dark moonlit beach with Carter. He was photographing me. The flash of the bulb was blinding. Instead of the usual click and whirr of the camera, the flash was punctuated with a loud deafening crack.

Carter's dark figure was outlined with a moonlit edge. I could not see his features, but I knew who it was. Every blaze of light from the camera made it harder for me to focus my eyes. I heard crazy laughter surrounding us. I wasn't sure where it was coming from. I was scared. I shivered wildly, feeling wet and cold. I could not stop my shaking. I heard someone call my name...

I felt something metallic and hard against my cheek, but it was so difficult to focus. I felt pain. Where was it coming from? I couldn't find it. I weaved in and out of the dream several times before I was able to surface from the depths of it.

I woke on cold metal that felt damp. Bright light flashed intermittently, and thunder rolled. It was my head that was hurting, I realized. My hands and knees, also. I reached a hand up to feel a lump at the back of my head, as the lightning blinded me again. There was a hard, dry crust on the bump. My teeth chattered. I opened my eyes and tried to sit up. Things began to swim in and out of clarity, but I managed to get myself upright.

I was in a round brick room on a metal floor. There were windows all the way around. I could only see ebony skies, through the rain pelted windows that surrounded me. A metal railing and stair on one side of the room went down through the floor. In the middle of the round room sat a large glass and metal object that was mounted to table-like support.

The lightning flashed again and lit up the room. I stood up and made my way over to a window. It was hard to see through the rain-streaked glass. Another flash lit up the landscape and I could see that I was a long way above the beach and ocean below. I was in a lighthouse. Maybe even the one I had seen with Charles on our tourist day, but I didn't know for sure.

I had no idea what time or day it was. I went over to the stairs and looked down into blackness. I inched my way down into the void, holding tightly to the railings. When I was down below floor level, I reached a small platform. I felt around and found a gate handle. It was padlocked shut. I was stuck at the top of the lighthouse in the storm. I wouldn't have made it very far even if the gate had been unlocked and I knew it. I was a mess.

I made my way back up the staircase. At least there was a tiny bit of light from the dingy windows. I wanted to stay in that light. I looked around again at my surroundings. I found a folded-up cloth tarp on a table. I unfolded it and wrapped it around me. It smelled musty. It wasn't very soft but maybe it would warm me up a bit. I walked back over to a window and looked down again. In the flashes of light, I could see the rocky beach below. The waves pounded against the shoreline. I had no idea what to do next.

Was the captor who put me up here going to return for me? Or had he dumped me off not caring what happened to me? I wasn't sure which thought was worse. I didn't know if this lighthouse was in use or open to tourists. How long would it be before someone found me? My heart was pounding so hard in my chest that it scared me. A panic attack was going to take me. I couldn't let that happen. I needed to focus on something. I needed to try and find a way out. Trying and failing was better than doing nothing. I had to think.

I thought back to the Junkanoo parade and all the things that had happened. My captor must have hit me on the head from behind as I was getting into his car. My suitcase was gone. He had made me put it into his trunk. It was what he had wanted all along, but I remembered that I had escaped with one small piece. One maybe very important small piece. It was so important that it had been hidden in a secret location in the lining of the suitcase.

I dropped the tarp and fumbled with sliding the wet sweater off my arms in a brilliant flash of lightning. I shivered even harder as it came off. After my arms were out, I reached in the sleeve feeling around for paper. Nothing. Had my kidnapper found it? No, try the other arm I chided myself. I found it and it was surprisingly dry.

I pulled out the thick envelope and carefully opened it with shaky fingers. There were several pieces of paper stuffed into it. I made my way closer to the window as the lightning and thunder struck. The thunder rattled the windows. This was not the best place to be in a storm such as this. I was so scared, but I had to know what was in that letter. It gave me focus.

I looked around and found an old flashlight on the table. It worked but it flickered like the batteries were running low. I didn't have much time.

There was a small slip of paper that appeared to be a receipt for a room at the Montague Hotel. The room number was listed, and I guessed it would match up with the room number where Arthur Murray's body had been found. The registered guest signature was that of Angela Merriweather. The date was June 5th, 1956. It was hard evidence in the death of Arthur Milton Murray. The rest of the papers were a handwritten letter from my Great Uncle Walter, dated the same day as Angela's letter…

November 2, 1960

There is one particular event in my lifetime that goes beyond regret and disappointment. It is something that I have hidden from all. I have never forgiven myself for what happened on June 5th, 1956 on the Island of Euphoria. This event occurred at the Montague Hotel where I was employed at the time.

I tried to sit down and write a letter to Angela Merriweather. All I could come up with was a weak plea for forgiveness, that I doubt I will send. But I must release this burden of shame that has weighed me down for so long, even if only to paper that no one will ever read.

I was so happy to end up in what I thought to be paradise. That is truly what the Island of Euphoria was for me, at least in the beginning. We were worlds away from the mainland. The rich and famous would come down and things would get really out of hand, but always with tasteful discretion. I was the Vice President and right-hand man to Arthur Murray at the Montague Hotel. He was a great man, known for his philanthropy, we became fast friends. We were inseparable.

I knew he had a wife and kids back home, but when he was on the Island, it was always anything goes for the two of us.

We lived in the moment back then. He was Dean Martin to my Jerry Lewis and the ladies loved it. I became concerned when I noticed him spending more and more time with one of the locals who worked at the hotel. He had broken our unwritten rule. Have fun and move on, no entanglements.

The girl seemed lovely enough. She quickly worked her way up the pecking order at the hotel as she and Arthur grew closer. Everyone working at the hotel knew. Whispered rumors were heard in the hallways. One day she was cleaning rooms and a month later she was the mermaid in the pool behind the bar. A month after that she was hosting parties with me in the Jungle Room. A week after that she was serving champagne in the Winner's Circle at the Hobby Horse racetrack when Arthur's horse won. Of course, people talked.

I never confronted Arthur about the situation, but I found myself jealous of all the time he was spending with her. I was missing my partner in crime. It surprised me greatly since I had been so good at pushing people away and drowning myself in the drink. He had become like family to me.

I found myself spending more and more time with Angela as well, as she moved up the ladder of hotel employees. The more I was around her, the less I liked her. There was a dark streak in her that became more dominant as her position grew at the hotel. Arthur was not around all the time, and she kept it hidden when he was.

I walked in on her yelling at some maids one day, as if she were their boss. Only weeks before they had been her equals. She even slapped a customer who had tried to give her direction. Anyone else would have been fired on the spot. But Angela had Arthur's protection and he always smoothed things over for her.

I was eager for Arthur to grow tired of her, but I soon found out he was in over his head. Arthur came to me one day and confided that Angela had told him she was pregnant with his child. That was the writing on the wall. I had no idea how our world would be changed forever.

He told me that she had reserved a suite and they were going to get together to talk. Of course, a scandal would ruin a person in those days. He said he knew of a place where she could go to remedy the situation. He wanted me to meet with them to help talk some sense into her. He wanted me to back him up. I was shocked that he would want me to get involved with something so personal, but I couldn't turn down my friend.

I met Arthur in the room that night. We had agreed to meet early and discuss matters. Arthur arrived before I did. He had been drinking, but that was okay because I was already drunk too.   He winked when he saw me come in and then he grabbed a glass and filled it for me.   We sat on the couch and drank in silence.   I didn't know what to say.

He was so distraught.   He did not want his wife or family to find out.   I was afraid he might do something desperate when Angela arrived.   When she did finally arrive, things escalated quickly.   She had entered the room carrying a large teddy bear, happy as a lark.   I knew things would not go well.   He tried to reason with her.   He wanted her to get rid of the baby, but she expected him to leave his family and be a father to their illegitimate child.

When he told her that was never going to happen, she flew into a rage.   She threatened to tell his family and the whole world.   He charged at her and grabbed her by the throat.   I had been quiet so far, but the physical altercation moved me to action.   I grabbed him and pulled him off her.   They were yelling and screaming at each other.   Once she was freed, she began picking up loose objects and hurling them at Arthur.

The rocks glass caught Arthur on the side of the head, cutting him as it broke.   He fell to the ground, hitting his head on the edge of the desk when I pushed him back to keep them apart.   There was blood everywhere from the head wound.   When she ran out of objects to throw, she grabbed the ice pick off the table and stabbed him with it. Her temper was out of control. It shocked me.

She was hysterical when I ran to her and grabbed her. She even stabbed me a couple of times in the shoulder. I slapped her face and then I restrained her until she calmed. Arthur was covered in blood, his eyes stared at the ceiling with a vacant gaze. He was dead. My dear friend was gone, and I put the blame on myself for not doing more.

She pleaded with me to help her as she cried into my shoulder. I did help her too because I felt so responsible. It had all happened so fast. I was there to keep things from getting out of hand and I had failed miserably. I had let my closest friend down and he paid the ultimate price for it.

In our state of panic, we pulled down the curtains and wrapped his body up. Then we lit everything on fire in hopes of destroying any evidence that would link us to the crime. I wiped the blood from the ice pick and then I went and found the room receipt as well, from the front desk. It was a comp'd room, in Angela's name and handwriting. Of course, no one dug too deeply into the matter, especially the cops. Arthur was well known, and no one wanted to rake his name through the mud, especially his own family. People talked and the rumors flew. He brought it on

177

himself some said.   It was so easy for them all to dismiss him, even the ones who had claimed to be his friends when he was alive.

That was it.   Angela and I avoided each other for the remainder of my time on the Island.   No one was ever arrested. It became the unsolved mystery of the decade.   I quickly went downhill after it happened.   I was soon fired and begging old chums for jobs.   That is how I ended up in Arizona at a rundown hotel that I wouldn't even recommend to my worst enemy.   My drinking grew out of control, but it was the only way to drown out my demons.

After Arthur's death, the weight of all my past hurts and sins overwhelmed me.   They crushed me.   I am too ashamed to ever tell this horrible story, but I had to get it out.   I thought about burning these pages as I wrote them, but I just don't have it in me. Arthur deserved so much more.   My death could be coming soon now.   I am too weak and old to make amends for my sins.

I will leave this letter, along with the room receipt, in my case that was given to me by the staff of the Montague Hotel as a going away gift.   It will serve as a record of the events that occurred, and of my participation.   Maybe someday I will be brave enough to let the truth be known, for Arthur's sake.

G. Walter Fender

I folded up the papers and stuffed them back into the envelope. I laid the envelope on top of my sweater that was now on the table. What was I supposed to do with this knowledge? My great uncle and Angela were both long gone. Should I tell Brooks about this? About his Mother, the murderer? Or did he already know? Did he know he was Arthur's illegitimate son? And what about the family of Arthur Murray? Surely this knowledge would not help Arthur's heirs rest any easier.

I was deep in thought when I heard a noise from below. Someone was in the lighthouse with me and it sounded like they were coming up the steps to where I was. I turned off the flickering flashlight. I heard the metal gate on the platform below being opened as the chain and padlock were removed. Was it the man who had brought me here unconscious? I scurried over to the old light on the table. I knelt down behind it so that it was between me and the staircase. I was sure my ragged breathing and chattering teeth would give me away. I had to get it under control.

A shadowy figure with a flashlight ascended through the stair opening. He stopped when his waist was at floor level.

"Sunny?" he said in a whisper.

My body tensed up. I couldn't answer. He started moving upward again as a gust of wind rattled the windows in their frames. He stood framed in front of a window when a flash of lightning lit up the room and I saw then that it was Carter. The thunderclap followed a split second after the flash. Relief washed over me, and I called out his name. I tried to stand back up and almost fell over. I had been coiled so tightly that my whole body felt shaky and weak. I had dug my nails into the wood table without even realizing it.

He rushed over to me and grabbed me and pulled me toward the windows, holding me out at arm's length to give me the once-over in the dim glow of his flashlight.

"You are a mess Queenie. Look at you. Your hands and knees...are you okay?"

"Yes," I said even though I felt like I was swaying with the ocean below.

"You're shivering. We have to get these wet clothes off."

He pulled the strings at my shoulders and my sundress slid to the floor with a flop. Then he whipped off his sweater and pulled it down over my head and fished my arms out through the sleeves. He grabbed the old tarp off the floor, the one I had used earlier, and he wrapped that around me as well. He pulled me down on to his lap as he sat on an old wood box that was up against the wall. He had his arms wrapped around me, trying to warm me up. My teeth clicked in my head.

"I was so mad when I saw you with Brooks at the Junkanoo parade. I couldn't believe you were with him again," he said, as he rubbed my shoulders.

"Wait...what?"

"You were with Brooks in the alley...the night of the parade. I saw you. I stopped and talked to you"

"No...it was a stranger and he had a gun at my back. He wanted my suitcase."

"You are delirious," he laughed. "Didn't you know that was Brooks behind you in the mask?"

"No. But why?" That was all I could think to say. Carter shifted and pulled me closer.

"I don't know but I saw you walking with him. I was mad at first because you told me you were done with him. I walked away but then I decided I needed to get some answers and I couldn't leave things that way between us. I tried to find you both again, but I was too late. And then I saw him hit you from behind and push you into a car, but I couldn't reach you before he drove off and I had no car to follow in. I was at least a block back when I saw you. That was two days ago. I couldn't believe he would do such a thing. I contacted the police. They found him...but not you. I was so worried after...well..."

"What?" I said as I tried to sit up, but my world began to sway in and out of focus again.

"Just relax," he said as he pulled me back into his arms. "You should rest."

"What's wrong? What happened? After what?"

"Well...the police arrested Brooks."

"Why?"

"For murder."

"What?" My mind was reeling. I couldn't think straight.

"They arrested him for the murder of the girl that they found on the beach near your hotel. I guess they found some of her stuff in his room when they searched it looking for you. I thought I would never see you again. I thought maybe he had killed you too. I have known him my whole life and I never thought him capable of something like this."

"But why? Why would he do it?"

"I just don't know. No one knows. But you are safe, and he will finally get what he deserves."

"But how did you know I was here?"

"Lucky guess really. This place has been shut down for years. Brooks and I both had keys from a friend. His dad was the caretaker here. We all had a copy of the key. We used to have parties and bring girls up here back in high school. I didn't think to look here right away, though. It took me a while to find the key too. I am so sorry. I need to get you out of here. I am going to get you to a hospital and have you checked out, okay?"

"Wait...I don't understand any...why...the detective...then...is Charles safe?"

"Shhh...you're not making any sense. Rest," he said.

I tried to ask more questions, but the words weren't coming to me. He pulled me closer and I turned my face into his neck. He felt warm and safe. He smelled of campfire and cologne. Everything was swaying again, and the lightning flashed around us.

The lightning bugs, like the ones I had seen at the ruins of the Montague Hotel, were floating around the lighthouse, trying to get in. I could hear them hitting the windows alongside the raindrops. They were everywhere. I wondered if Carter was seeing them. How could he not? I tried to ask him. His arms gently squeezed me tighter as he whispered in my ear, and the world went black as the bugs and rain pelted the glass.

DOUBT
December 30, 1988

The brightness of the gray light woke me. I smelled antiseptic and cleaner. I thought I was back in my grandmother's hospital room, but I couldn't hear her raspy breathing that I had grown accustomed to. I realized I was the one in the hospital bed this time, with a needle in my arm and bandages on my hands and knees. Carter had kept his word and brought me in.

My eyes adjusted slowly and when I finally opened them, I found myself staring at my adopted mother and father. That brought me back to reality fast. My adventure had turned into a real disaster and all the memories came flooding back. I couldn't believe they were here. I tried to tell myself I should be glad they had come all this way for me, but it still felt like failure.

"There's our girl," Mom said. "You really gave us quite a scare, you know. We have been so worried. What the hell have you been doing on this Island?" Dad put a warning hand on her knee, but she wasn't having it. She had been sitting in this hospital room mulling over a lot of things for quite some time, I guessed. Once I woke up, she wanted her answers. I would give her that, this was on me.

"We called David when we got the word that you were hurt and in the hospital. I only found out when I tried to call you at your hotel. I was shocked to hear that you had broken up with David. We flew out on the first flight we could find. It cost an arm and a leg too. And you know I don't like hot weather since I got heatstroke two years ago. What have you been doing here? Are you seeing someone else? What has gotten into you? Well? What do you have to say for yourself?"

I had no idea what to say and that was the truth. I laid there speechless. My inability to speak did not keep her quiet for long.

"You really have nothing to say for yourself? I am so disappointed in you. We took you in when you weren't even a baby. Do you know how hard it is for a kid to get adopted, especially at four years old? Most people want a newborn. We gave you everything and now you're pissing it all away. You dumped a great guy. You will probably lose your job because you are too busy partying in the Caribbean and spending all your grandmother's money. You need a good wake up call. We are taking you home as soon as you get out of here. Maybe there is still a chance of piecing things back together at home, if you're lucky."

"Enough! Shut up for one minute." I yelled. I was so done with her. She had a way of always throwing things back in my face. It drove a wedge between us that I did not think would ever be removed. She wasn't the first mother I had distanced myself from. I knew deep down there was a good heart in her, but she kept it so well hidden with her hurtful words. She never filtered what came out of her mouth, she always spoke whatever was on her mind.

"Of course, I realize how lucky I was to end up with a normal family. I use the word normal loosely because there really is no such thing. You have both given me so many opportunities that I am grateful for, but right now I just need your support and your trust, not your judgment. And just so you know, David broke up with me, not the other way around. It may end up being a good thing, but I am not sure yet. I really did not come here for a vacation…there is so much more to it than that. This is not the time to get into it. So much has happened. Just give me some time…okay? You will have to trust me. I am not going to let you talk to me like this anymore. This is my life now."

Now it was my adopted mothers turn to remain silent, which was an unusual occurrence. I was glad for that but at the same time, I felt bad. I had never stuck up for myself so forcefully to her before. It did not feel as good as I always imagined that it would, all those years as I held it all in. I could say anything to Dad, but I had to hold my true feelings back with her. I could never let her see them. Thank goodness Dad was always there to keep her from going too far. I don't know what I would have done without him.

I think it had something to do with allowing myself to relive the Bad Day. I had allowed myself to see that day through a grown-up's eyes. I allowed myself to grieve and to stop the self-blame. I felt stronger and more confident with that weight released. It had profoundly changed me; in the way that moving from innocence to adulthood does. I could never go back to who I had been.

"Look…have they said anything to you about when I will get out of here? The doctors I mean," I asked, hoping to change the subject.

"No. You've been in here two days already. They wanted to wait until you woke up before they decided. They are giving you fluids through the IV. You were dehydrated, and they said you had a slight concussion. You got hit pretty hard on the back of the head."

"Mom, will you talk to them please?" I knew this would be a task that was right up her alley. She was a nurse and she never let Dad go alone to a doctor's appointment. He would never ask the right questions or get enough details for her. Besides, it would be a good distraction for her.

"Okay, yes, I will go check." Her anger at me had eased up with the redirection. She left the room.

Dad and I gave each other knowing glances.

"Sunny, what is really going on here?" Dad asked. "Does it have to do with that old suitcase you were carrying around before you left home?"

"Yes," I said, as my eyes teared up. Dad was a man of few words and he always got to the heart of it.

"What was in there?"

"A lifetime. The belongings of one of my biological relatives. He had some unfinished business here on this Island and I was trying to settle it for him. I wanted to do something good for my biological family even though they are not around to see it. It's turned out to be more for me than them if I am honest."

"I see, I guess. Well, you do what you have to and finish this, we'll be here," he said, and it was the end of his questions on the matter. "We couldn't get a room at your hotel, there was a convention going on, but we got a room nearby. We talked to your hotel to make sure you still have a room there. We explained the situation. We called the airline too. They said you had moved up your return date already, but you missed that flight. We told the airline we would call them when we knew more and reschedule. They will be charging you more too, I'm afraid. You can join us at our hotel, if you want. Up to you. We'll get it all worked out when you are ready."

"Thanks, Dad. Thank you for coming here. I think I will keep my room if that is okay. You and Mom should go do some sightseeing or something. Please…go. I might be hanging out here for a while yet today. Go have some fun. Mom needs it. It really is beautiful here."

"Sunny, I just want you to know that I am proud of you for sticking up for yourself…with your Mom I mean. She needs to let you live your own life. I know it's hard to believe sometimes, but she has good intentions."

Mom interrupted our conversation as she came back into the room with news. The doctor would be doing rounds soon. He would check me out one more time and then I would be free to go if everything was okay. My parents looked tired but relieved. I pleaded with them again now that they were both in the room. I gave them the names of some of the beaches that I had visited along with some other tourist spots. Thanks, Charles.

I was surprised that I was able to talk them into going to do something fun. They could see that I was alright. It had been a long couple of days for them I guessed. Besides, Mom probably realized that it would be better for the two of us to get some space from each other. I promised them I would call their hotel and leave a message when I was back at my hotel. I also assured them that I could find a ride although I wasn't exactly sure about that part.

They both came over to the bed and took turns giving me a hug before they left. Mom was quiet, and I could tell she was still hurt and mad, but she would have to learn to deal with it. It was her turn to bottle up her emotions for a change. I wasn't going to let her do what she was so good at anymore, at least not to me.

🌴 🌴 🌴

After they left, I looked around the room. My charm necklace from Charles' grandmother sat on the bedside table. My sundress was folded on a chair. I didn't see the sweater that I had been wearing. I remembered putting the letter and room receipt on top of the sweater in the lighthouse. Carter must not have seen any of the items and left them there.

I wanted to go back and find the papers and my sweater, when I was out of the hospital. The contents of it came rushing back at me, but I did not get to dwell on it for long. There was a knock on the door and then Roger Hodair walked in. I had been expecting the Doctor.

"Hello Sunny. How are you doing? I hope I am not bothering you."

"No, no. Come in, please. How did you know I was here?"

"Well, word gets around. You are the talk of the Island. You and Brooks I am afraid," he said looking slightly embarrassed.

"Oh," was all I could think to respond. I felt embarrassed too. I never liked to be the center of attention under any circumstance.

"You missed most of Junkanoo too. It was a great party. We had a good turnout at the Historical Society. Thanks so much for sharing your Uncle's items with us."

Tears welled up in my eyes at the thought of my lost suitcase. I think I managed to cry every day since landing on this Island, except for the time I was unconscious maybe. It struck me that the suitcase and all its contents were most likely gone for good.

It had meant so much to me and now it was all gone. It was the catalyst for this whole journey. Would the blonde be dead, or Brooks be in jail if I had not come to this place? My inner voice would have jumped all over this if she had still been speaking to me. I hadn't heard from her since the night on the beach with Carlos.

"Hey, what's wrong? I came to cheer you up and wish you well. I didn't mean to make you cry. Here, see, I got you this jolly little teddy bear. He's a kind soul," he said as he held it out for me.

"I'm sorry. It's not you, really. I just lost my uncle's suitcase and all its contents. Actually, it was stolen from me. It's probably been destroyed or who knows what by now."

"Well...I have photo-quality reproductions of most of it. I could get Carter to make extra copies of everything for you," he said hopefully.

"Oh my gosh. I never thought of it. That would be amazing. Thank you, Roger."

"No worries."

"I would pay you for the copies too of course."

"We can work that out later. You just get better and get yourself out of here. I will take care of it. Scout's honor, although I never was a boy scout. I preferred the chess club."

"Thanks. Roger, do you know anything about what is going on with Brooks Laughton?"

"Not much I'm afraid. The authorities are staying tight-lipped on everything right now. Even my contacts at the police station aren't talking and they always talk to me. Rumor has it that they found some of the dead girl's belongings in his hotel room. You do know that he was the one that kidnapped you and locked you in the old lighthouse, right?"

"Yes...Carter told me when he found me. I just can't believe he would stoop to murder. I know he is a real jerk and full of himself but kidnapping and murder just seem unimaginable. Especially murder. What do you think?"

"Well, I don't really know. I know there were pictures of his mother in your old suitcase. I had pictures of her as well of course, but I don't know if he knew that. I just can't imagine him stooping to murder. He had the world in the palm of his hand. Good looks, fame, lots of beautiful women. Why do you think he was so concerned with your uncle's suitcase?"

"Great uncle and I don't really know either," I lied. I had my suspicions. Brooks had to know what happened to Arthur Murray and he must have known that his mother and Walter were both in on it. Why else would he have wanted the suitcase so badly? Murray had to be his father. He was afraid there was evidence in the suitcase that would tarnish his mother's name and prove who his father was I guessed. But why would he kill the blonde? That seemed totally disconnected from the suitcase.

"Well, if they can't make this murder rap stick then just add it to the long list of unsolved homicides and mysterious deaths that have occurred on this Island. For the number of people living on this little rock, the amount of tragedies that have occurred is really quite astounding.

"Let's see, there was a young girl that had just graduated from high school in the sixties or seventies, I forget which. They never found her as far as I know. Some said she ran off, others suspected foul play. There was a couple that disappeared in a boating accident around then too. Those two really stand out, but there were others. Anyway, it sounds like they do have a pretty tight case this time. They are keeping it under wraps so that they don't screw it up somehow, I would guess. Too bad you and I aren't on the case, eh? The couple on the boat…they were Carter's parents you know. Very tragic."

"What? He told me his parents were retired in Miami."

"Well…I guess he would. He has never been one to talk about it, ever. He probably just said that because it was easier than the truth. They found the burned-out boat floating in the ocean, but they never found the bodies. I think he has always held on to the hope that they would eventually be found, alive that is."

"That is awful."

"Yes, well, sorry to end on that note but I must be going now. You take care and please stop by when you are up to it. Before you leave the Island, okay?"

"I will. Thank you."

Roger exited, and I was alone again, briefly. I didn't have much time to dwell on what Roger had said before another knock on the door pulled me out of my thoughts. The door opened and in walked Charles with some daisies in his hand, fresh dirt and roots dangling. I was so happy to see him. His smile immediately brightened my day. He walked over and sat on the edge of my bed beside me and held out the flowers. I reached over and pulled on the bill of his faded Yankee's cap. Then I grabbed the flowers and put them into the jug of water on my bedside table. It was meant for drinking, but I thought I would make better use of it as a vase.

"I heard what happened to you," he said shyly.

"I'm fine, really. I can't wait to get out of this place."

He abruptly stood up and grabbed my moonstone necklace off the bedside table. He put it back around my neck, fumbling with the clasp a little. He finally managed the clasp even with his one bad hand.

"You need to keep this around your neck for protection. Don't ever take it off, okay?"

I was touched by his concern and his faith in his grandmother's charm. He was a good kid. I would truly miss him when I went back home.

"I will keep it on, I promise."

"When you get out of here, I have some more places for you to see."

"You got it. Anywhere you want to go, okay?"

The door to my room swung open again and in walked Carter. He stopped when he saw us and smiled.

"Well, hello," he said as he reached out a hand to Charles. "I have not officially met you yet, but I have heard a lot about you. I am Carter and you must be Charles. Have you been taking good care of our Sunny here?"

"Hello...yes," he said looking down at his shoes. He looked uncomfortable. He did not return the handshake. Maybe because that would require his right hand, the bad one. Carter withdrew his hand and turned toward me.

"And how is our star patient today? Glad to see you awake."

"I'm doing good. Look...Carter...thanks for everything you did. I don't know what would have happened to me if you wouldn't have come looking for me. You saved my life."

"Now, don't talk like that. Come on. Would you like some food or water or something? What can I get you?"

"I'm really hungry actually. Starving."

"I will go see what they have down in the cafeteria, okay? Your doctor should be in any minute. I saw him in the hallway just now."

"Ma'am, I'll be going now. I'll see you soon," Charles said. He seemed in a hurry to leave.

"Okay, bye Charles. Oh, and thanks for the flowers."

After they left, I looked out the window. The storm was gone but the skies still looked gray and gloomy. Maybe there was worse weather to come. I hoped not after being up close and personal with a storm in the lighthouse. I shuddered at the thought.

The doctor came in to check me out. He never even looked at me, just studied my chart. Then he mumbled something to the nurse, and she removed the IV needle from my arm. She told me I was good to go whenever I was ready. They left, and Carter came back with a cup of soup and a sandwich. I was so grateful for some food. It was the best tasting soup I had ever had, even if it was from the hospital cafeteria.

Carter sat and watched me eat in silence. I was too hungry to worry about manners, but I didn't eat it all for fear of making myself sick after going so long without food. I pushed the tray table away when I was done and let out a big sigh. I needed to let the food settle before I started worrying about getting dressed and leaving the hospital.

"Feeling better?" Carter asked.

"Yes, thank you."

"Well, it's been quite a ride, Queenie."

"I know. I meant what I said, thank you for everything."

"You're welcome."

"Carter?"

"Yes?"

"Any news on Brooks?"

"No news on that I am afraid, but really…you shouldn't be concerning yourself with all that right now."

"But I just have this feeling like maybe he didn't kill that girl. Why would he? Why kill her? Do you think he was in love with her? He obviously liked her a lot. A crime of passion maybe? But he had so many others…"

"Look, I told you once before, none of us know what lies in another's heart or mind. I have known him my whole life and I could not tell you the answers to your questions. You need to let this go. The police will get to the bottom of it, I promise. Besides, he is dangerous. Remember the night of the Junkanoo Parade? He kidnapped you for Christ's sake," Carter said, running a hand through his hair, agitated with the discussion.

"But I just don't understand…I guess you're right, but I wish I could ask him a few questions to get things straight in my mind, that's all."

"What? What about us, Queenie? If there is a chance for us, you need to let this go. I told you that before too. He was just using you this whole time. He physically attacked you for Christ's sake. Why do you still care what happens to him?"

"I just want to talk to him. Maybe I can get my suitcase back. Besides, I discovered something about his mother that I wanted to talk to him about."

"What about his mother?" Carter asked, moving a step closer.

"I prefer to talk to him about that first."

"Okay, I see."

"But you've known him your whole life. Doesn't that count for something? No one deserves to rot in jail if they didn't commit the crime," I said, pleading my case.

"All I know is that he has always been given everything on a silver platter and he has always taken it for granted. He doesn't deserve any of it. The fame...the fortune...Angela. He hasn't worked hard for anything in his life and he takes advantage of everyone around him. He uses people to get ahead...but it looks like now he will finally get what he deserves."

"None of that matters if he didn't do this thing. Wouldn't you want to help him if you could? If he is truly innocent of murder?"

He glared at me, with anger burning in his eyes. That was my answer, all the answer I would get. It was obvious that his hatred for Brooks ran deep. When he finally responded, he did not reply to my question.

"And just how are you going to prove his innocence or guilt? Do you know something that the police don't know? Are you going to get out that magnifying glass again, Sherlock? That hasn't really done you much good now, has it?" he said in a mocking tone. He could flip that emotional switch so easily when he wanted to. It really hurt sometimes.

"I don't know," was all I could come up with.

"I'm really disappointed that you want to keep pursuing this. I thought we were done with it for good, but I see you have made your mind up already, haven't you? You are making the wrong choice is all I can say. You should be scared of him, not trying to help him. Come on, get dressed and I will take you back to your hotel, okay?"

With that, he left my hospital room and went out into the hallway to wait. I was frozen, wondering if he was right. But I didn't see it as choosing Brooks over him. I just wanted the truth. I didn't know exactly why I felt so strongly about Brooks' innocence. Maybe I felt sorry for him after learning about what happened with his mother and father, and that my uncle was involved. Maybe it was more misplaced guilt for actions of my unknown family. Actions I had no responsibility for. I couldn't let it go.

I stood up to put the sundress back on, feeling unsteady, then grabbed my purse off the table. That was all I had come in to the hospital with. Someone had washed the dress. It smelled like sanitizer and it felt rough. There were still a few faded blood stains on it from when I had crawled around in the alley the night of the parade.

I let Carter drive me back to my hotel, he gave me a chilly goodbye when we arrived that sounded much too formal. I didn't know if I would see him again or not after that.

I made my way up to my room and dutifully called my adopted parents to let them know that I was back at the hotel. They asked if they could bring me dinner and I said no. I told them I was going to rest. Mom didn't say much when she was on the phone; she still held a grudge against me for calling her out at the hospital. There was nothing to be done about that.

I laid awake for many hours that night with the covers pulled up tight under my chin as I thought over what I was going to do and what I was going to say the following day. It played over and over in my mind several times.

SUSPECT
December 31, 1988

I was groggy when I woke up, and sore, but it felt good to be back in a familiar bed, even if it was not my own bed back home. It was earlier than I thought it would be. That was good. I hadn't thought to set an alarm. I scrambled around the room looking for some presentable clothes to wear. I was glad I had made it to the laundromat the other day. But in the end, I found a pair of capris and a button-down shirt that I had not worn yet. It was the least casual outfit that I had brought.

First, I would call Mom and Dad. I had no idea how it would go. I called their hotel and was quickly transferred to their room phone. Dad answered. That was good.

"Hello?"

"Hey, Dad."

"Hi Sunny. How are you feeling? Did you sleep well?"

"Yes, really good. I am going to grab some breakfast and then I think I will just lay low today. Probably nap and watch TV. Did you and Mom do some sightseeing? What are your plans today?"

"We did play tourist yesterday afternoon. This is a beautiful place, but we really need to think about heading home soon."

"I need another day. I'm not up to traveling yet."

"Well, I think I can hold off your mother one more day, okay? And then we can sit down and talk about getting back home."

"Thanks, Dad. You're the best."

"Bye Sunny. Get some rest, promise?"

"Promise, bye Dad."

I felt calm and focused again. I put on some makeup and put my hair up in a ponytail. I checked the phone book and map and then I grabbed a light sweater and my little purse. The clouds were still sticking around, and I didn't know what to expect. I made my way downstairs and grabbed a quick breakfast and coffee. I had to fill out more paperwork for a new rental moped. It was ready at the front door by the time I walked outside.

I put on the helmet and hopped on. I started it up and headed for the bridge that connected the resort to the rest of the Island. I knew the area I needed to go to and hopefully, my destination would be easy to spot once I was in the vicinity.

When I got to the general area, I went street by street until I found it. I pulled up right out front of the police station and turned off the moped. My pulse was racing, I took the front steps two at a time. I was committed and there was no turning back. I just prayed that they would let me see him.

I walked into the station. It was a wide-open space with lots of desks and bright fluorescent lights. Hazy cigarette smoke hung in the air. There were cops typing away at some of the desks. I saw a couple guys in handcuffs on a bench along the wall, waiting to get processed. I walked up to the desk that was closest to the door. The cop sitting there gave me a questioning look like, *this better be good cause I've seen it all before.* His receding hairline was graying. He wore an old polyester suit and glasses that barely hung on to the tip of his nose.

"Hello," I said holding out my hand. He just glared at me and said nothing.

"I would like to see Brooks Laughton…or Samuel Merriweather I mean. You're holding him here?" It came out more like a question as my voice went up in tone under the scrutiny of his stare.

"Nope, not going to happen. You know how many women have been in here trying to see him? And don't try to sell me some story about you being his girlfriend. I been hearing it all day long, lady. Besides, I know he only dates blondes."

"Oh…well, actually I'm his cousin…and he's expecting me," I blurted it out, surprising myself with my boldfaced lie. I had to get in.

"Now that's funny. That is a new one. I have no message about any relatives coming to visit."

"Well, I just flew in and I am his only living relative…well, me and my two sons that is," I said, hoping I sounded convincing.

"Now Miss, I guess I did hear that he had a cousin…what did you say your name was?"

Damn. What was her name? I had to get the name right if I wanted any chance of getting in to see him. Was it Martha…or Marilyn…or…

"Marlena. My name is Marlena. Please, can I see him?"

"Marlena what?"

"Manderson," I said, remembering the name of the town that my aunt lived in.

"Sounds right, let me do some checking," he said with a sigh. "Wait here, I'll be right back."

It worked; I couldn't believe it. I was going to get to talk to Brooks. The cop came back shortly and motioned for me to follow him. I was led to a small room with high windows that had bars on them. There was a rough, old picnic table in the middle of the room and a large mirror on the wall opposite the door. I sat down and waited for five minutes or so.

There was a buzz and the door opened. Brooks was led in by a uniformed cop. He was wearing a black and white striped prison uniform. Brooks curious expression turned to exasperation when he saw me. He looked tired and his usually slicked back hair was ruffled. The cop pushed him down across from me and uncuffed one hand. The open handcuff was secured down to a metal bar on the table. It made me feel a little safer given the way he was looking at me. The cop said, "fifteen minutes," and then walked out.

"What the hell are you doing here? They told me my cousin was here," he said, with anger.

"Yeah…look…I'm sorry but I need to talk to you, I need some answers."

"I don't owe you anything. What the hell are you talking about? Guard!"

"Wait! Please. Why did you kidnap me? Why did you want my uncle's suitcase? Carter said it was you."

"I don't know what you are talking about," he said, smugly.

"Well, the kidnapping charges are a laugh compared to murder, I guess. Look, I might be the only person on this Island that thinks there is a chance, just a chance, that maybe you didn't kill that girl. So, give me a break here. Let's talk," I said, as anger crept into my voice. I didn't have time for his stand-off attitude.

"Okay…okay. Maybe I was interested in your suitcase. Maybe I got curious because you were talking about my mother and people and places from the past. Maybe I just wanted to know what was going on because it involved my family. Would that be so bad if it were the case? I didn't mean to hurt anyone, I just wanted to scare you a little. Get you to drop it. Who wouldn't be concerned?"

I stared back at him looking deep into his eyes. I was afraid to ask the question that was dancing through my brain. I was afraid I already knew the answer. Did he know that his mother had killed his father? How could he not? Would he really have kidnapped me and stolen the suitcase if he wasn't worried about that information getting loose?

"What did you do with my suitcase?" I asked instead.

"Look, I am not admitting to anything, but you shouldn't waste your time trying to find it," he said a little too haughtily.

"Oh, well maybe you didn't realize that Roger Hodair at the Historical Society made copies of every single document and photo that were in the suitcase. So, nothing is really lost at all, thank goodness for that."

That caught his attention.

"Look…I left this Island a long time ago. My mother has been dead even longer. I just wanted to keep the past behind me. You know the paparazzi and the tabloids would be all over this story of my humble beginnings. I just want my mother's memory to rest in peace. Besides, they have plenty of other things to write about, trust me."

"You know, I used to admire you and my Great Uncle Walter. I wanted to be like you both. I wanted that lifestyle. You used me and tricked me into thinking I could get it. It was all just a lie. You never had any interest in me. The funny thing is now I see that you're the one who has been living the lie. You and Walter. Always the life of the party. Always the center of attention. But the reality is that you were both using your lifestyles as a cover to hide the pain and heartache that neither of you wanted to deal with. You both used it to keep yourselves…your real selves, isolated. Neither of you ever really liked yourselves very much, did you? How ironic is that?"

He slammed his free hand down hard on the table and I instinctively leaned back as far as I could on the rickety picnic bench. I had hit a nerve, but I couldn't stop myself as the words poured out of me.

"Maybe my little life is a joke to you but at least it's real and not a cover-up. It's a life worth living. What about yours?"

I looked at him; really looked at him. For the first time, I could see past the good looks and the sophisticated charm. I saw a scared little boy with no father. I felt sad for him and I felt sad for Walter. Both of them, wasting their lives away because they were too scared to be real with another human being. I realized that I had been heading down that same path since I had arrived on the Island. Why would I ever want to be anything like either one of them? There was still time to change course.

I decided not to bring up what his mother and my great uncle had done to his dad. I didn't know how much he really knew, but he was hurting enough already. There was a deep ache in him that might never go away. He had been trying to outrun his past all these years. Just like the pain and guilt that Walter had never let go of. Just like the past that I had been lucky enough to get out from under.

I wondered if Brooks would ever be able to escape it? That was his real prison, the one that he had put himself in. It was wasted guilt for something he had no control over. Like my guilt over what happened to Bobby…and for what Walter had done. Would Brooks be able to learn what my uncle had not? That he would never be able to drink away the heartache. That there wasn't enough booze or women or drugs for that.

Brooks was right, they were all long gone. What good would it do to dredge it back up? Let sleeping dogs lie. I thought of my grandmother as I said it to myself. She had been good at forgetting. I think he saw the pity in my eyes and his anger dissipated. It surprised me. He put his head down in his hands and was silent.

"I am going to get up and walk out of here now and not come back. You are going to be here for who knows how long. I think you're a jerk, but I don't think you're a killer. Can you tell me what evidence they have on you? If there is any way I can help, I will try. I really don't believe you belong in here."

He lifted his head and looked at me with red, weary eyes. He looked at me as if he had never seen me before in his life. Maybe since I couldn't deliver the letter to Angela, or right the wrong Angela and Walter had done, maybe this was a way for me to do something good to balance the scales. I knew in my heart that I was right about Brooks' innocence. Even after all he had done to me.

"Well, they said they found some jewelry of hers in my hotel room, a cross necklace. They had a photo of her wearing it. They also found a jacket of mine in her room with her blood on it…and my fingerprints were on a glass…and there were some witnesses that had seen us together. I think that was it."

My mind latched on to the cross necklace. Something stirred at the back of my brain, but I couldn't latch on to it…I didn't want to.

"Boy, it doesn't sound like much, but I am no lawyer."

"Well, I won't lie, she did spend time in my room, but I don't know how her necklace ended up in the drawer of my bedside table. She never took it off. And I was never in her hotel room.

"The funny thing about the jacket…it was the same one I gave to you on the Yacht. When you were cold. It was a custom tuxedo that I had made for parties and award shows and such. It had a special label in it with my name embroidered on it.

"I had given it to you and asked you to drop it off at the hotel desk in the lobby. When I asked for it the next day after the yacht party, they said that you did drop it off but that someone had already picked it up. None of the hotel staff seemed to know who had picked it up, though. The police didn't put much stock in it. They think I lied about picking it up, along with everything else. Do you know anything about it?"

"I left it at the lobby desk for you the same night you gave it to me. I don't know any more than that, really."

"I did see a photo of the glass they found with my fingerprints. It was one of the champagne flutes from the Yacht party. Anyone could have grabbed it from the Yacht after I had set it down. The police didn't believe me on that one either though.

"You know…I really did feel affection towards her. She was a sweet girl. They showed me photos…it was awful. She had been strangled and her neck was bruised…there was blood on her head…it was horrific. No one should have that happen to them," he said as he broke down.

He finally let that smiling façade slip. His grief poured out. He had probably been holding it in since before he was arrested. Everyone had already judged him for the crime, and they were ready to throw the book at him. He didn't deserve this. I felt certain of it the more I spoke with him.

Thoughts formed in my brain, trying to push forward. Images swirled in and out of focus like the images on Walter's 8mm film. I wasn't sure what to make of them. If I let them come forward, they might take me someplace that I didn't want to go. Even so, the pieces were beginning to fall into place. Once again, I shoved the thoughts back.

The cop came back in and unhooked Brooks from the table and then re-cuffed his free hand. Then the cop pulled him up off the bench and walked him to the door. Brooks stopped and turned around.

"I'm sorry, Sunny. The gun was a movie prop…and I was going to come back…you know that, right?" With that, he was gone, as the cop pulled him out of the room.

I made my way back to the front of the police station. I stopped to thank the officer at the front desk, the one who had let me in. He just rolled his eyes at me.

"You want to thank me? Do me a favor and don't come back," he said.

🌴 🌴 🌴

I walked outside into the cloudy, gray day. When I saw my moped, I stopped cold for a moment. I thought I had gotten a ticket but then I realized it was just a business card. Someone had squeezed the brake handle and put the card in against the wire, and then let the brakes go to hold it in place. I squeezed the brakes and took the card out. It had a big indentation in it from the handle.

It was the business card of the detective who had been following me. I guessed it was an invite to go and see him. Ironic since he had been so quick to get rid of me before. Why the change of heart I wondered? I climbed on the moped and pulled the helmet onto my head. There was no excitement or terror, just tiredness. I wanted to see what I could do for Brooks, no matter how much of a long shot, but I thought I better answer the invite first.

I buzzed along on the little bike. I remembered the way back to the office of the detective, even though I had only been there once. I parked in the parking lot and went into the brick building. When I arrived at the detective's door I knocked. He opened the door and waved me in this time. It was just as messy as the last time I had visited. The spilt coffee stain had dried into the orange shag carpet.

"I see you found the card I left for you. I wasn't sure if you would get the meaning of my invitation. Were you visiting your imaginary boyfriend at the police station?"

"You tell me, Dick Tracy."

"Let's just get this over with. I have two envelopes here. You get one of them depending on your answer to my offer. Someone wants you to go away, really bad, and I am not just talking about myself."

"What do you mean?"

"Someone is willing to give you ten thousand dollars if you will leave this Island as soon as possible. No more questions and no more snooping around. What do you say?"

I was shocked. The offer hit me like a slap in the face. I had to admit that it was awfully tempting, but I thought about my promise to try and help Brooks. But still, I could use the money to replenish my inheritance and make a hefty contribution to Charles' college fund. I didn't know what to make of his offer.

"Who are you representing with this offer?" I asked.

"Look, I wouldn't tell you even if I knew but the truth is, I don't know. I started getting anonymous letters after you arrived on this Island. Each one contained payment and directions. I did what was asked. There was nothing unusual about it except for the unknown identity of my client, that and the fact that anyone would bother to keep tabs on you. Though this last letter has crossed this whole episode into the Twilight Zone. You would make me and others very happy if you would agree to this. We all win. Don't tell me you wouldn't like to get your hands on that cash."

I was frozen. I wasn't sure what I should do. I wanted to be done with all this and get back to my life. I found myself truly ready to jump in headfirst, into the real world back home, after all I had been through on the Island.

Brooks, Carter and Charles…wouldn't they all be better off if I left? If I stopped stirring things up on this Island. If I had never stepped foot on this Island. I was no detective. What could I expect to accomplish for Brooks? But I just kept seeing the image of Brooks with his head in his hands, in jail, alternating with the image of Charles' smiling face. I had some unfinished business.

"Come on lady, I don't have all day. What's it going to be?"

"I am not ready to leave just yet."

"Suit yourself," he said as he tossed one of the envelopes at me. I picked it up off the floor and began to rip it open.

"NO, no, no! You take that damn letter and get out of here. The less I know about all this the better. As a matter of fact, I am done with this case. I don't get paid enough to deal with you. Good day," he said with a huff.

I walked out of his office wondering why he disliked me so much, but could I really blame him? I had insulted his detective skills more than once and that was his livelihood. Oh well. I guess it wouldn't hurt my feelings not to see him again either. After I was outside and sitting on the moped, I finished opening the envelope.

Inside I found a tourist brochure for the Cliffside Fort and Gardens. It was in color. I didn't understand. I unfolded it and found writing on the inside in black marker. It was in big block letters. All it said was:

10 PM – COME ALONE. I HAVE INFO FOR YOU.

A chill ran down my spine. I knew it was not a good idea, but I felt compelled to follow through with it after everything that I had already been through. I needed answers. I hoped I could resolve everything by finding out who sent this and what they knew. Thoughts swirled around in my head, like leaves stirred up by the wind. Maybe it would be information that could help Brooks. I had to find out.

I started up the moped and headed off down the street with the brochure under my hand as it rested on the handlebar. I was winding my way back to the tourist market which was near the road to my hotel. If I was going to do this, I had to do it alone. I didn't want to put anyone else in danger. I couldn't tell anyone what I was going to do.

I turned a corner and saw Charles in front of me, there with some friends. He saw me as well and jumped out in front of my moped. I almost hit him as I squealed the tires when I squeezed the brakes.

"Watch where you're going crazy lady driver," he exclaimed with a smile. "Hey…what are you doing driving around? Shouldn't you be resting or something? You just got out of the hospital."

"Hi, Charles. I am doing much better," I said with a forced smile. He saw the brochure in my hand and grabbed it.

"Hey, you want me to take you here? Wait a minute…what is this?" He had unfolded the brochure and was now looking at the writing on it.

"What is this? Wait, you can't go. This sounds dangerous. I will go with you."

"NO!"

"But you can't go alone."

"No. I appreciate you wanting to go with me, but if something happened to you, I would never forgive myself."

"But you need me to look out for you ma'am."

I smiled, despite the seriousness of the conversation. He was so sweet to want to help but his grandmother's warning came to mind. I could not put him in any more danger. Hanging out with me was not in his best interest. I had to put my foot down on this one.

"Charles, I know you would do this in a heartbeat, but you need to promise me that you will stay away tonight. How about tomorrow we do some sight-seeing? I'm afraid tomorrow will be one of my last days here and I couldn't think of anyone better to spend it with. I am heading home soon. I will really miss you, kid," I said as I tugged on that old faded Yankees cap that he always wore.

"Okay, I guess. Make sure you keep your protection charm on, okay?"

"I will – promise. And I will make another contribution to your college fund too, before I leave."

"Okay," he said, not smiling.

"Why don't I believe you?"

"Scout's honor…"

With that, he took off down the street. I could see that he wasn't happy about it and I didn't believe for one second that he had ever been a boy scout. He was right. I should not do it alone. Why was I being so brave and so foolish? Maybe there was someone I could ask for help but first I decided to make one more stop before heading back to my hotel.

I had to ask for directions from some locals on the street. Their directions were clear, and I found my way to the lighthouse where I had been imprisoned by Brooks. It wasn't near as scary in the daytime, and without a storm raging. I climbed the steps, crossing my fingers and hoping to find the door unlocked. I was in luck. It was unchained when I reached the platform with the door. I walked the final staircase into the top windowed room. I looked around, but my sweater and the letter were both gone. I guess I shouldn't have been surprised.

I took off once again and made my way back to my hotel, feeling bad that I had lost the only evidence that could clear up Arthur Murray's death. Maybe it was for the best I tried to tell myself. Let sleeping dogs lie.

🌴 🌴 🌴

I found some food and turned on the TV back at the hotel, but I was too anxious to really watch or eat much. I was still mulling things over. I thought about giving my folks a call when the phone rang.

"Hi Sunny. It's David. I didn't think I would be able to reach you, but I was hoping I might. How are you doing? Your parents told me you were hurt. What's going on?"

"I am fine…really…whatever they said it was probably blown out of proportion. Especially if you talked to Mom."

"What happened?"

"Let's just say I had a run in with a disagreeable type. I got robbed...and kidnapped."

"That sounds more than a little serious."

"Trust me, I don't think he was trying to hurt me. He just wanted...my purse. Luckily someone found me."

"But you can't know for sure what his intentions were. You are so lucky."

"Well, he's in jail now, so case closed." I didn't mention that he was in jail for the murder of someone else.

"I'm glad you're okay. I felt bad about our last conversation. I mean it's still over, but you deserved better. I have been feeling like a jerk since we talked. And when I found out about all this...I felt even worse. We really can still be friends if you are willing."

"You know, I think you're right. It needed to happen. You are a nice guy, but we just didn't have that spark, did we? But you were there when I needed someone. When I was going through it with my grandmother. And when I was struggling through college. Hell, ...you were the one who pushed me into going away to college. I am so grateful. You have always been there. It means a lot to me. You have been a true friend. You deserve good things and happiness in your life. How could I stay mad? I'm not mad anymore, okay?"

"Thank you. I hope we can meet up and talk when you get back, okay?"

"Sure...and thanks, David. Thanks for everything you've done for me over the years."

"Hey now, don't sound so serious. I will see you when you get back, okay?"

"Okay, bye."

I was in a much better place when it came to David and that felt good. No tears this time. He was right about everything, but I had been afraid to let go and admit to myself that he was right. As the saying goes, when one door closes another door opens. I had to trust in that and trust in myself. I needed to make another phone call. I needed to call my parents.

David was right about my tone of seriousness. I was scared about what would happen at ten. I couldn't deny it. Putting myself in danger was not my smartest move, but I could not turn back. What if I never saw any of them again? I had to say bye and tell them I loved them one more time. But this had to be finished, one way or another before I left Euphoria. To the end, I thought as I pulled a beer out of the mini-fridge. I would quit when I left the Island. I needed some liquid courage.

I dialed up the number for my parent's hotel and asked for their room. They were not in. I felt relief. I left a message saying I was going to bed early and putting out the 'do not disturb' sign on the door. I would call them first thing in the morning. Then I said I loved them, and I said my goodbye. I was proud of keeping it together with David, but I wasn't sure if I would have been able to do the same with them. Even as angry as I was at Mom. That would have raised the alarm.

Charles had been right about not going alone. The more I thought about it the more I knew it was the right thing to do. I decided to make one more phone call. I really hoped Carter would be home. I knew he was mad at me, but I hoped he would still be willing to help. If he was willing to help me, it would push my doubts about him away for good.

The doubts that had tried to come forward in the police interrogation room. The image of a broken cross necklace in Carter's desk drawer at his studio would not leave my mind. I felt sure of his innocence as much as I was sure of Brooks. Lots of people wore cross necklaces. The phone rang a few times and then he answered.

"Hello?"

"Hi…Carter…it's Sunny."

"Oh, hi. What are you up to?"

"Well, I have a favor to ask. Are you busy tonight?"

"Yeah, but nothing I can't do later. What's up?"

"This will sound crazy."

"I don't think you could surprise me anymore."

"Okay. Someone wants to meet up with me tonight at 10 PM. They left me an invitation today. I think this could clear everything up for me. I need to do this before I leave."

"Wow. I guess you can still surprise me. This sounds ridiculously dangerous. You can't seriously be thinking to do this, can you? It's too dangerous."

"Well, that is why I'm calling you. Would you be willing to go with me…so I don't have to do this alone?" I asked as I twirled the cord of the phone around my fingers in nervous anticipation of his answer.

"Have you told anyone about this? Have you talked to the police?"

"No," I said. I thought about my run-in with Charles, but I had convinced him to stay away, I hoped.

"Maybe you should talk to the police."

"No. It might scare them off, whoever they are. The person that wants to meet."

"Well we know it can't be Brooks, he's tied up at the moment."

"I know, but maybe he had someone helping him all along. Or maybe this person has some information that could help him get out of jail."

"Aahh, still trying to save the world, and Brooks. But why would they contact you with this info?" he asked.

"I don't know. Maybe they don't want to go to the cops themselves? Maybe they are afraid of getting dragged into it."

"You have quite an imagination, you know that? Must be all those mystery novels. Maybe they want to silence you. Have you thought about that? I'll go with you. I've kept you safe this long. I want to see you make it off this rock, one way or another."

"Thanks, Carter," I said as I let the phone cord drop from my fingers.

"How about I meet you there…where did you say you were meeting?"

"The old Cliffside Fort and Gardens."

"See you at ten."

Click.

After I talked to him, I knew I had made the right decision. It was stupid to consider doing this alone, and even dumber to consider him a suspect as I had. He would never suggest I call the police if he was guilty. Just like he had talked me into calling the police about Bikini Blonde's identity. I felt a sense of relief after talking to him.

I went down to the lobby and found some dark colored clothes in the store along with a flashlight. Then I was back in my room picking at my cold dinner and trying to focus on the television. The only thing that really settled me was another beer. I didn't want to get carried away though. I needed to be clear headed, plus I needed to cut back or maybe quit altogether after this trip.

I planned to leave around eight, so I could get there early and scope out the location as best I could in the dark. I was mad at myself for not thinking to do this earlier in the day when I would have had the advantage of some sunlight. It would have been the smart thing to do since I was not familiar with the area. I guess I wasn't as focused as I tried to tell myself.

My anxiety level soared as it got closer to eight. Finally, it was time to leave. I grabbed my small bag and the flashlight and headed down to the lobby. Throngs of people moved through the lobby with party hats and noise makers. I realized it was New Year's Eve. How had I missed two holidays in a week's time?

I walked outside and saw my moped sitting in front of the doors, there was a young boy sitting on it. It was Charles. I was furious and happy at the same time. But I couldn't let him go with me.

"Charles! No way. You cannot go with me. Did you sneak out of the house? How did you get here? Your parents are going to be furious. Your grandmother is going to be furious with me."

He did not say anything. He just stared at me with the most determined look possible. There was something so grown up in that look. I could see that there would be no way possible to convince him not to come along. I didn't want to waste time arguing with him. I knew it was wrong and I knew I would regret it, but I shook my head in agreement anyway.

I hopped on the bike behind him, handing him the helmet. We rode in dark silence to the site of the fort. It was high up on some bluffs looking out over the ocean and far from the civilized portions of the Island. It must have made a good lookout point in the days when it was still operational. The moonlight was strong enough for me to get a look at it, but wisps of clouds cluttered the sky, threatening to take over. There was a chill in the air as we sped down the empty road that wound to the top of the cliffs.

The fort was surrounded by a maze of gardens that had several paths leading up to it. That was good. We could use the trees and bushes for some cover. I really wished I had come by during daylight hours to get a better look. I motioned for Charles to park. We hid the bike in some shrubs, and I turned to look at Charles.

"Charles, I have let you come this far. Now I need you to do something extremely important. You have to stay here, near the bike. Find a spot where you can see me and watch."

"But ma'am…"

"No buts. This is important. If something happens, I need you to get on that moped and go right to the police station. You have the most important job. Whatever you do, you must stay clear, so you can go to the police if necessary. Don't try to rescue me, got it? No matter what happens. I want you to stay safe. Agree to it or you can take the moped and leave right now."

"Okay I guess," he said dejectedly.

"Promise me."

"Okay…I promise."

"Okay, good. Now I am meeting someone else here. Do you remember Carter from the hospital?"

"Yes."

"He will be here too. He is here to help," I said, but Charles looked doubtful. "Charles, can you climb this tree? It might give you a good view of what is going on and give you some cover."

"Yeah, sure."

He shimmied up the tree and easily climbed to about fifteen feet off the ground. I smiled up at him, giving him a thumb's up and telling him to be quiet and careful, and to stay put. I walked along the garden paths. The crunch of my feet on the rock mulch, and my heavy breathing were the only sounds that echoed in my ears. The moonflowers were out in full bloom. They glowed eerily and their scent mingled with the other garden flowers. Their heady floral aroma overwhelmed me.

All the paths of the garden radiated outward like rays from the sun. When I reached the center, I saw a circular plaza at the heart of the garden that held a stone water fountain. It was a beautiful garden and the trickle of the water soothed me. I wished I could come back under different circumstances. Carter was sitting on the edge of the water fountain with his hand in the water. He turned and looked at me as I walked up to him.

"Hi, Queenie."

"Hi. Thanks for coming."

"I've been here a while, and I've been walking the grounds. No sign of anyone yet."

"Okay. That's good. Let's keep looking and try to stay out of sight. Maybe we can spot him before he spots us."

"Sounds good," he said as he stood up and stretched. He walked off and I went the other direction. I turned and looked toward Charles in his tree and I gave a thumbs-up. I hoped he was seeing me because he was very well hidden, and I couldn't see him at all.

We circled in silence many times without any other sign of activity. We walked through the gardens and up to the fort along the bluff and then back again. After about the tenth time around,

Carter stopped me on the lookout area by the fort. He tapped his watch and whispered.

"It's ten forty-five already. I think your mystery man is a no-show," he said, with a shrug of his shoulders.

🌴 🌴 🌴

I was cold and tired, and I could not disagree. This had all been a waste of time. I was going to leave this Island and never know the truth. Who was I to think I could help Brooks anyway? I looked down on the cold empty sea below the cliffs that was laid out in front of me, bathed in sparkling moonlight. Such a dark and lonely sight. This was it. This was the end of it all. Back to the real world for me. I would never get all the answers.

Carter came up behind me and put his hands on my shoulders. He pressed his lips to my neck and kissed me. It made me shiver. He moved his hands down to my waist and then he kissed the side of my cheek.

"Can we forget about all this now and move forward? It can all be over," he said softly.

He spun me around and pulled me into him. He kissed my lips. I thought back to Jenna telling me he was a good guy. He had helped me when I needed it most, but I was still hesitant. My body was reacting to his touches. His kisses were messing with my thoughts. I didn't know what I wanted anymore. I felt like I was falling, and I thought of Charles in the tree, probably watching us right then if he was still out there. I didn't want to kiss Carter with Charles watching over us. Besides, I needed time to think. I pushed Carter away. I felt him tense up.

"Damn it Sunny. You just can't let him go, can you?"

"No…no. That's not it at all…"

"This could have all ended right here, right now. Maybe we could have been happy together. I was willing to try. I realized you had no idea what was really going on when you called me tonight. You had no idea that I sent you the damn invite. I wanted to give you one last chance; to see which way this would all go. But you chose wrong. Over and over again. You chose him. You kept throwing him in my face. I really had feelings for you."

"No. I'm sorry. It's not what you think."

"It's too late. I can see that you won't let this go. I will not be made a fool of again. This ends tonight," he said with icy coldness. My heart was pounding in my ears.

"Okay, Queenie. You want to know the whole truth? You want to know all the secrets? Even Brooks doesn't know it all. But I will be rid of him now, forever. Don't look so confused, Sherlock. You came as close as anyone to the bottom of it all. You stumbled right into it, didn't you? You, armed only with your uncle's suitcase and some letters," he said, as his hands grabbed hold of my upper arms and dug in. He took a step toward the drop-off and pulled me along with him.

"What are you saying? I don't understand."

"You were right. Brooks was always trying to cover up his humble beginnings. The bastard child with a tramp for a mother and an unknown father. That would make the front page of the tabloids for sure. She was the talk of the Island back then. But there was something that you never got right. If you had done the math you would see that it never added up. Arthur Murray was not Brooks' father. He couldn't be. Brooks was born three years after Arthur died. Did you know that I am two years older than Brooks? Did you know that I was adopted just like you were? Only I was an infant when I was given up. Are you seeing where I am going with this?" he said as he took one more step toward the edge, pulled me along with him.

"But your parents moved away…or was that a lie? Roger Hodair said they died in a boating accident. Is that the truth?" I asked, not wanting to know the answer. The more I knew the less chance I had of getting away from Carter. I could see that clear as day now. Why was I always so naïve? But I had to keep him talking. I had to give Charles time to escape.

"Roger was right. I just preferred not to discuss it with anyone, so I started telling a different story. Not many people even remember it anymore, except for good, old Roger. He never forgets anything, does he? He's like an elephant. He's even helped me piece together things from my own past, but I doubt he realized it.

"I will never forget the day that my adopted family told me the news. It still plays over and over in my brain. I sometimes wonder how this story could have ended if I would have done things differently that day. I guess I'm as bad at controlling my emotions as my mother was.

"It was the first time that I ever flew into a black rage. I couldn't stop myself. I thought I would never pull myself back together. I was only sixteen years old then. We were out on the sailboat. It was my Dad's prize possession. He loved to take it out and head for open waters.

"My mom thought it was time that I knew about my adoption. She had brought along the documentation from the hospital. I was so shocked to see the birth certificate. There was no father listed and when I saw my birth mother's name...I couldn't believe it. Angela Merriweather was not just Brooks' mother...she was mine too. I am Brooks' brother. Well, half-brother. A fact that he still doesn't know, even to this day, and I intend to keep it that way.

"I was his friend when we were kids. That's true. As we grew older, we grew apart; I grew to like him less and less. He lied, and he was manipulative. Always so superior and smug. He was the last person on the Island that I would have wanted to call *brother*. Angela, on the other hand, was a beautiful lady but she never realized the truth either. She didn't know where I had ended up after she gave me away.

"He had our mother all to himself. No one knows who his father is, doesn't really matter now, does it? But I pieced together the mystery of mine. The letter that you had with you in the lighthouse confirmed what I already knew. Don't worry, it's gone now. I will never be able to ask Angela why she gave me up and decided to keep him two years later. That is something I will never know the answer to, I guess. But it's a question that has haunted me over the years.

"He didn't deserve her. If he only knew. He was always getting into trouble and causing her heartache. I would have been a much better son to her. I would have done right by her for sure. Do you see now why I said that he never deserved any of it? He never truly appreciated all that he had," Carter said as he moved another step closer to the edge, with me in tow.

"My adopted mother was surprised by my angry reaction to the news of my adoption and she tried to put her arms around me. I shoved her so hard that she fell over the edge of our little sailboat, surprising both of us. She wasn't wearing a life jacket. Dad jumped in immediately to help her. Well...the sails were up, and the boat was moving fast. I could have tried to bring down the sails, which would have taken a lot of effort for one young boy. But I froze instead," he said, pausing as he thought back on it.

"I was shaking with anger and my fists were clenched in tight balls at my side. I had cuts on my palms where my fingernails had dug in. I was glad they were in the water. They deserved it for lying to me. I sailed away from them without even looking back. Once I was close enough to shore to swim in, I set the boat on fire and jumped off.

"And then when I was a senior in high school, I was in love with a girl. Her name was Maria. I loved her as much as an untried teenager could love someone. We would go to the lighthouse together and watch the ships go by in the distance. The same lighthouse where I found you.

"We spent so many afternoons there, planning what we would do after graduation. I should have known better. Anything I showed interest in would be something that Brooks would go after on a lark. He never loved her the way I did. She was just a game and he loved the thrill of the chase. I found out they were seeing each other. I didn't understand how she could lie to me like that. I was furious," he said as he took another small step.

"I confronted her about it. She never denied anything. That was the second time the anger took me. She seemed surprised by my anger and that made my hatred grow even greater for her. We were up in the lighthouse again when I put my hands around her neck. I couldn't stop. I just kept seeing Brooks laughing in my mind. I took her body out to sea. That was where my parents had found their rest. It seemed fitting to me.

"No one looked too hard except for her parents. She had been threatening to run away to Broadway every chance she got. She wanted to go to New York to be a serious actress. Maybe that was what had drawn her to Brooks. He always had that ambition, just like our mother.

"Brooks and I were not her only boyfriends I found out. It hardened my heart even more toward her, and it kept me from being a prime suspect in her disappearance as well."

He was moving forward again, and my feet were losing traction on the loose rocks near the edge of the cliff. My upper arms felt numb where his fingers were dug in. I felt eerily calm though. There was no fight in me. Maybe it was shock, but I could do nothing except listen to his horrible tale. How could I have been so blind?

"After high school, Angela died and then Brooks left the Island. You know she had a bank account in Brooks' name with hundreds of thousands of dollars? He used to brag about it and what he would do with the money. It had sat in a bank for years collecting interest, untouched. It was deposited the year I was born. I figured it was a payout from the Murray family, to keep her mouth shut about her affair and pregnancy. She never touched it, even when she was sick with cancer. She could have used it for medical treatment instead of letting herself waste away. Too much guilt, I guess. Brooks was able to move on to bigger and better things with that money...with my money.

217

"I thought I was free of him when he left. Sure, I would hear about him and see him on the television occasionally, but as long as I wasn't face to face with him, I found an escape from my deep anger. But every time he would return to Euphoria, my anger was reborn.

"I made sure I knew his every move when he was back. I knew the only way I could ever hope to escape my anger permanently was to be rid of him for good. I couldn't kill him. That would be to easy. I wanted him to hurt and suffer for years as I had.

"I had to do something to him that would really get his attention. Something that would shake him to the core. Something worse than death for him. I wanted him to lose all that fortune and fame. I wanted him to become a bad memory that people would whisper about in a sad pathetic way. They would say *he had it all and it went to his head...he let it all slip away.* I knew what I had to do. I knew what a far harsher punishment it would be. For him to be forgotten...for him to lose everything...that would make him suffer far worse. I've planned for years..."

"Stop. I don't want to hear any more of this," I cried, but all he did was squeeze my arms tighter and take another step towards the drop. I knew what he meant to do, and I could do nothing. I was frozen.

"I really hated to kill the blonde. I didn't know her. There was no passion in it for me. It was hard, but I just thought of Brooks and all he has done over the years, and my rage grew. Then I made sure the evidence was in place. You know, it's funny, you gave me the perfect opportunity to contact the police when you went missing. That was an unexpected surprise.

"Everything came together so easily after that. I called the police and told them Brooks had kidnapped you after the parade. He was already on their radar after you tipped them off about the blonde. I had a pretty good idea of where I would find you, but I let the police take care of Brooks and search his room before I went to retrieve you from the lighthouse. Once they found the blonde's necklace in

Brooks' room, they took a closer look and found the jacket and champagne flute in her room.

"The bungling keystone cops were too dumb to put it together the first time they searched her room before you went missing. I went back and made sure the clues were far easier to find the second time. I handed them the case on a silver platter. Now Brooks is going to go away for a long time. His kidnapping of you was the nail in the coffin," Carter said with a laugh.

He was telling me things I had begun to piece together in my mind when I had talked to Brooks at the police station. Why had I been so stubborn? Why didn't I let myself see the truth then?

"I really hate to kill you too, you know that? I mean it. It sounds awful to say it out loud. I tried so hard to get you to drop all this, but you were just too infatuated with him. Just like all the others. But you were the only one to believe he might be innocent. Everyone else was so quick to throw the book at him. I tried to change your mind, but you wouldn't listen and now I can't let you ruin all that I put into motion."

"Please...don't do this. You're better than this. You can still change all this," I pleaded.

"Sure. What should I do, hand myself over to the cops? Give them my confession? That's not going to happen. I would be the one rotting away in a jail cell. I have managed to keep all these secrets for so many years now. It's almost finished. This ends with Brooks out of my life for good. Then I can be done. I'm sorry that you had to get caught up in all this. Brooks should have never got you involved. But now you know too much. I am really sorry," he said.

"You could throw me away so easily? And you made out Brooks to be the monster. I really did have feelings for you. I just have so many things going on in my life. I was trying to sort it all out. Things from my childhood and my family. That's why I hesitated. Not because of Brooks.

"I thought you would understand. I thought you would give me time, but you are not the person I thought you were at all. Jenna really believed in you too. I think a lot of people did. You're nothing but a phony. You're a much better actor than Brooks ever thought of being. How could you wear that mask for so many years? I was so blind," I said, as the tears fell down my face. Me and my stupid tears again.

My words gave him pause. His grip on my arms lightened as he took a step backwards, away from the drop-off. I was not sure what I had said that would give him second thoughts. Maybe it was mention of Jenna. She was as close to him as anyone. He was truly hesitating, and I began to hope. I was watching him work through his internal struggle when a dark figure came running at us. The stranger knocked Carter to the ground and fell on top of him. The stranger's hat went flying. I was shoved out of the way. The element of surprise had given the stranger the advantage.

They wrestled around on the ground, kicking up dust and rocks. The tables turned, and Carter was on top of his assailant. Carter had his attacker's arms pinned down to the ground over his head. I was able to get a better look at his face when they rolled over, but I already knew. It was Charles. He looked over at me with a defiant look on his face. My heart sank. Why did he have to come over here when he did? I might have been getting through to Carter, but now I would never know.

Carter had Charles completely restrained. He stood up and pulled Charles to his feet, twisting his arms around behind his back. He was glaring down at him.

"Damn it, Sunny. You dragged this kid into all this? What the hell were you thinking?"

Carter scooped down to pick up Charles' baseball cap, which he flung out to sea like a frisbee. Then Carter walked over to the edge of the cliff, dragging Charles along with him. When he got close enough, he gave Charles a hard shove and over he went, falling to the black waters below.

I heard nothing, except for the dull roar of the waves washing over the rocks. I waited for a splash, but nothing. I remembered Charles talking about cliff jumping with his buddies during our day at the beach. I dared to hope that he had made it down to the water safely. I was furious. I had to do something. I had to help Charles. Maybe in some small stupid way, it would make amends for my failure to help Bobby all those years ago. That irrational thought spurred me on.

I took a few steps back. Carter was looking down over the edge, trying to determine Charles fate. I ran as fast as I could toward the drop-off. I got to the edge and pushed off with all my might thinking of Charles's tips for cliff diving. Jump out away from the rocks, tuck your arms in.

I was floating in midair. I could hear yelling. Time moved in slow motion as gravity pulled me downward. I saw a lone firefly swirling around my face. Then there were hundreds of them churning around me as I fell. Surely, they couldn't fly fast enough to follow me down, but there they were. Did Carter see them from above? I pointed my toes and squeezed my arms in tight to my sides just like Charles had advised. I didn't want bruises under my arms. I prayed that I was not heading for the rocks.

I sliced my way into the cold water. I had been a little off kilter and I went in with a big splash. The lighting bugs had followed me down and they were all over, even in the water. I couldn't see anything in the dark waters except for the bugs, and I lost my sense of direction. I began to panic, flailing my arms around and trying to move in the direction I thought would lead to the surface. The fireflies grew brighter around me, and my lungs began to ache. I needed air. In the light of the fireflies, I suddenly saw movement.

There were two figures moving towards me. Walter and little Bobby were growing closer. Their faces came into clear view in the greenish glow of the bugs. But how could this be happening? They were smiling at me and I felt each of them grab on to one of my arms and pull me. Things were getting fuzzy. Walter and Bobby went in and out of focus a few times and then everything went black.

🌴 🌴 🌴

I woke up wet and cold on the hard-packed sand of the beach. Darkness surrounded me. I wasn't sure how long I had been unconscious, but it didn't seem like long. Charles and Carlos were looking down into my face and smiling.

I remembered where I was and what had happened. I looked up to the rocky bluff that jutted out over the water to my right. I could see the outline of the old stone fort, but there was no one up on the cliff now, at least no movement that I could detect.

"Are you okay, ma'am?"

"Yeah, you gave us a scare. What were you doing up there on the cliff?" Carlos asked.

"What are you doing out on the beach so late at night, Carlos? Wait, forget I asked that. I'm fine, really. I'm glad you're here," I said, as I sat upright. "How long was I out of it?"

"Just a few minutes or so, ma'am"

"Charles, I am so proud of you. What you did was so brave, but please, never do anything like that again. We really should think about getting out of here. Did anyone see where Carter went?"

"Wait a minute...Carter Davis is here? Where is he? What's he doing out here? I don't understand any of this," Carlos said.

"We don't have time to discuss it right now. Let's go. Carlos, do you have your car nearby?" I asked.

"Sure. Let me pack up my stuff."

Carlos began gathering up his things and that left me alone with Charles. I reached out and gave him a big hug. I was so grateful for him and the uncontrollable tears were in my eyes again. I was so glad he was not hurt. I would jump a million times more if I had to. If it would keep Charles safe. I would never let Bobby drown again on my watch. I would sacrifice myself for both of them.

"Charles, thank you for what you did. You know, your cliff diving tips totally saved me." I wanted to tug on the bill of his baseball cap, but it was gone thanks to Carter.

"No worries."

"Charles, did you see anything when we jumped or when we were in the water?"

"Like what?"

"Anything out of the ordinary? Bugs? Lights?"

"No, nothing."

"Okay. Well, let's get going. Let's see if Carlos needs help," I said disappointedly. Was I imagining the lightning bugs? It hadn't been the first time.

Carlos had already taken all his belongings up to the car in the parking lot. He was moving things around within the car. Probably making room for Charles and me. Fear came over me. We were out in the open in the parking lot. There were trees and bushes around the edges that became a black void in the darkness of the night. Lots of places to hide.

"Hey Carlos, we should really get going now. My moped is over by the gardens, but I can come back for that tomorrow. I just want to get out of here if you don't mind," I said looking around nervously.

"Sure, no problem. Hop in."

I let Charles jump into the front passenger seat and I slammed the door for him. I climbed into the back, behind Carlos' seat. Carlos opened his door to get in but before he could I heard a loud and sickening thud. His body crumpled to the ground. Carter was standing over him with a big rock in his hand. My heart dropped, and panic took over.

My door was still open, and Carter was reaching in to grab at my feet and legs. I kicked at him as hard as I could. He slapped my feet, trying to dodge the blows I was sending his way.

"Charles, get out!" I yelled as I inched my way back across the car seat. I was trying to make it out the passenger side and away

223

from Carter. I heard Charles open his door and jump out. I got enough traction for one good kick and I saw Carter go flying backwards. He tripped over Carlos and ended up on his back on the ground.

Charles opened the door behind me, and I fell out of the car with a thump landing painfully on my tailbone. The adrenaline was going, and I was back up on my feet instantly. I grabbed on to Charles' good hand and we took off running for the cover at the edge of the parking lot. That might buy us a few minutes to regroup. I looked back over my shoulder and saw Carter's shadowy figure was still on the ground. That was good. There was nothing I could do for Carlos. I prayed he would be okay until we could find some help.

We made it to the trees and I instantly turned left, pulling Charles along with me. When we were deep into the brush and away from our entry point, I thought it would be okay to stop for a minute. I motioned for Charles to stop. I was breathing hard, but Charles was not winded at all. I could hear Carter calling after us.

"Sunny. Come out come out wherever you are. Are we really going to do this? Be reasonable. Let's talk," Carter shouted.

He sounded angry and crazy. I hadn't heard him like that before. It scared me. He had been so good at keeping it under control. I wanted to yell to him and tell him he should have found a bigger cliff to push us off. I knew that would anger him even more if I taunted him like that. Bad idea. I was afraid he had already crossed over into one of his black rages as he called it. Besides, I didn't want to give away our exact location now that we had some cover. He kept calling and mocking us. Daring us to come out.

"Charles, what's around here? Is there someplace close by that we can make it to on foot?" I asked in a whispered hush.

"We are a long way from any place. I don't know."

"What about houses?"

"We would have to go back by the fort, but it is a pretty small path and we'd have to go back towards that guy."

WALTER'S SUITCASE

"No, we don't want to cross paths with Carter. We would have to head right toward him or make a big loop around. We need to move in the opposite direction."

"Well...there is another place I know where we could hide. It's close by here. Might be a little tough to get there in the dark, but I think I can find it."

"I trust you, Charles. Let's go. We have to keep moving."

It sounded like Carter was moving away from us. That was good. I let Charles lead the way. He was hard to keep up with in the darkness, he moved quickly through the trees and brush. Branches scraped at me as we went, but I was grateful for the concealment. It was quiet now. Carter had stopped calling for us. That meant he was focused on finding our trail. I prayed he was not as familiar with this area as Charles was.

Charles was picking up the pace and the trees seemed to be thinning. He stopped short and I plowed into the back of him. The force of it knocked him over and I stumbled, landing on top of him. I stood up and reached out a hand. He was back up and looking around in the dimness.

"We're close, I know this place."

We were moving again, and we quickly reached a clearing. I couldn't see much in the moonlight, but Charles knew where we were. He stopped and looked at me.

"My friends and I do a lot of cliff diving, but we also do some cave diving too. This is one of our spots. See that hole in the ground? You have to trust me on this. It is a lot shorter than the cliff you jumped off at the fort. Much easier. There is a deep underground hole at the bottom. Even at low tide, the water is plenty deep enough."

I could see it. It was about ten feet in diameter. Just a hole in the ground, but in the dark, it was impossible to see down into it. I was scared. I had so many questions. How would we get out of the hole once we went in was the most important thing that came to mind but there was no time for questions when I heard a noise behind us. I turned to see Carter stumble out into the clearing. He fell onto his knees as he broke through the trees.

"Trust me and jump out hard to the middle of the circle."

Charles grabbed my hand and we both ran and jumped through the hole and into the darkness below. My body tensed up. I didn't know what to expect. He was right, the jump was a lot shorter than the cliff at the fort. We landed with a splash and Charles was giggling from the rush of it when we both surfaced. I never wanted to take a jump like that or the other again.

The cave below the hole was big. Much bigger than the hole above. The rough sides of the cave arched up to the opening in the ground. The surface of the water was maybe twenty feet below the ceiling above, but it was hard to tell for sure in the darkness.

Only an indistinct light filtered into the cave from the hole overhead. It disoriented me. We swam over to the side and climbed up on to some rocks. The rocks were wet and slippery, I found it hard to keep my footing. I was glad for the long shirt and pants I had on as I fell flat on the rocks a couple of times. Charles knew exactly where he wanted to go.

"This way," he said. "The tide is low enough now. There is a tunnel to the side that goes to another cave where we can get out. It's a tight squeeze, though. Even with low tide, we might have to hold our breath a couple of times."

I did not like the sound of that. A tight squeeze for Charles might mean impassable for me, but I didn't have time to dwell on it. Carter fell through the hole above with a shout, hitting a stalactite on the way down. It broke off and crashed into the water with him. I heard him surface as he moaned and cursed in pain. He must not have seen the hole before he stumbled into it.

Charles found the spot he was looking for and waved me closer. We silently squeezed into the hole in the side of the cave. I was hoping Carter was too distracted to see us go into the wall. It might take him a while to find the opening and that would buy us some time to get away.

We inched along silently. Charles kept reaching back to see if I was still with him. We were shrouded in blackness. I knocked my head on some rocks. In the tighter spots, rocks grabbed at my clothes and skin, ripping and scratching. I thought I heard movement behind me, but it was hard to tell as sounds bounced strangely off the hard surfaces of the cavern and tunnel. Every noise echoed. The water level crept upward, getting closer and closer to my chin as we moved forward. I knew it would be over my face soon. I had to stop. Panic took me, my breath came hard and ragged. Tears were burning my eyes.

I felt Charles hand in mine again as he reached back to me in the darkness. He squeezed my fingers questioningly with his good hand. I had to get ahold of myself. I had to keep going. I had to trust him. We had come this far. I moved forward again, and the cave began to widen. I stretched my arms out to the sides to reach the cave walls around me, as the tunnel opened up. I was so grateful for the reprieve.

"Get ready to hold your breath. It's short, I promise. Just don't stop, keep moving," Charles whispered.

Luckily it was even wider where the water went above our heads. I took a deep breath when the water was just below my mouth, and then went under. I had more room to move and I was able to get through fast. In a matter of seconds, the ground moved upward, and I was above water again. I inhaled a deep breath inward. Much deeper than I really needed. I was so glad to inhale that stale mineral air in the blackness.

We kept moving forward for what seemed like forever. The tunnel was narrowing again, the water was rising higer. It was almost up to my chin and my knees were up to my chest as I did an awkward crab crawl. Charles reached back with a reassuring hand.

"Sunny, this is the worst part. It is tight, and you will have to hold your breath longer this time. Just keep going as fast as you can. Follow me close. I will be right in front of you, okay?" he whispered back to me. Something about how he said it frightened me. I realized I was shivering hard. My teeth chattered. My flight instinct tried to take control, but I knew I could only go forward with Carter somewhere behind me.

I moved onward, as far as I could before gulping in a deep breath and going under. All I could hear was the thundering sound of my heartbeat in my ears. I needed to focus to get through this but what welled up inside of me was a wave of hatred for Carter. It was his fault that we were risking our lives crawling through this tunnel. What he set in motion put Charles in danger again. The anger tightened like a knot in my stomach. The pain of it gave me focus. I could not let him win.

I made good progress, there was still air in my lungs. But I felt an inconceivable terror as I wondered whether my lungs would hold out long enough, or if I would end up a body wedged in this tunnel. A body for some diver to come and retrieve. I had to push those thoughts back and keep going. Charles had stopped and reached a hand back. That was good. He must have been able to stop and get a breath. I was so close but the way through was getting so small. I felt pinned. I tried twisting and turning in different directions to see if I could find a better angle to make it through. Panic was rising. I needed air, fast. The more I struggled the more jammed in I felt. The walls were closing in around me.

Charles must have sensed my panic. He grabbed my arm with one hand and was gently stroking my forearm with his bad hand in an effort to calm me. I realized I was writhing and thrashing against solid rock. I stopped all movement. He began to pull on my arm, pulling me downward instead of straight forward. It was working. The walls widened ever so slightly as I moved down. I was getting through, but my lungs were hurting, and everything was growing fuzzy in my brain. Charles kept on pulling me, little by little. I heard Bobby calling for me. He was telling me to move but I knew that was impossible. He couldn't talk. Then he was in front of me putting his hands on my face and whispering to me. A green glow surrounded him.

Charles was squeezing my arm hard, he brought me back to reality. I was almost through it when I felt something grab a handful of my hair from behind. Was I caught on a rock? No, something was actively pulling me backwards. It had to be Carter, but how did he catch up so fast? That thought sent a new wave of adrenaline through me and I pushed myself forward as hard as I could, hitting my head on some rocks again. Some of my hair was ripped out of the back of my head as I moved forward, but I didn't care, as long as I could pull free of his grasp.

I was free of Carter at last, and the water. I breathed in deep. I began to cough. I felt something warm on my forehead where I had hit the rocks. It was hurting. I realized I had scrapes and bruises all over from the tight crawl. I had to forget about that and keep moving. There was no way Carter would get through. He was much bigger than me. I hesitated. I didn't want anyone to die but if I tried to help him then what would happen to me? What would happen to Charles? Charles was pulling on my arm again.

"He's right behind us. Go…go," I said to Charles softly as I pushed on his back.

PLANTATION
January 1, 1989

I t only took a couple more steps and we were free of the wall and passageway. We stumbled into another cavern. It was smaller than the first and one side of it was carved away and open to the sea. Ocean waves washed gently against the rocks as they poured into the cave. We made our way across the slippery stones, heading to the opening. I fell a couple of times and Charles was right there to pull up on my shaking form.

Once out of the cave we walked across more rocks to get to the sandy beach. A thick row of trees and brush followed the edge of it for as far as the eye could see in the dim moonlight. It seemed so bright out in the open compared to the gloom of the grotto. KA-BOOM! I heard a cannon shot, and then the sky filled with an explosion of twinkling lights that left white hot forms in my vision. Midnight had arrived to usher in a new year.

We made the beach and kept on moving, walking along the shoreline as fast as we could. Charles seemed fine, but I hobbled and limped along with each step. Every muscle in my body was balled up into thick knots. My feet felt heavy in my water-logged sneakers. I could sense that he was holding back to keep pace with me. KA-BOOM! Another blast lit up the sky. The fireworks hovered over the ocean, at least a couple of miles down the beach, maybe more. I wasn't sure.

I tried to push myself to go faster. There were no houses or buildings in view, and I had no idea how far away civilization was. I didn't know how much ground we had covered since leaving the fort. KA-BOOM! Again, a large blast shook the ground as the sky exploded.

Charles was a few steps ahead of me and he turned to reach his good hand back to me. That's when I heard a sharp crack and saw Charles spin around in a circle before hitting the ground hard. I barely avoided landing on him again, as I went down. I thought the loud sound might be another firework, but there was no flash of light to follow it. I crawled over to him and looked into his face. His eyes were open in a grimace. His jaw was clenched in agony.

"Charles, what's wrong? What happened?"

"I think I got shot," he said in pure disbelief.

"What…where?"

"My arm."

I gently ran my hands along his shoulders and down his arms. He winced when I found the wound. His skin was warm and sticky below the shoulder of his bad arm. I scrambled around to find a rough rock that I could use to tear off a strip of my shirt hem with.

I didn't know much about first aid, but I tied a strip of my shirt around his upper arm above the wound to apply pressure and hopefully slow the bleeding. I told him to keep the cloth tight and I dragged him toward the edge of the beach, into the thick brush. I had to hide him and try to lure Carter away. It was me he was after.

"Charles, stay here, out of sight, okay? I will be back, I promise you."

I jumped up and took off running again. I looked behind me, but I couldn't find Carter. I moved over to the side of the beach that was along the water's edge and away from the trees. Another firework rattled the trees. Carter must have seen me then, he started shouting at me.

"Damn it Sunny. Look what you made me do? I didn't want any of this. The gun was my last resort. No way to make a gunshot wound look like an accident, is there? Oh well. I can still make your death look like one at least. The boy's death will probably be blamed on gang violence or drugs. Might take the police a while to find him out here, though," he said with a crazy laugh. He had gone over the edge and there was no turning back. Maybe ever.

I glanced back over my shoulder as I ran. I was surprised by how close Carter was. He was a dark outline on the beach like in my dream at the lighthouse, kicking up sand as he went. He hobbled at a surprising pace. He crept along like some monster from a horror flick. Seeing him made me speed up as the adrenaline rushed in. I had to get him away from Charles. I knew he would go back for him after he got to me. I didn't care what he did to me, but I would not give up without a fight, for Charles' sake. I didn't know how bad Charles' wound was, but I had to get him some help. I was his only hope. That thought spurred me on.

I ran at top speed, which was not that impressive. I had too many bumps and bruises to move any faster. I thought back to watching Brooks run along the shore. I wished like hell I could run as fast as he had. It was getting hard to breathe and I had a nasty stitch in my side that was threatening to drop me at any minute.

I looked back over my shoulder and there was Carter. He wasn't any further back, but he wasn't any closer either. That was good. His yelling and laughter had died down as we went. I couldn't make out anything he was saying anymore. The running was affecting him too.

Ahead in the distance, I could see dark structures taking shape, but they turned out to be some crumbling stone buildings along the edge of the beach when lit up by another firework. Ruins of something big left behind by time. The largest piece looked to be an old windmill with busted up sails and some narrow stone steps that spiraled around the outside of it. There was a stone chimney or smokestack of some kind that was taller than the windmill and soared skyward at an abnormal angle. I wondered why it hadn't been torn down already, before it falls. It was all abandoned. There would be no support to be found within those walls.

I arrived quickly at the ruins and ran inside a small hut with no roof for shelter, praying Carter had not seen me. It was hard to hear anything over the pounding of my heart and my staggered breathing, but I did hear him stumble into the compound on the crushed gravel. He slowed down. That was not a good sign. He was walking around and looking into buildings. I saw a flashlight beam bouncing around. I felt trapped. He was getting closer. There was a second door on the opposite side of the hut, and I scampered through it as quietly as possible.

I stayed in the shadows as I tried to get away from him. Panic was coming at me hard. I didn't know what to do. Would I die on this Island? How long would it be before anyone found me if he carried me up those stone steps and dropped me into that crumbling windmill? How long would it be before someone found Charles' lifeless body in the brush after he bled to death? I had to push those thoughts away. I had to keep it together and go on the offensive. That's when I saw the fireflies swirling around the windmill. They were only there for a brief moment and then they flew off at an unbelievable pace. I had to follow them.

I kept moving in the darkness. I picked my way over to the windmill and then I started up the stone steps that wound around it. There were no railings and the steps were about two feet wide. I tried not to look down. I worked my way up to the top, or what was left of it. I ducked under the sails as I wound around the building. Most of the roof was gone, only the exposed walls remained. They were thick and made of large round stones. The walls were at least a foot wide.

I found a spot were the stones were especially loose at the top. I hoisted myself up on to the narrow ledge of the crumbling wall and then I waited. Another loud boom and flash shook the old windmill. It seemed like hours before I saw Carter standing at the bottom of the exterior steps, but in reality, it was a matter of minutes.

I waited until he was half-way up the steps and on the same side of the wall as me before I began to rain down loose rocks on him. Some hit him directly and others bounced off the stone steps. He went down to his knees with his hands up trying to protect his head. He almost went over the edge. Almost. He managed to hold onto something and keep himself from falling. My plan was failing, and I was running out of ammunition.

He was on his feet again and moving upward. He shined his flashlight up in my direction and then back down to his feet. I had one last stone to push and it totally missed him. He was getting closer. I had screwed up everything.

"Sunny, why are you doing this? Come on…let's be done with all this. You know how this will end. I promise to make it painless…for you…and the boy," he said as he lumbered up the steps. His speech was slurred and hard to understand. I was frozen in place by my fear.

Step by step he inched towards me, ducking under the sail of the windmill, until his face was level with mine. He finally saw me and shined his light into my eyes and then back down at the steps under his feet. He put a hand out to steady himself on the wall. He looked horrible. He was battered and bleeding. His clothes were shredded. His right eye was swollen up so much that I wondered if he could see through it. I almost allowed myself a moment of compassion for him once again, but I quickly shoved the thought away. He didn't deserve it.

He held out his hand to me. He motioned for me to come down off the wall. That tightly coiled spring in my gut felt like it had unwound. I grabbed his hand and hopped down. The steps were too small for both of us to fit on one. I was standing on the step below his with my hand in his. The fireworks lit up his face for a couple of seconds and it sickened me.

We were face to face, just him and I under a tropical web of stars. I sensed him hesitating as he looked down at me. I wished I could know what was going through his mind at that instant. I kept seeing glimmers of humanity within him, or maybe it was just wishful thinking on my part.

"Goodbye Sunny," he said as he let go of my hand. He put the hand back on the wall and leaned backwards a little as he kicked a leg out at me, it connected with my stomach. He knocked the wind out of me with his kick, and I felt myself falling backwards. My arms flailed outward in slow motion, and I managed to grab onto a rusty piece of metal that was protruding from the stone wall. I regained my balance even though I could feel the rusty metal biting into my palm.

Carter had lost his balance with the kick and I saw my chance. I lunged upward at him as hard as I could on the narrow steps. In his unsteadiness, the impact pushed him over the edge. He managed to grab onto my arm as he went over the side. I was down on my hands and knees across three different steps. His weight hanging off my arm was slowly pulling me over with him. I grabbed onto the rough stone steps but there was nothing to hang on to.

His hands were sliding down my arm and I pulled as hard as I could, shaking and trying to get free of him. He finally let go of me and grabbed onto the side of a step. He was dangling in mid-air. I rolled onto my back and squeezed up against the round stone wall, trying to get as far away from the edge as I could.

That's when the fireflies came and circled round his head and face. They were everywhere all at once. I knew he was seeing them this time for sure. He began to laugh as his hands gave way in release from the stone step he was clinging too. He swatted in vain at the bugs on his way to the hard ground. The sky lit up with another explosion.

He didn't stop laughing until he hit the earth below with a sickening thud. The fireflies had followed him down, but they quickly dispersed after he landed. Then everything was silent. I laid on my back on the step until I had recovered my breath. Tears were running down my face. This was not what I had ever wanted but it was inevitable.

It took me a long time to get down the steps. I was unsteady, and my sight blurred from my tears. I got to the bottom and then I walked over to where Carter's body lay. Several flashes of light rained down on his form. The fireworks finale had started, and the show was coming to an end. One of his legs was bent back at an awkward angle and I tried to focus on his face, so I wouldn't see it.

I kneeled beside him and sat in silence, for how long I am not sure. I was dazed but I needed to get myself moving again. I thought of Charles and it moved me. I stood up to go and I heard Carter take in a deep breath and then he grabbed my ankle. He wasn't dead, but he was so weak that I easily pulled my leg away from him.

"I...can't...move...my legs won't...move."

"Don't move. Stay here. I'm going for help."

"No...don't leave."

I took off running again, leaving him lying there. I had to find help. I went back to the beach and ran along the water as fast as I could, hoping I was going in the right direction. This island couldn't be that big, could it? Slowly a light came into focus in the distance. I hoped it was not more fireflies messing with my brain. It steadily grew bigger until I reached the outskirts of civilization. I saw it was the porch light of a shanty on the beach. There weren't any other buildings around. There was a gravel road leading up to it and a beat-up taxi cab sat in the driveway.

I ran up to the door and began pounding, not caring what time of day it was. A toothless, elderly man answered the door in yellowed undershirt and unzipped slacks. He was rubbing his eyes and looking at me funny.

"Hey. You know what time it is? What's wrong? What happened to you?"

"Please...I need your help. My friend is hurt. He's down the beach," I said pointing back to the way I had just come from.

"Okay, okay. Let me get my cart. We go look. Look for your friend. Is he at the old sugar plantation?"

"No…past that."

He went around to the back of his house and into a shed. He came back around driving a golf cart covered with bumper stickers. I hopped in and we took off down the beach. It was close to sunrise by then. Dawn began to peel away night's veil, revealing an orange tinge at the eastern end of the sky. He sped along in the golf cart near the edge of the ocean.

We cruised by the sugar plantation. The first light dripped down the crumbling stones. I was able to get a better look at the place. It was so much more deteriorated than I had realized in the darkness. I was lucky I hadn't brought down the entire windmill when I climbed it.

I was trying to retrace my steps as we drove further. I knew we were getting close but the events of the last few hours seemed like an eternity away. I began yelling for Charles. I jumped out of the cart and ran over to the brushy edge of the beach when I thought we were getting close. I walked along calling his name. The golf cart trailed behind me in the sand.

I heard movement in the brush and then I heard a weak 'here' as Charles reached out to me. He was alive. Tears again. Again, with the tears. I didn't care. They were tears of joy. The man in the golf cart came over to help me and we gently pulled Charles away from the brush and onto the sand.

In the spreading light, I could see that the wound to his arm was not as bad as I had feared in the blackness of the night. I was grateful for that. We got him on his feet and then over to the golf cart. The old man did not ask any questions and that was a good thing. I was not sure what I would have said.

We headed down the beach, back toward the man's hut. As we passed by the plantation, I asked him to stop the cart. I jumped out and ran over to the windmill. Over to the ground where I had left Carter lying. He was gone. I didn't see him anywhere, but he had left his mark. It looked like something large had been dragged along the gravel. Something that left smeared blood behind. I followed the trail. It led down to the beach. The shallow bloody trench in the sand went down to the water and disappeared.

He was gone. Forever. He had gone to be with his adopted parents and his high school girlfriend. Maybe it was his way to make amends for all the horrible things he had done in his lifetime. He gave himself to the ocean that had taken the rest of them. Whatever it meant to him in his sick mind, I was glad he was gone.

I got back into the golf cart with Charles and the old man. I put an arm around Charles, and I looked out to the water where a beautiful sunrise of oranges and pinks was exploding across the sky to welcome the new year. Charles was safe now. That's what mattered most.

RESOLUTION
January 1, 1990

I t took me one full year to finally get on with my life after all that had happened on the Island of Euphoria. One year to the day, as a matter of fact, I called a college friend and asked her to put in a good word for me with her boss. It was my New Year's resolution, to reenter the world of the living. That was all it had taken to finally move forward, after being on hold for so long. I interviewed on the phone and I was offered a job the very next day.

I rented a truck and Dad helped me pack everything back up. Mom and Dad weren't happy about me leaving again, but they understood, and they didn't give me any grief. Not even Mom. Dad made the trip with me and helped me find a studio apartment to call my own. We unloaded everything and then he left me alone in my maze of taped up boxes. I sat down on a box and cried.

I had not cried in the year that I had been back home. I had moved back in with my parents after returning from the Island. The police had found Carter's broken body in the ocean. It verified my story and Brooks was released and back to his old ways. I had temporarily checked myself out of the human race in that year, except for my monthly letters to Charles.

The first letter I sent included a new Yankees baseball cap to replace the one lost in the ocean. I promised to stay in touch with him and to keep contributing to his college fund. I planned a trip back to the Island for his graduation when that day came. I was looking forward to that day more than anything. It kept me going in that long year.

I had heard no word from my biological mother, who was still in New Jersey. Now that I was in New York it would be easier to catch up with her. I wasn't sure if I was ready for that, yet. But maybe the day would come when we could find some sort of peace. Only time would tell. I knew it would be up to me to make that move.

When I was done crying, I took a long hot shower in my new apartment. I stared out the window of my third-floor walk-up. The lights of New York City were coming to life all around me. Millions of people surrounded me, and I still felt all alone. I decided to call my friend and see if she wanted to meet up for a coffee; no more alcohol for me. She did.

I finished getting ready and walked down the stairs and out into the night air of the city that never sleeps. The chilled breeze took my breath away. I thought I saw a flash of something out of the corner of my eye but when I turned to look it was gone. I hadn't seen any fireflies since leaving the Island. In some strange way, I thought the light might be a sign from Walter or Bobby. Maybe now they were trying to tell me that I was finally where I belonged.

I met my friend, Diana, at a coffee shop. We ordered some pastries and coffees. We reminisced about our college days and talked about her office. I was truly excited to be starting work. Her enthusiasm was contagious. Her bubbly personality reminded me of Jenna. I found it impossible to be sad around her. I felt better than I had in a long time.

"Hey, I have to meet my boyfriend at nine," she said. "We're going to the movies. Do you want to come with us? It's a new action thriller with that Brooks Laughton. My boyfriend never lets me pick the movie, but as long as I have some eye candy to look at, I won't complain."

"Thanks...but I'm really more of a book person. Besides, it's getting late. I'm beat from moving. You should go. Thanks for everything. See you Monday at the office, okay?"

We said our goodbyes and I made my way back to my tiny apartment. Hearing Diana talk about her boyfriend made me think of David. We never did get together after I got back from the Island. That was okay. He had moved on and now I was moving forward too. I unlocked my door and turned on the overhead light. My grandmother's couch was piled high with boxes, so I sat on a dining chair. I thought about going to bed, but I was not feeling that tired yet. Maybe it was all the coffee.

I reached down and ripped off the tape from the nearest box. It was full of books. Right on the top of the pile was the tattered old copy of *The Book of Virtues*. The same book I had read from to my grandmother as she lay in her hospital bed so long ago. I picked it up and rifled through the pages. Something fell out, spiraling to the floor like a seed pod from a sycamore tree. Another of my grandmother's literary booby-traps. I bent down and picked it up. It was a glossy clipping from the pages of some unknown magazine. There was a color photo at the top that showed a small bowl of pottery woven with veins of gold. The blurb under the photo said:

kintsukuroi

(n.) (v. phr.) Japanese in origin; "to repair with gold"; the art of repairing pottery with gold or silver lacquer and understanding that the piece is more beautiful for having been broken

I read the clipping and smiled. The simplicity and depth of it hit me hard. I would never get to ask her about it or discuss it with her, but it was enough to find it tucked away inside her favorite book for safe keeping. It was too good of a thought to remain hidden between the pages of a book, though. I taped the clipping onto my bathroom mirror and then I crawled under the covers and shut my eyes as the night sounds of the city lulled me to sleep.

THE END

SHERYL COLEY

AUTHOR'S NOTE

THANK YOU so much for embarking on this journey with me. I truly hope you have been entertained. I hope you found yourself transported to the fictitious Island of Euphoria, in the Bahamas, for a little sun and sand with Sunny McQueen. It has been a wild ride. I am so happy to have shared this with you.

& PLEASE if you have enjoyed this novel, would you take the time to leave me some feedback on the Amazon website, and tell your friends about this book. It would be sincerely appreciated. As a self-published author, I rely on you. I would love to hear from you too! Find me on Amazon or Twitter.

Sheryl Coley
@WaltersSuitcase on Twitter

Made in the USA
Middletown, DE
13 January 2021